Elizabeth Hoyt is a *New York Times* bestselling author of more than seventeen lush historical romances including the Maiden Lane series. *Publishers Weekly* has called her writing 'mesmerizing.' She also pens deliciously fun contemporary romances under the name Julia Harper.

Elizabeth lives in Minneapolis, Minnesota, with three untrained dogs, a garden in constant need of weeding, and the long-suffering Mr. Hoyt. The winters in Minnesota have been known to be long and cold and Elizabeth is always thrilled to receive reader mail.

You can write to her at:
PO Box 19495, Minneapolis, MN 55419
or email her at:
Elizabeth@ElizabethHoyt.com.

Visit Elizabeth Hoyt online:

www.elizabethhoyt.com
www.twitter.com/elizabethhoyt
www.facebook.com/ElizabethHoytBooks

C334013530

By Elizabeth Hoyt

Maiden Lane series:

Wicked Intentions
Notorious Pleasures
Scandalous Desires
Thief of Shadows
Lord of Darkness
Duke of Midnight
Darling Beast
Dearest Rogue
Sweetest Scoundrel
Duke of Sin
Once Upon a Moonlit Night (novella)
Duke of Pleasure

Elizabeth Hoyt

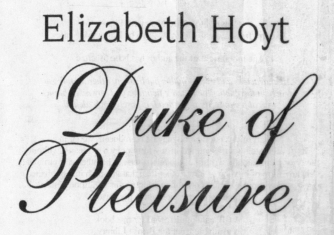

Duke of Pleasure

*A
Maiden Lane
novel*

piatkus

PIATKUS

First published in the US in 2016 by Grand Central Publishing,
A division of Hachette Book Group, Inc.
First published in Great Britain in 2016 by Piatkus

1 3 5 7 9 10 8 6 4 2

A CIP catalogue record for this book
is available from the British Library.

ISBN 978-0-349-41235-1

Printed and bound in Great Britain by
Clays Ltd, St Ives plc

Papers used by Piatkus are from well-managed forests
and other responsible sources.

Piatkus
An imprint of
Little, Brown Book Group
Carmelite House
50 Victoria Embankment
London EC4Y 0DZ

An Hachette UK Company
www.hachette.co.uk

www.piatkus.co.uk

For my editor, Amy Pierpont, who is, quite possibly, The Best. ;-)

Acknowledgments

Thank you to my beta reader, Susannah Taylor, who, despite all evidence to the contrary, consistently tells me that I shouldn't give up writing and become a professional dog walker instead; to my editor, Amy Pierpont, who hasn't yet torn out all her hair due to my egregiously missed deadlines; to my assistant, Melissa Jolly, without whom I would have lost my fracking mind, oh my dear god; and to my darling husband, Mr. Hoyt, who brings me cappuccinos every morning whether I deserve them or not.

And a special thank you to Facebook reader Bernadette Bernstein for naming Pudding the puppy!

Thank you all.

Duke of
Pleasure

Chapter One

*Now once there were a White Kingdom and a Black
Kingdom that had been at war since time began....*
—From *The Black Prince and the Golden Falcon*

JANUARY 1742
LONDON, ENGLAND

Hugh Fitzroy, the Duke of Kyle, did not want to die tonight,
for three very good reasons.

It was half past midnight as he eyed the toughs slinking
out of the shadows up ahead in the cold alley near Covent
Garden. He moved the bottle of fine Viennese wine from his
right arm to his left and drew his sword. He'd dined with the
Habsburg ambassador earlier this evening, and the wine was
a gift.

Firstly, Kit, his elder son—and, formally, the Earl of
Staffin—was only seven. Far too young to be orphaned and
inherit the dukedom.

Next to Hugh was a linkboy with a lantern. The boy was
frozen, his lantern a small pool of light in the narrow alley.
The youth's eyes were wide and frightened. He couldn't be

more than fourteen. Hugh glanced over his shoulder. Several men were bearing down on them from the entrance to the alley. He and the linkboy were trapped.

Secondly, Peter, his younger son, was still suffering nightmares from the death of his mother only five months before. What would his father's death so soon after his mother's do to the boy?

They might be common footpads. Unlikely, though. Footpads usually worked in smaller numbers, were not this organized, and were after money, not death.

Assassins, then.

And *thirdly*, His Majesty had recently assigned Hugh an important job: destroy the Lords of Chaos. On the whole, Hugh liked to finish his jobs. Brought a nice sense of completion at the end of the day, if nothing else.

Right, then.

"If you can, run," Hugh said to the linkboy. "They're after me, not you."

Then he pivoted and attacked the closest group—the three men behind them.

Their leader, a big fellow, raised a club.

Hugh slashed him across the throat. The leader fell in a spray of scarlet. But his second was already bringing his own club down in a bone-jarring blow to Hugh's left shoulder. Hugh juggled the bottle of wine, seized it again, and kicked the man in the balls. The second doubled over and stumbled against the third. Hugh punched over the man's head and into the face of the third.

There were running footsteps from behind Hugh.

He spun to face the other end of the alley and another attacker.

Caught the descending knife with his blade and slid his sword into the hand holding the knife.

A howling scream, and the knife clattered to the icy cobblestones in a splatter of blood.

The knife man lowered his head and charged like an enraged bull.

Hugh flattened all six foot four inches of himself against the filthy alley wall, stuck out his foot, and tripped Charging Bull into the three men he'd already dealt with.

The linkboy, who had been cowering against the opposite wall, took the opportunity to squirm through the constricted space between the assailants and run away.

Which left them all in darkness, save for the light of the half moon.

Hugh grinned.

He didn't have to worry about hitting his compatriots in the dark.

He rushed the man next in line after the Bull. They'd picked a nice alley, his attackers. No way out—save the ends—but in such close quarters he had a small advantage: no matter how many men were against him, the alley was so cramped that only two could come at him at a time. The rest were simply bottled up behind the others, twiddling their thumbs.

Hugh slashed the man and shouldered past him. Got a blow upside the head for his trouble and saw stars. Hugh shook his head and elbowed the next—*hard*—in the face, and kicked the third in the belly. Suddenly he could see the light at the end of the alley.

Hugh knew men who felt that gentlemen should never run from a fight. Of course many of these same men had never *been* in a real fight.

Besides, he had those three *very* good reasons.

Actually, now that he thought of it, there was a *fourth* reason he did not want to die tonight.

Hugh ran to the end of the alley, his bottle of fine Viennese wine cradled in the crook of his left arm, his sword in the other fist. The cobblestones were iced over and his momentum was such that he slid into the lit street.

Where he found another half-dozen men bearing down on him from his left.

Bloody *hell*.

Fourthly, he hadn't had a woman in his bed in over nine months, and to die in such a drought would be a particularly unkind blow from fate, god*damn* it.

Hugh nearly dropped the blasted wine as he scrambled to turn to the right. He could hear the men he'd left in the alley rallying even as he sprinted straight into the worst part of London: the stews of St Giles. They were right on his heels, a veritable army of assassins. The streets here were narrow, ill lit, and cobbled badly, if at all. If he fell because of ice or a missing cobblestone, he'd never get up again.

He turned down a smaller alley and then immediately down another.

Behind him he heard a shout. Christ, if they split up, they would corner him again.

He hadn't enough of a lead, even if a man of his size could easily hide in a place like St Giles. Hugh glanced up as he entered a small courtyard, the buildings on all four sides leaning in. Overhead the moon was veiled in clouds, and it almost looked as if a boy were silhouetted, jumping from one rooftop to another...

Which...

Was insane.

Think. If he could circle and come back the way he'd entered St Giles, he could slip their noose.

A narrow passage.

Another cramped courtyard.

Ah, *Christ.*

They were already here, blocking the two other exits.

Hugh spun, but the passage he'd just run from was crowded with more men, almost a dozen in all.

Well.

He put his back to the only wall left to him and straightened.

He rather wished he'd tasted the wine. He was fond of Viennese wine.

A tall man in a ragged brown coat and a filthy red neck-cloth stepped forward. Hugh half-expected him to make some sort of a speech, he looked that full of himself. Instead he drew a knife the size of a man's forearm, grinned, and licked the blade.

Oh, for—

Hugh didn't wait for whatever other disgusting preliminaries Knife Licker might feel were appropriate to the occasion. He stepped forward and smashed the bottle of very fine Viennese wine over the man's head.

Then they were on him.

He slashed and felt the jolt to his arm as he hit flesh.

Swung and raked the sword across another's face.

Staggered as two men slammed into him.

Another hit him hard in the jaw.

And then someone clubbed him behind the knees.

He fell to his knees on the icy ground, growling like a bleeding, baited bear.

Raised an arm to defend his head...

And...

Someone dropped from the sky right in front of him.

Facing his attackers.

Darting, wheeling, spinning.

Defending him so gracefully.

With two swords.

Hugh staggered upright again, blinking blood out of his eyes—when had he been cut?

And saw—a boy? No, a slight *man* in a grotesque half mask, motley, floppy hat, and boots, battling fiercely with his attackers. Hugh just had time to think: *Insane*, before his defender was thrown back against him.

Hugh caught the man and had another thought, which was: *Tits?*

And then he set the woman—most definitely a *woman* although in a man's clothing—on her feet and put his back to hers and fought as if their lives depended on it.

Which they did.

There were still eight or so of the attackers left, and although they weren't trained, they were determined. Hugh slashed and punched and kicked, while his feminine savior danced an elegant dance of death with her swords. When he smashed the butt of his sword into the skull of one of the last men, the remaining two looked at each other, picked up a third, and took to their heels.

Panting, Hugh glanced around the courtyard. It was strewn with groaning men, most still very much alive, though not dangerous at the moment.

He peered at the masked woman. She was tiny, barely reaching his shoulder. How was it she'd saved him from certain, ignoble death? But she had. She surely had.

"Thank you," he said, his voice gruff. He cleared his throat. "I—"

She grinned, a quicksilver flash, and put her left hand on the back of his neck to pull his head down.

And then she kissed him.

* * *

ALF PRESSED HER lips against Kyle's lovely mouth and thought her heart might beat right out of her breast at her daring.

Then he groaned—a rumbling sound she felt in the fingertips on his nape—and tried to pull her closer. She ducked away and out of reach, skipping back, and then turned and ran down a little alley. She found a stack of barrels and scrambled up them. Pulled herself onto a leaning balcony and from there shinnied up to the roof. She bent low and tiptoed across rotten tiles, some broken, until she was nearly to the edge of the roof, and then lay flat to peer over.

He was still staring down the alley where she'd disappeared, daft man.

Oh, he was a big one, was Kyle. Broad shoulders, long legs. A mouth that made her remember she was a woman beneath her men's clothing. He'd lost his hat and white wig somewhere during his mad dash away from the footpads. He stood bareheaded, his coat torn and bloodied, and in the moonlight she could almost mistake him for a man who belonged in St Giles.

But he wasn't.

He turned finally and limped in the direction of Covent Garden. She rose and followed him—just to make sure he made it out of St Giles.

The one and only time she'd met Kyle before this, she'd been dressed in her daytime disguise as Alf, the boy who made his living as an informant. Except Kyle had wanted information on the Duke of Montgomery, who had been *employing* Alf at the time.

She snorted under her breath as she ran along the ridge of a rooftop, keeping Kyle's shorn black head in sight. Insulting, that had been—him thinking she'd inform on the man paying her. She might not be a lady, but she had her honor. She'd waited until he'd bought her dinner and outlined what he wanted to hire her for—and then she'd turned the table over into his lap. She'd run from the tavern, but not before thumbing her nose at him.

She grinned as she leaped silently from one rooftop to another.

The last time she'd seen Kyle, he'd worn potatoes and gravy on his costly cloak and an angry expression on his handsome face.

Down below, his stride was increasing as they neared the outskirts of St Giles, his boot heels echoing off the cobblestones. She paused, leaning on a chimney. There were more lanterns set out here by the shopkeepers. She watched as Kyle crossed the street, looking warily around, his sword still in his hand.

He didn't have need of her to see him home to whatever grand house he lived in. He was a man well able to look after himself.

Still, she crouched there until he disappeared into the shadows.

Ah, well. Time to go home to her own little nest, then.

She turned and ran over the shingles, quick and light.

When she'd been a child and first learned to scale buildings, she'd thought of London as her forest, St Giles her wood, the roofs her treetops.

Truth be told, she'd never seen a forest, a wood, nor even treetops. She'd never been out of London, for that matter. The farthest east she'd ever traveled in her life was to Wapping—where the air held the faintest hint of sea salt, tickling the nose. The farthest west, to Tyburn, to witness Charming Mickey O'Connor being hanged. Except he hadn't been, to the surprise of all that day. He'd disappeared from the gallows and into legend like the wondrous river pirate he was. But wild birds—free birds—were supposed to live in forests and woods and treetops.

And she'd imagined herself a bird as a child on the rooftops, free and flying.

Sometimes, even as a world-weary woman of one and twenty, she still did.

If she were a bird, the roofs were her home, her *place*, where she felt the safest.

Down below was the dark woods, and she knew all about the woods from the fairy tales that her friend Ned had told her when she'd been a wee thing. In the fairy-tale dark woods were witches and ghouls and trolls, all ready to eat you up.

In the woods of St Giles the monsters were far, far worse.

Tonight she'd fought monsters.

She flew over the roofs of St Giles. Her booted feet were swift and sure on the shingles, and the moon was a big guiding lantern above, lighting the way for her patrol as the Ghost of St Giles. She'd been following the Scarlet Throat gang—a nasty bunch of footpads who'd do anything up to and including murder for the right price—and wondering why they were out in such force, when she'd realized they were chasing Kyle.

In her daytime guise as Alf, she had a bad history with the Scarlet Throats. Most recently they'd taken a dislike to her because she refused to either join them or pay them to be "protected." On the whole they left her alone—she stayed out of their way and they pretended not to notice her. But she shuddered to think what they would do if they ever found out her true sex.

Letting a lone boy defy them was one thing. Letting a woman do the same?

There were rumors of girls ending up in the river for less.

But when she'd seen the Scarlet Throats chasing Kyle like a pack of feral dogs, she'd not thought twice about helping him. He'd been running for his life and fighting as he went, never giving up, though he'd been far outnumbered from the start.

The man was stubborn, if nothing else.

And afterward, when their enemies lay at their feet, groaning and beaten, and her heart was thumping so hard with the sheer joy of victory and being *alive*, it'd seemed natural to pull his pretty, pretty lips down to hers and kiss him.

She'd never kissed a man before.

Oh, there'd been some who'd tried to kiss *her*—tried and succeeded—especially when she'd been younger and smaller and not so fast, nor so swift with a kick to the soft bits of a man. Despite that no one had gotten much beyond a mash of foul tongue in her mouth. She'd been good at running even when little.

No one had touched her in years. She'd made sure of it.

But the kiss with Kyle hadn't been like that—*she'd kissed him*.

She leaped from one roof to another, landing silently on her toes. Kyle's lips had been firm, and he'd tasted sharp, like wine. She'd felt the muscles in his neck and chest and arms get hard and tight as he'd made ready to grab her.

She'd hadn't been *afraid*, though.

She grinned at the moon and the rooftops and the molls walking home in the lane far below.

Kissing Kyle had made her feel wild and free.

Like flying over the roofs of St Giles.

She ran and leaped again, landing this time on a rickety old half-timbered tenement. It was all but fallen down, the top story overhanging the courtyard like an ancient crone bent under a big bundle of used clothes. She thrust her legs over the edge of the roof, slipped her feet blind onto one of the timbers on the face of the building, and climbed down into the attic window.

If St Giles was the dark wood, this was her secret hidey-hole nest: half the attic of this building. The sole door to the room was nailed firmly shut, the only way in by the window.

She was safe here.

No one but she could get in or out.

Alf sighed and stretched her arms over her head before taking off her hat and mask. Muscles she hadn't even realized were tensed began to loosen now that she was home.

Home and safe.

Her nest was one big room—big enough for an entire family to live in, really—but only she lived here. On one wall was a row of wooden pegs, and she hung up her hat and mask there. Across from the window was a brick chimney where she'd left the fire carefully banked. She crossed to it and squatted in front of the tiny hearth—a half moon not much bigger than her head, the brick blackened and crumbling. But this high up it drew well enough, and that was the important thing. She stirred the red eyes of the embers with a broken iron rod and stuck some straw on top, then blew gently until the straw smoked and lit. Then she added five pieces of coal, one at a time. When her little fire was burning nicely, she lit a candle and stood it on the rough shelf above the fireplace.

The half-burned candle gave a happy little glow. Alf touched her fingertip to the candlestick's base and then to the little round mirror next to it. The mirror reflected the tiny candle flame. She tapped her tin cup, a yellow pottery jug she'd found years ago, and her ivory comb. Ned had given her the comb the day before he'd disappeared, and it was perhaps her most precious possession.

Then she picked up a bottle of oil and a rag from the end of the shelf and sat on a three-legged stool by the pile of blankets she used as a bed.

Her long sword was mostly clean. She stroked the oiled cloth along the blade and then tilted it to the candlelight to check for nicks in the edge. The two swords had cost most of her savings and she made sure to keep them clean and razor sharp, both because they were her pride and because in the dark woods they were her main weapons as the Ghost. The long sword's edge looked good, so she resheathed it and set it aside.

Her short blade was bloodied. That she worked on for a bit with the cloth, humming to herself under her breath. The cloth turned rust red and the sword turned mirror bright.

The sky outside her attic window turned pale pink.

She hung up her swords in their scabbards on the row of pegs. She unbuttoned her padded and quilted tunic, pat-terned all over in black and red diamonds. Underneath was a plain man's shirt and she took that off as well, hanging them both up as she shivered in the winter-morning air. Her boots she stood underneath the pegs. Her leggings, also covered in black and red diamonds, hung neatly next to the shirt.

Then she was just in her boys' smallclothes and dark stockings and garters. Her shoulder-length hair was clubbed, but she took it down and ran her fingers through it, mak-ing it messy. She bound her hair back again with a bit of leather cord and let a few strands hang in her face. She took a length of soft cloth and wound it around her breasts, binding them flat, but not too tightly, because it was hard to draw a deep breath otherwise. Besides, her breasts weren't that big to begin with.

She pulled on a big man's shirt, a stained brown waist-coat, a tattered pair of boys' breeches, and a rusty black coat.

She put a dagger in her coat pocket, another in the pocket of her waistcoat, and a tiny blade in a thin leather sheath under her right foot in her shoe. She smashed an old wide-brimmed hat on her head and she was Alf.

A boy.

Because this was what she was.

At night she was the Ghost of St Giles. She protected the people of St Giles—her people, living in the big, dark woods. She ran out the monsters—the murderers and rapists and robbers. And she flew over the roofs of the city by moonlight, free and wild.

During the day she was Alf, a boy. She made her living dealing in information. She listened and learned, and if you wanted to know who was running pickpocket boys and girls in Covent Gardens or which doxies had the clap or even what magistrate could be bought and for how much, she could tell you and would—for a price.

But whether the Ghost or Alf, what she wasn't and would never be, at least not in St Giles, was a woman.

WHEN HAD THE Ghost of St Giles become a woman?

Hugh hissed as one of his former soldiers, Jenkins, drew catgut thread through the cut on his forehead.

Riley winced and silently offered him the bottle of brandy.

Talbot cleared his throat and said, "Begging your pardon, sir, but are you sure the Ghost of St Giles *was* a woman?"

Hugh eyed the big man—he'd once served as a grenadier. "Yes, I'm sure. She had *tits*."

"You searched her, did you, sir?" Riley asked politely in his Irish accent.

Talbot snorted.

Hugh instinctively turned to shoot a reproving glance at

Riley—and Jenkins tsked as the thread pulled at his flesh. *Damn* that hurt.

"Best if you hold still, sir," Jenkins quietly chided.

All three men had been under his command at one time or another out in India or on the Continent. When Hugh had received the letter telling him that Katherine, his wife, had died after being thrown from her horse in Hyde Park, he'd known his exile was at an end, and that he would need to sell his commission in the army and return. He'd offered Riley, Jenkins, and Talbot positions if they elected to return to England with him.

All three had accepted his offer without a second thought.

Now Riley leaned against the door of the big master bedroom in Kyle House, his arms folded and his shoulders hunched, his perpetually sad eyes fixed on the needle. The slight man was brave to a fault, but he hated surgery of any sort. Next to him Talbot was a towering presence, barrel-chested and brawny like most men chosen for the grenadiers.

Jenkins pursed his lips, his one eye intent on the stitch he was placing. A black leather eye patch tied neatly over the man's silver hair covered the other eye. "'Nother two, maybe three stitches, sir."

Hugh grunted and took a drink from the bottle of brandy, careful not to move his head. He was sitting on the edge of his four-poster bed, surrounded by candles so that Jenkins could see to stitch him up.

The former army private could sew a wound closed with better precision than any educated physician. Jenkins was also capable of extracting teeth, letting blood, treating fevers, and, Hugh suspected, amputating limbs, though he'd never actually seen the older man do the last. Jenkins was a man of few words, but his hands were gentle and sure, his lined face calm and intelligent.

Hugh winced at another stitch, his mind back on the woman who had moved so gracefully and yet so efficiently with her swords. "I thought our information was that the Ghost of St Giles was retired?"

Riley shrugged. "That's what we'd heard, sir. There hasn't been a sighting of the Ghost for at least a year. Course there's been more than one Ghost in the past. Jenkins thinks there were at least two at one point, maybe even three."

A hesitant voice piped up from a corner of the room. "Beggin' your pardon, Mr. Riley, but what's this Ghost you're talking about?"

Bell hadn't spoken since they'd entered the room and Hugh had all but forgotten the lad. He glanced now at Bell, sitting on a stool, his blue eyes alert, though his shoulders had begun to slump with weariness. The lad was only fifteen and the newest of his men, having joined Hugh's service after the death of his father.

Bell flushed as he drew the attention of the older men.

Hugh nodded at the boy to reassure him. "Riley?"

Riley uncrossed his arms and winked at Bell. "The Ghost of St Giles is a sort of legend in London. He dresses like a harlequin clown—motley leggings and tunic and a carved half mask—and is able to climb and dance on the rooftops of London. There are some who say he's nothing but a bogeyman to scare children. Others whisper that the Ghost is a defender of the poor. That he goes where soldiers and magistrates dare not and runs out the footpads, rapists, and petty thieves who prey on the most wretched of St Giles."

Bell's brows drew together in confusion. "So . . . he's not real, sir?"

Hugh grunted, remembering soft flesh. "Oh, he—or rather *she*—is real enough."

"That's just it," Talbot interjected, looking intrigued.

"I've spoken to people who have been helped by the Ghost in years past, but the Ghost has never been a woman before. Do you think she could be the wife of one of the former Ghosts, sir?"

Hugh decided not to examine why he didn't like that particular suggestion. "Whoever she was, she was a damned good swordswoman."

"More importantly," Jenkins said softly as he placed another stitch, "who was behind the attack? Who wanted you dead, sir?"

"Do you think it was the work of the Lords of Chaos?" Riley asked.

"Maybe." Hugh grimaced as Jenkins pulled the catgut. "But before I was ambushed I was at the Habsburg ambassador's house. It was a large dinner party and a long one. I got up to piss at one point. I was coming back along the hall when I happened to overhear a bit of conversation."

"Happened, sir?" Riley said, his face expressionless.

"Old habits die hard," Hugh replied drily. "There were two men, huddled together in a dim corner of the hallway, speaking in French. One I recognized from the Russian embassy. No one official, you understand, but certainly he's part of the Russians' delegation. The other man I didn't know, but he looked like a servant, perhaps a valet. The Russian slipped a piece of paper into the servant's hand and told him to take it quickly to the Prussian."

"The Prussian, sir?" Jenkins asked softly. "No name?"

"No name," Hugh replied.

"Bloody buggering hell." Talbot shook his head almost admiringly. "You have to admit, sir, that the man has bollocks to be passing secrets to the Prussians in the Habsburg ambassador's house."

"If that's what the Russian was doing," Hugh said cautiously, though he had no real doubts himself.

"Did he see you, sir?" Riley asked.

"Oh, yes," Hugh said grimly. "One of the other guests bumbled up behind me calling my name. Drunken fool. The Russian couldn't help but know that I'd heard everything."

"Still, there would be very little time to find and hire assassins to target you on your walk home from the dinner," Talbot said.

"Very true," Hugh said. "Which brings us back to the Lords of Chaos."

Jenkins leaned a little closer now, his one brown eye intent, and snipped a thread before sitting back. "Done, sir. Do you want a bandage?"

"No need." The wound had mostly stopped bleeding anyway. "Thank you, Jenkins." Hugh caught Bell trying to smother a yawn. "Best be off to bed, the lot of you. We'll reconvene tomorrow morning after we get some sleep."

"Sir." Riley straightened and came to attention.

Talbot nodded respectfully. "Night, sir."

"Good night, Your Grace," said Bell.

Then all three were out the door.

Hugh picked up a cloth, wet it, and wiped the remaining blood from his face, wincing as the movement reminded him of the bruises up and down his ribs.

Jenkins silently packed his surgical tools into a worn black leather case.

Hugh glanced at the window and saw to his surprise that light was glowing around the cracks of the curtains. Had it been so long since he'd staggered home from St Giles?

He crossed to the window and jerked the curtain open.

The bedroom looked over the back garden, dead now in winter, but it was indeed light outside.

"Anything else, sir?" Jenkins asked behind him.

"No," Hugh said without turning. "That will be all."

"Sir." The door opened and closed.

Outside, a slim figure trotted down the path between the house and the gate that led to the mews. For a moment Hugh stilled before he realized it was the bootblack boy who worked in the kitchens. He felt his upper lip curl at his own folly. The Ghost of St Giles would hardly be haunting his garden, would she?

He let the curtain fall and strode out of his bedroom.

Katherine had named this town house Kyle House. He'd always thought the name pompous, but she'd insisted on it. She'd said it was the name of a great house—a dynastic house. He'd been newly married and still besotted with her when he'd bought the place, so he'd acquiesced, and the name had stood even as their marriage had fallen.

There was a moral there somewhere. Perhaps to not name houses. Or, more probably, to never let passion for a woman sweep away reason, self-preservation, and sense, for that way led to devastation.

Of nearly everything that he'd held dear and that had made him a man.

He passed two maids carrying coal buckets and shovels in the corridor and nodded absently as they curtsied. Made the stairs and took them two at a time to the third floor. It was quiet here. He prowled down the hall past the nursemaids' rooms and opened the door to the bedroom his sons shared.

It was a pretty room. Light and airy. Katherine had been a good mother. He remembered her planning this room. Planning the upper floors when she'd been big with Kit and all had seemed wonderful and new and possible. Before the shouted arguments and her hysterical tears, the disillusionment, and the stunned realization that he'd made a monstrous and permanent mistake.

And that he couldn't trust his own judgment.

Because he'd truly believed himself in love with Katherine. What else could he have called the wild, joyous ecstasy of pursuing her? The complete visceral satisfaction of making her his wife?

Yet barely three years after he'd wed her, all that grand passion had turned to ashes and bitter hatred.

Oh, what a beautiful, fickle thing was love. Rather like Katherine herself, in fact.

Hugh sighed and went into the boys' bedroom.

There were two railed beds, but only one was occupied.

Just turned five years old, Peter was still prone to nightmares. Hugh wasn't sure if his son had experienced them before Katherine's death, but now the boy had them several times a week. He lay curled against his elder brother, red face pressed into his side, blond hair tufted under Kit's arm. Kit was sprawled on his back, openmouthed, his black curly hair flattened sweatily against his temples.

If last night's assassins had succeeded, his boys would be orphans now. He shook off the thought with a shudder, and his mind turned to the Lords of Chaos. They were a terrible secret club that met irregularly to revel in the worst sort of debauchery. Once a man joined he was committed to the Lords for life. Most members didn't know the other members, but if one Lord revealed himself to another, the second Lord was bound to help the first man in any way possible. Hugh had reason to believe that the Lords of Chaos had infiltrated the government, the church, the army, and the navy.

Which was why the King wanted them stopped.

When Hugh had begun his investigation into the Lords, he'd been given four names by the Duke of Montgomery:

William Baines, Baron Chase
David Howzell, Viscount Dowling
Sir Aaron Crewe
Daniel Kendrick, the Earl of Exley

Four men who were aristocrats and members of the secret society. In the two months since, he'd quietly looked into the four men, attempting to discover how the Lords were organized, who the leaders were, and when they met and where.

He'd found out none of these things.

None.

Why then would they try to assassinate him? It seemed far more likely that tonight's attack had been the result of political intrigue on the Continent. Wars abroad, rather than a vile secret society that preyed upon the most innocent of victims here in England.

There was no reason at all to link this to the Lords of Chaos.

And yet he could not quite banish the suspicion from his mind.

Hugh grimaced and silently left the bedroom.

In the hall he turned and made for the stairs again, climbing this time to the floor above—the servants' quarters. He walked along the long corridor, lined with doors on either side, passing a startled scullery maid, and then tapped on one of the doors on the left before opening it.

Bell shared a room with two of the younger footmen. Both of the footmen's beds were empty, for they would already be up and about their work at this time of the morning, but Bell's tousled brown head just peeked beneath his blankets.

Hugh winced at the sight, hating to wake the boy so soon

after sending him to bed, but this couldn't wait. He touched Bell's shoulder.

The boy woke at once. "Your Grace?"

"I have a job for you," Hugh said. "I want you to find a St Giles informant for me. His name is Alf."

Chapter Two

❦

*No one could remember why the White Kingdom hated
the Black Kingdom, nor why the Black Kingdom loathed
the very mention of the White Kingdom's name. The
beginnings of the war were lost to time and suffocated
in blood. All anyone knew was that the war was endless
and without mercy. . . .*
From The Black Prince and the Golden Falcon

Alf strutted down a street in St Giles an hour later.

When she was a little girl, running with a gang of boys
and hiding her sex from all but Ned, he used to instruct her
on how to act like a boy. *Walk with your legs wide and with
a long stride*, he'd tell her. *Pretend you own the street. Look
strangers in the eye like a little tough. They might cuff you
for your cheek, but they won't think you a girl, and that's the
important thing. That's the thing that'll keep you safe.*

Now it was second nature, like a skin she drew on in the
morning: the disguise of Alf the boy. He was younger than
her real age—only fifteen or sixteen—and even though she'd
lived all her life in St Giles, no one seemed to notice that Alf
the boy hadn't aged in the last half-dozen years or so. Alf

smirked to herself. But then one more cocky boy making his way in the world alone in St Giles wasn't something of note.

She turned onto Maiden Lane, shivering a bit. She'd stuffed her coat with rags and wore a pair of fingerless gloves, but her ears were cold despite her hat. Up ahead the Home for Unfortunate Infants and Foundling Children stood out from the surrounding buildings, simply by being clean, straight, and new. She ducked down a narrow alley and around the back to the kitchen door, where she mounted the steps and knocked.

A pretty blond woman in a mobcap opened the door.

Nell Jones, the home's head maidservant, eyed her and pursed her lips. "Morning, Alf. I'd ask you in, but I know it's no use."

Alf shrugged. She disliked taking charity, and if she stepped in the home's kitchens she'd be offered breakfast. No point in getting too close to people, Ned had endlessly repeated. They always wanted something from you sooner or later. Best to do things for yourself rather than rely on another and be disappointed. "Can I see 'er?"

"Of course."

Even before Nell finished speaking, Alf could hear Hannah's running footsteps.

"Is it Alf?" The little redheaded girl peered around Nell's skirts and Alf couldn't help the curl of her lips at the sight.

Hannah was six now, freckle-faced and plump, but when Alf had first met her, almost two years before, the little girl had been thin, frightened, and unsmiling. Hannah had been taken by the lassie snatchers—a gang that put little girls to work in slave shops, laboring over the making of stockings. Alf had rescued her with the help of the then Ghost of St Giles and had brought Hannah to live at the only safe place for children in St Giles—the Home.

Ever since, Alf had tried to visit the girl several times a week. "And 'ow are you, 'Annah?"

"Go on," Nell said to the little girl. "Better step out to talk to him and not let the cold in."

Hannah came out on the step, accompanied by a smaller girl. This one had dark hair and a thumb stuck in her mouth. Both girls were wrapped in shawls against the cold.

"'Oo's this?" Alf asked, crouching down to the smaller girl's level.

"Mary Hope," Hannah said. "She follows me everywhere and she hardly says anything at all. Sometimes I have to speak *for* her."

Mary Hope glanced up at Hannah and grinned around her thumb.

"Ah," Alf said, trying not to smile. "'Ow old are you, then, Mary 'Ope?"

Mary held up five fingers.

"No you're not," Hannah scolded. "Your birthday's not for another fortnight, Nell says. You're only *four* now."

The correction didn't seem to bother Mary, though. She simply nodded and leaned against Hannah.

The bigger girl gave a great put-upon sigh and wrapped her arm around Mary. "Mr. Makepeace is teaching us to read. Well, he's teaching me and the big boys and girls. Mary and the little ones just play, mostly."

"What're you reading?" Alf asked, amused.

"The Bible," Hannah said, sounding a little glum. "But Nell sometimes reads the broadsheets to us, and she said that when we're good at reading we can read them ourselves— though," Hannah amended conscientiously, "she says as how some bits aren't for little girls' eyes."

"Aye, well, keep at your reading," Alf said sternly. "You'll need it to get any sort of good position, understand?"

Hannah nodded solemnly. "Yes, Alf."

"Good girl." She fished in her pocket and brought out a shiny shilling. "That's for studying 'ard."

Hannah's face lit up in a grin. "Thank you!"

"And one for you, Mary, as well." She placed another shilling in Mary Hope's grubby little fist. "Mind you don't lose it. Put it somewheres safe."

"We will," Hannah said, and uninhibitedly threw her arms around Alf's neck.

Alf closed her eyes. This was such a lovely thing, this sweet girl's touch, so fleeting, so momentary. For a second she was no longer a boy but a woman longing with all her heart and soul for the feel of pudgy arms about her neck. What she wouldn't give to have this always. She felt the whisper of a damp kiss, and then Hannah stepped back, already bouncing with excitement over her shilling.

Mary leaned forward and pressed her warm, damp cheek against Alf's.

Then the little girls giggled as the door behind them opened.

Nell shooed them inside as Hannah yelled her good-byes for the both of them.

The door closed, and Alf was alone again in the cold.

She sighed and stood slowly, wiped her face with one gloved hand. Sometimes she thought about what it might be like if she didn't have to say good-bye to Hannah each time she saw the girl. If they could spend more than just a few hurried minutes together.

But that wasn't possible. Not here. Not now.

Not with the life she led.

Alf shook herself, straightened her shoulders, and set off back the way she'd come, striding briskly.

St Giles was waking up by the time she stepped back out onto Maiden Lane. Porters and peddlers were making their way to the better parts of town. Those who begged and cajoled and sang for a living shuffled along, an outgoing tide as timeless as the Thames's. The money was in other parts of London, not here. St Giles was where the poor lived and fucked, bred and died, but it wasn't where they made their pennies.

She nodded to Jim the ragpicker, jerked her chin at Tommy Ginger-Pate, the leader of a gang of street sweeper boys, and stopped to help old Mad Mag, who'd dropped her basket of whisks and brooms. Mad Mag either cursed her or thanked her when the basket was picked up. It was hard to tell because Mag had most of her teeth gone and talked in a strange country accent no one hereabouts could understand.

Alf smiled in any case and went on her way, whistling through her teeth. She turned on Hogshead Lane, jumped the reeking, half-frozen puddle standing just round the corner, and came to the One Horned Goat. Up over her head swung the wooden sign showing a mean-looking goat, no horns on its head but a big ugly prick between its legs.

She pushed open the door to the tavern.

Inside, the place was quiet. Most were either already awake and gone about their business for the day or sleeping off last night's drink, depending.

Archer, the tavern keep, didn't bother glancing up as Alf entered. He poured a tankard of small beer, skewered a sizzling sausage from the fry-pan on the hearth, and slapped it on a slice of bread. Alf sat just as the tavern keep set the lot down on a table in front of her.

"Ta," Alf said, shoving five pennies at the keep. She took a gulp of the beer. The One Horned Goat's beer was warm, sour, and well watered, and there wasn't a better wake-me-up in St Giles.

Archer grunted and tilted his greasy head, his bulging

eyes rolling to the corner of the room. "Lad as says 'e 'as a message for 'e."

Alf took a bite of the tasty sausage and stale bread and chewed, glancing at the corner. A boy sat there, his legs spread wide, his face defiant and a little scared. He looked about thirteen, maybe fourteen. She'd never seen him before. He might be new to London. He was definitely new to St Giles.

She got up, still chewing, her tankard in one hand, the bread and sausage in the other, and walked over.

The boy's eyes widened as she neared.

Alf smirked at him. She hooked a foot around a chair and sat across from him, then took a swig of her beer and eyed him as she swallowed.

"Alf."

The boy just stared at her. He had big blue eyes and curling brown hair he'd tried to slick back into a tail, although it hadn't quite worked. Pretty wisps of hair curled at his temples and at his nape and ears. One glance and she could tell that he hated his curls. He needn't have worried, though. Right now his ears and nose and chin were all too big. They matched his hands and elbows and, for all she knew, his feet as well—he was at that age when he was growing all out of control. But in a couple of years, when he had reached his full height? Then, *then* he'd have to worry.

Because then he'd be handsome.

And in the dark woods of St Giles *handsome* made you either the monster or the little boy who'd lost his way.

Right now, though, he was only a gangly lad still staring at her.

She stared right back and took a big bite of her bread and sausage and chewed slowly.

With her mouth open.

He frowned.

She swallowed and sighed. "Got a moniker?"

Spots of bright pink bloomed on his face. "Bell."

She nodded. "'Eard you gots a message for me."

Bell leaned across the table as if he had the King's secrets to impart. "My master 'as a job for you."

"'Oo?"

"The Duke of Kyle," he said, sounding proud.

"Yeah?"

She took another bite, thinking and making *damned* sure her face didn't show anything. A *duke*. She'd not known Kyle was a duke. But more importantly, why was he calling for her so soon after last night? Had he somehow recognized her under her Ghost mask?

She could feel a jittering under her skin as she asked, "What kind of job?"

Bell frowned again. "Didn't say. You got to come and 'Is Grace'll tell you."

"Oh, *'Is Grace*, is it?" Alf grinned.

Bell sounded awed at the title.

She'd met both the Duke of Wakefield *and* the Duke of Montgomery. The first was like a stone statue of a soldier, all pride and stiff bearing, as if his blood ran as cold as rain in December. The second was mad and dangerous, and as like to thrust a dagger in your gut as hand you a guinea. And despite all that they were but men. They ate and they shit and they could be killed like any other man.

Dukes and night soil men both pissed standing up, as far as she could see. The only difference was where their piss landed.

But if *this* duke had found her out—had realized that the Ghost was not only a woman but was also *Alf*—he might very well get her killed. She ought to send this boy on his way. Get out of the One Horned Goat and disappear into St

Giles. Lie low for a bit until she was absolutely sure the danger was past.

If there *was* danger.

Because that was the problem, wasn't it—she couldn't be sure. He might only be sending for her for information. For a job.

He had been attacked in St Giles last night, after all.

And damn it, she was curious.

Alf drained her ale in three gulps, slammed down her tankard, and stood with the remains of her breakfast in her fist. "Let's go, then."

She waved her bread at Archer in farewell as Bell scrambled after her.

Outside the sun still wasn't out, and Alf pulled her coat tighter around herself, shoving the rest of her bread and sausage in her mouth. "Which way?"

Bell put on a tricorne and headed west without a word.

Alf shrugged and stuffed her fists under her arms, keeping stride with the boy.

He wore a brown coat—nice cloth, hardly worn—and his shoes were newly polished, too.

"Been working for the duke long, have you?" Alf asked.

The boy ducked his head and glanced sideways at her. He was her height, but spindly like a stork. "Fortnight."

"Yeah?" They jumped over a half-frozen dead rat in the channel running down the middle of the lane. "How'd you get the work?"

He frowned. "You ask a lot of questions."

She grinned at him. "It's my job, innit?"

"My pa was under 'is command," Bell muttered. "In the army."

"Was."

Bell looked down and hunched his shoulders as they

passed two butchers' apprentices arguing. "Pa died of the fever last autumn. Lost 'is leg in India two years ago, 'e did, and was poorly ever since. My ma died when I was but ten, and I hadn't family to take me in. My pa said the duke would take care of me if 'e couldn't, so I wrote to the duke and 'Is Grace said as I could come to London and work for 'im. So I did."

"Ah." A man who took care of his people, then, was Kyle. "Where're you from?"

"Sussex."

"And do you like working for 'im?"

Bell looked at her blankly. "I guess?"

Alf laughed at that. "You'd know if you didn't."

They trotted for a bit more as the streets became wider and cleaner, the houses straighter and nicer, and the people better dressed.

At last Bell jerked his chin at one of the tall white buildings, all polished windows and heavy stones. So clean you could eat right off the sparkling front steps if you had a mind to.

Of course they didn't go up *those* steps.

No, they went down into the well where the servants' entrance was and knocked.

A footman answered, a tall fellow in sky-blue-and-purple livery, looking quite smart. If she didn't know better, she might've mistaken him for the duke himself.

But she did know better.

Alf cocked her hip and grinned up at him. "Come to see the duke, I 'ave, good sir. 'E's expecting me."

The footman's broad brow wrinkled in confusion. He'd probably been hired for his looks and his height, not his intelligence.

"Who is it, Gibbons?"

A giant of a butler loomed behind the footman. He had a white wig, a slab of a nose, and a carbuncle face, all pitted and red. He looked down his nose at them and raised one bushy black eyebrow.

Bell seemed to shrink a little.

"'Ow do," Alf said to the butler. "Was just telling Gibbons 'ere that 'Is Grace is expecting me."

The butler's mouth pursed as if he'd accidentally drunk vinegar instead of wine, but he nodded. "This way."

He turned inside.

Alf winked at Bell and followed the butler, and they all tromped through the house. Belowstairs the walls were painted green and the floor was bare wood, which was normal enough. But then they went through a door and entered where the masters lived and everything changed. The walls were the blue of the sky when the sun came out in summer. There were carved bits on top of the blue that were painted white and sometimes gold. The first time Alf had seen such a thing it'd been in the Duke of Montgomery's house, and she'd been altogether perplexed. Why put gold on the wall? It had seemed to her like a terrible waste. She'd even tried prying a piece off, just to see if she could. That was when she'd found out that the gold was very thin, almost like paper. Which meant aristocrats took *gold* and made it into *paper* and then glued it to their *walls*.

Madness.

The floor was wood here, too, but there the similarities ended. Here the wood was many-colored and fitted cleverly into an intricate pattern and polished. Alf had the childish urge to linger and study the floor—except she knew the snooty butler wouldn't bother to stop and wait for her. They passed pretty carved tables, just sitting against the hallway walls for no reason at all. There were paintings of horses and trees and dogs, and even a statue of a man with the legs of a sheep. He had little horns on his head, and she wanted to turn and stare, but the butler had halted before a door.

Alf straightened.

Kyle must be behind that door. He'd sent for her. After she'd kissed him last night. Did he know? Had he recognized her, even in the mask and in the dark?

Her heart seemed to be thumping hard against the bindings covering her breasts.

The butler threw open the door. "Begging your pardon, Your Grace, but Bell is here and he's brought a ... visitor."

Alf made sure to smile sweetly to the butler as she passed him.

It was a big room with books in cases from ceiling to floor on three walls. At the side of the room nearest the door they'd entered was a hearth with a fire and a chair. Only one chair, though. Maybe Kyle didn't like company.

He'd been sitting there, in his red leather chair, but he stood and turned to face them as they entered.

Kyle looked nothing like a duke or even a proper aristocrat. He was tall, with big, bulky shoulders, like an Irish prizefighter—the ones who fought bare-chested and bare-knuckled, sweating before shouting crowds. He wore a white linen shirt and neckcloth and a blue coat and gray waistcoat, but she wondered what he looked like under all that nice clean pressed cloth.

What his chest might look like naked and wet with sweat.

Last night his head had been bare, shorn black hair half-covered in blood. This morning he wore a white wig, curled and powdered, but the wig didn't cover the cut on his forehead. Black stitches like spider legs disappeared under the hairline, with specks of dried blood at the edges, reminding her again of a common brawler.

He was a duke.

She knew that now. Bell had told her, and she'd seen the gold on the walls and the paintings of horses and the ridiculously snooty butler. But his eyes were black, framed by curling lashes, and he hadn't shaved and he looked like a highwayman with cynically twisted thick lips. He looked like one of those rogues the molls in St Giles loved to sing romantic ballads about in the taverns. A man born to hang.

A man born to break a woman's heart.

She met his black eyes and cocked her head, waiting.

"Alf," he said, his voice rasping and deep, making her quim clench under her boys' smallclothes. "I was attacked last night in St Giles by hired ruffians. I want you to find out who they were and, more importantly, who hired them."

And her heart fluttered and fell like a bird shot from the sky.

He didn't remember her from last night at all.

Not at all.

That was good.

That was *good*, and she needn't feel disappointment.

She took a deep breath, puffed out her chest, and stuck her fist on her hip, making *damned* sure her lips didn't tremble when she answered him. "And what'll you be paying me, guv, for I don't work for nothing, more's the pity."

She heard a gasp from Bell. The boy had come to stand a little behind her.

Kyle didn't smile or frown or wince or react at all to her lip, and for a moment she thought she might've gone too far.

Then he said, still calm, still blank-faced, "I already paid you in a dinner, if you'll remember."

She shrugged. "Didn't finish it, did I?"

He mimicked her shrug. "Not my fault."

She smirked at that, feeling lighter. She liked a quick wit, she did. "S'pose most did end in your lap, if I recollect aright."

"Yes, it did," he said, dry as week-old bread. "I wasn't quite sure why you reacted so violently to my offer of money."

"As it 'appens, I don't inform, guv," she said gently. "I were already in the Duke of Montgomery's employment and you wanted me to spy on 'im. I don't accept a cove's coin and then turn around and sell 'im out."

Kyle eyed her with interest. "You're loyal."

"As long as you treat me fair and as long as you pay me, I'm your man, guv, 'eart and soul and all my loyalty." She grinned at him. "That good enough for you?"

He lifted a black eyebrow in what looked like amusement. "Very well, imp."

He took a small purse from his pocket and tossed it to her.

She caught it and opened it. The coins inside were silver. She looked up again and raised her eyebrows.

He met her gaze. "The same again when you bring me back information."

"Right." She stuck the purse inside her waistcoat. "Tell me about these ruffians."

"They attacked me near Covent Garden and chased me into St Giles." He turned to stare into the fire, that beautiful wide mouth twisting down again. She'd pressed her lips to those lips last night. Tasted his breath and felt the thud of his heart. "There were at least a dozen. Maybe more. Their leader had a long knife—as big as my forearm—and wore a red neckcloth."

He didn't mention the Ghost. Did he think her unimportant? Or was there another reason for keeping her secret?

She whistled. "'Oo's your enemy, guv? That's a lot o' coves to send after one man."

"I don't know." He glanced at her. "That's what I've hired you to find out."

"Fair enough." She eyed him. "Anything else you can give me to 'elp my search?"

He looked at her expressionlessly. "Such as?"

She shrugged carelessly, holding his black gaze. "A description of the men. Anyone 'oo might've been about?"

"I didn't see the men that well. I was with a linkboy, though, when I was first attacked. I'd hired him near Covent Garden. Blond. Fourteen or so. Perhaps five and a half feet. He had on a green coat."

"Ta, that'll 'elp. If that's all—" Alf began, but the door to the library opened behind her before she could finish.

"Lady Jordan to see you, Your Grace," the big-nosed butler intoned.

The lady who walked in was about Alf's own size, but that was where any similarity ended. The woman was older than she, nearer Kyle's own age, with hair the color of the gold on his walls. Pure and bright and pinned into a pretty knot at the back of her head.

You never saw hair that color in St Giles.

The lady wore a white silk gown printed in tiny blue and yellow posies. The overskirt had two halves, ruffled and embroidered all along the edges. It parted down the front and was held together over the stomacher by a row of three blue bows.

It was a pretty gown. A pretty gown for a pretty, feminine woman.

Alf set her jaw. Ned had once told her that envy could eat your insides clean away like a rat trapped in a box. Until now she'd never known exactly what he'd meant.

The lady glanced at Alf, her blue-gray eyes widening in puzzlement. "Hugh, who is this?"

Alf looked between her and Kyle and thought, *Of course she knows his true name.*

They belonged together.

Both aristocrats. Both pretty and clean and living in the kind of house that was papered in gold and able to wear white, white silk.

Alf held her head high, because that was what Ned had taught her all those years ago. *Never let them see you cry,* he'd said. *Never show them your weakness.*

So she grinned at Kyle and at the lady in her pretty white dress and strutted out his door.

To do the job she'd been hired for in filthy, rotten St Giles.

Chapter Three

*The White Kingdom was ruled by a powerful sorceress,
descended from kings and warriors. She had taken
as her consort her best general and from him had five
children, all golden eyed and golden haired. The Black
Kingdom was ruled by a ruthless warlock. He had but
one child, a son as black in hair and eyes as his name....*
—From *The Black Prince and the Golden Falcon*

The urchin gave Iris Daniels, Lady Jordan an impudent wink
as he strutted from the room. She stared after him, her brow
knitted. Something about the way the boy walked was...
odd. She shook her head and looked at Hugh.

He had his hands outstretched to her, his diplomat's smile
firmly on his lips, as he said, "Good morning, my lady."

She took his hands, cocking an eyebrow at his formality.
"Good morning, darling Hugh."

He bent over her knuckles in greeting and rose again,
which was when she noticed the ugly wound above his left
eye.

Her own eyes widened in concern. "Your head—what
happened?"

His mouth tightened in what looked like irritation, and she felt a familiar twinge of hurt. Was it so horrible to want to know what things affected a friend?

"It's nothing, I assure you," he said to her as if she were a girl of six and not a woman of seven and twenty. "Come. I know you wish to visit with the boys. Shall we go up and see if they've breakfasted yet?"

She pressed her lips together and nodded, remembering to smile brightly at the last, for they *were* friends—or at least she thought they were. The trouble was that it so hard to tell sometimes. Hugh Fitzroy was such a secretive man in many ways. He kept his thoughts and his emotions very close to the vest, and though they had something of an understanding that would lead one day in the vague future to marriage, it was at times like these that she wondered if she was perhaps making a mistake.

James, her late husband, had also kept his emotions and thoughts under tight control and entirely apart from her, his wife.

Theirs had not been a happy marriage.

But James and Hugh were not the same man, and it was not fair to either to compare them, Iris reminded herself as Hugh led her up the grand staircase to the upper floors of Kyle House. Though both men had been army officers, James had been more than twenty years her senior, and she his third wife. James had been a brooding, quiet man, more comfortable, she'd always suspected, in the company of other gentlemen than that of the fairer sex.

Hugh seemed to enjoy the society of both sexes. She'd seen him smile and tell amusing stories and, of course, when he'd courted Katherine he'd been dashing and intent on her. Despite that, though, he'd always seemed to keep some piece of himself aloof. As if he'd watched and studied and took note of those around him even when he'd been in the midst of passionately pursuing Katherine.

Perhaps that was because of his parentage. For he wasn't truly like any of them, was he?

"Blast," Hugh said, drawing Iris out of her musings as they made the third floor.

She glanced at him and saw his heavy brows were drawn together just as a crash and a scream sounded from the nursery farther down the hallway.

Iris picked up her skirts at the same time that Hugh dropped her arm and strode down the hall to the nursery room door.

She hurried after, catching up as he opened the door and snapped, "*Peter.*"

Inside the nursery the little boy was lying on the floor, red-faced, his fists clenched, his heels beating the wooden boards, as he screamed at the top of his lungs. One of the nursemaids stood over him slapping him repeatedly on any limb she could reach.

Iris gasped. "Stop that at once!" She couldn't hear her own voice above the commotion in the room.

Christopher sat against the wall, his hands clapped over his ears, his face scrunched up, yelling over and over, "Shut! Up! Shut! Up!"

The younger nursemaid quailed at the far corner of the room, her hair half-down about her face.

Hugh grasped the older nursemaid by the arm and thrust her into the corridor. "*You.* You are dismissed."

He closed the door on the woman's protesting face.

He crossed to Christopher and picked him up, ignoring the boy's struggles, and took him into the adjoining bedroom, passing Iris on the way. "*Come.*"

"But Peter—"

"I will take care of him. Once he starts screaming like

this he continues for quite some time. I need you to see to Kit."

She trotted after him, as obediently as a terrier called to heel. One part of her brain thought that this must be the voice he used with his men, his voice of command, for it certainly was most effective.

He set poor Christopher on one of the boys' beds, gave Iris a single intent look, and turned back to the nursery, shutting the door between the rooms.

Iris sat on the bed beside the boy and took a deep breath. She was trembling. She'd known that Peter had thrown terrible tantrums since Katherine's death, but to actually witness one...Hearing such sounds from a beloved child was very distressing.

She looked at Christopher.

He'd stopped yelling, but he was sitting on the bed, his arms wrapped around his knees, silently weeping.

She drew his slim form into her arms.

He held himself stiff for a moment and then all at once he came undone, his limbs relaxing and falling apart as he tumbled into her lap.

She laid her cheek against his dark curls and simply held him, eyes closed. She didn't know what to do. No one, it seemed, knew what to do.

None of them had been prepared for Katherine's death.

Katherine had been her greatest friend ever since they'd been girls of ten. They'd lived near each other as children, and though Katherine had been vivacious and always surrounded by beaux while Iris was quiet, much preferring a book to a party, they'd stayed friends as they'd grown up and married.

And found their respective marriages not entirely happy.

She'd loved Katherine. Loved her quick, sometimes cutting wit. Loved the way she'd thrown her head back in private and laughed, full throated and overly exuberant. Loved that she knew Iris's sad weakness for soft licorice sweets—knew and pandered to her weakness by supplying said soft licorice sweets.

Iris swallowed against the choking thickness in her throat.

No one knew or cared that she liked soft licorice sweets now.

Katherine had had faults. She knew that. How could such a star shine so brightly and not have faults? It simply wasn't possible. But Katherine had adored her sons.

That had never, ever been in doubt.

And because of her love, and because Iris had loved Katherine, she would care for Christopher and Peter to the best of her ability for as long as they needed her.

The screaming from the nursery suddenly stopped, the cessation of sound leaving an odd, almost ringing sensation in her ears.

Iris breathed a sigh of relief.

Christopher stirred. "I hate him."

Her heart constricted. "Don't say that. I don't think he can help it, dear. He misses her so. I know you do, too."

"No." He yawned, pulling away from her, and lay down on his bed, his eyes closing sleepily. "Not Peter. *Him*."

And his cherry-red lips puffed out on the next breath as he fell asleep just like that.

She stared at the boy. Stunned. *Horrified*, if truth be told. How could he hate his father? Hugh had never done anything to earn such rejection, surely?

Except he'd not been there for most of the boys' lives. He'd been away on the Continent and in the army for three years.

And they couldn't comprehend why.

She raised her hand, wanting to comfort, but fearful of waking the child. Uncertain.

Not for the first time she felt her acute inferiority: she was a poor, dull substitute for the radiant mother they'd lost.

In the end she let her hand drop to the side of the bed, and as she did so, she felt an odd hardness under the coverlet.

She pulled the edge of the coverlet back, careful not to disturb Christopher, and looked. Under the boy's mattress, stuck between it and the bed frame, was the corner of a book, bound in red leather. She drew it out. The book was thin, hardly bigger than her hand. She turned it over, but found no mark.

But when she opened it, she saw familiar handwriting:

Katherine, Duchess of Kyle
    Her Diary
    May 1741

HUGH TOOK PETER into his arms, grasping at a kicking leg, winced as a flailing hand caught his still-tender ribs, and ignored the blow to his cheek. He picked up his son bodily and turned and sat on a chair in the corner as the child continued to scream, loud and awful. He paid no heed to the sound and kept himself contained, showing neither the frustration nor the anger he felt. He was the adult, Peter the child.

He could outlast the boy.

The little boy's wails were growing quieter.

Hugh tucked Peter's sweaty head under his chin and held the boy. He could almost admire his son's determination to make his rage known to all.

Peter gasped, choking wetly, and the screaming stopped simply because he couldn't draw breath.

Hugh took a handkerchief out of his pocket and gently wiped Peter's face.

"No!" The child started struggling again, although weakly, as he'd worn himself out. "No! Go away."

"No. I won't," Hugh said, calm. He held the handkerchief to Peter's nose. "Can you blow?"

His son responded noisily.

Hugh finished wiping the boy's face and wadded the handkerchief, then placed it in his pocket.

Peter had gone limp, sagging in exhaustion against him.

Hugh wrapped one arm across the boy's belly and stroked his hand over Peter's forehead, brushing back his sweaty hair, and felt the first sharp stab of a headache beginning behind his right eye.

He closed his eyes and wondered if his sons would ever recover from their mother's death.

From his own absence in their life.

He'd met Katherine eight years ago when he'd been four and twenty and she a dashing, beautiful nineteen. She'd been the daughter of the Earl of Barlowe, the acknowledged swan of the season, and the first sight of her had lit a madness inside him. It was as if he were drunk on her, on her wit, her spark, the way she teased and made him hard. And she, she was equally intoxicated with him, his title, and his uniform. They'd been a terrible brew, the two of them, though at the time he'd not known it.

All he'd been aware of was the most intense joy and excitement he'd ever experienced in his life. A feeling of freedom and hope that would have made him immediately suspicious had he been thinking with his brain instead of his heart and his cock.

After all, he knew well enough that love didn't lead to happiness.

But he'd disregarded his own past and the counsel of what few close friends he had and had married Katherine within months. That first year they'd fought and loved, and it was as if they lived locked inside an iron prison, their passion heating the walls to burning, neither of them able to get out, each unable to let the other go.

She'd become pregnant with Kit almost right away.

His birth, delighting them both, had cooled their fiery arguments slightly, but only for a little time. When Peter was born, his sweet, golden son, Hugh suspected that Katherine had been taking lovers for over a year.

By the time Peter was two she was no longer bothering to hide her liaisons from him and Hugh no longer bothered to rage.

He could've beaten her. Could've taken to drink or shot himself. Could've banished her to the country to rot in obscurity. Could've called out her lovers one after another and killed them in illegal duels until he was killed himself. He could've tried to ignore her and taken a mistress. Pretended he didn't hear the barely hidden laughter from other men who knew him for a cuckold.

He could have gone insane.

He did none of those things. Instead he left. He'd already been discreetly working for His Majesty—doing the sort of undertakings that couldn't be done through official channels—and his type of work would be quite useful on the Continent. So he'd gone abroad, traveling as an officer assigned to various army regiments, but engaged in much more sensitive matters. Once on the Continent, he contacted his men of business and through them informed Katherine of his terms: He would, of course, continue to support her and his sons. He asked only that she attempt to be discreet and, more importantly, not have any children while he was out of the country. He requested that she keep him apprised of their son's lives with regular letters, and in turn read his missives to them.

As it turned out, she was a much better mother than wife, or possibly they simply got on more civilly with his solicitors as intermediaries. Katherine had faithfully sent him long letters about Kit and Peter, and Hugh had spent three years tramping all over the Continent, both in the battlefield and in ballrooms.

The only thing he'd had to give up for such peace was his sons.

His. *Sons*.

He tightened his arm around Peter and bent to kiss the boy's forehead. Hugh had walked back into Kyle House after those three years a stranger to his sons. Peter hadn't recognized him. Kit had known him only from a miniature Katherine kept. The younger boy had been confused and fearful, the older had stared at him with frank hatred.

His sons.

Never again. He'd lost far, far too much because of a witless passion two parts lust and one part heady stupidity. When he married a second time, to the calm, gentle woman who even now was comforting Kit, it would be for friendship and companionship. A mother for his children and a mistress for his home.

Peter stirred sleepily in his arms. "Papa?"

Hugh opened his eyes. "Yes?"

"When're you leavin' again?"

Peter had asked him this question before. He gave the boy the same answer he always gave. "I'm not leaving."

Peter clutched Hugh's waistcoat, his face bent downward, playing with one of the buttons. "Kit says you're gonna leave."

He tried to think of the words to say to make a little boy believe in him. A little boy who had already lost a mother and still didn't really know him.

In the end he said the only thing he could, inadequate though it was. "I won't. I promise."

"YOU'RE GETTING SLOW, old man." Alf grinned that evening as she skipped back quickly, like a bird in flight.

Godric St. John didn't even crack a smile. St. John wasn't much for smiles—not unless it was at the sight of his lady wife or his little girl babe—but his ice-gray eyes narrowed and he lunged at her with his sword and if she didn't know any better she'd think he was bent on gutting her on the spot.

Good thing she *did* know better, then.

She brought her own practice sword up and parried his attack pretty as you please, then slipped under his arm, turning in a cunning move to drive her sword up into his exposed armpit.

Or it *would've* been a cunning move if St. John's sword weren't pressed into the padding at her throat.

Alf wrinkled her nose at the sword tip as she dropped her practice sword in surrender. The long room they dueled in was at the top of Saint House, the wooden floor bare, the only ornaments the swords and protective padding hanging on the wall. As far as Alf knew, the sole thing the room was used for was dueling.

"What," said St. John, not breathing fast at all, which was a bit of an insult, considering the man was practically old enough to be her *father*, "was your mistake?"

"I-did-not-anticipate-my-enemy's-movement-and-furthermore-*under*estimated-'is-intelligence," she said all in one breath, because *really* every one of her so-called mistakes was pretty much the same. "But seems to me that unless I meet *you* in a St Giles alley one night I'm not going to 'ave this 'ere *mistake* with any other opponent."

St. John sighed and lowered his sword. "This isn't a game. I only agreed to help you learn to fight with the swords so that you could better defend yourself, but if you continue to go out there, full of foolish arrogance, it's only a matter of time before you're injured or killed."

Alf scowled at St. John's harsh words, spoken in his usual maddeningly even tone. Two years ago she might've shown him a rude finger, cursed him for a thick swell, and stomped out of the room.

But this man had been the former Ghost of St Giles. He was the one who had helped her save Hannah from the lassie snatchers. Had sought her out over weeks and months and patiently talked to her, even when she'd rebuffed him again and again. Until, in a fit of frustration, she'd finally demanded he teach how her to use the swords so that she could become the Ghost of St Giles herself now that he'd retired.

She'd figured he'd refuse and that'd be the end of it.

He hadn't.

Instead he'd let her into his own home and taught her how to hold a sword. How to thrust and parry. How to angle her hips and slide her legs. When she was ready he'd introduced her to an elderly woman who had sewn her Ghost costume, and helped her purchase her swords. And he'd done all that knowing she was a *woman*. A woman with no name, no money, no family, a woman who came from the dung heap that was St Giles.

He'd asked nothing at all in return—not money or sex or anything else.

Alf had never met anyone like St. John in all her life.

She might be a little in love with him.

Not *love* love, mind. But love like the way she loved the sky and Hannah and the rooftops.

He was special and wonderfully strange, was Godric St. John.

So when he gave her *that* stare and raised his sword again, she picked up her sword and looked chastened.

Or at least tried.

But then there was a commotion belowstairs, and though nothing changed in St. John's face, something lit within him, and she knew their sparring was over for the day.

His lady wife was home.

"I beg your pardon," he murmured, sounding absent-minded already.

She sighed, trying not to feel resentful of the woman she'd never met, and went to hang her sword on the wall and untie the padded waistcoat she wore for practice.

"Would you like to stay for dinner?"

She looked up at his invitation because he'd never asked that before. Not when his wife was about.

"And what would you tell 'er?" She couldn't help it. She felt herself scowl like a child. After all, if his wife hadn't come home, they'd still be practicing.

His eyebrows rose. "I'd introduce you, of course. Megs does know who you are."

She stiffened. "You told 'er."

"I don't keep secrets from my wife," he said, sounding so reasonable. "Alf, don't look like that. Megs would never tell anyone, she promised me. She knows how important your disguise is."

She shook her head, moving away. It didn't matter what he said. What promises had been made. What mattered was that he'd *told* her.

That he'd trusted her secret to his wife.

That she, Alf, wasn't anyone special to him.

That shouldn't hurt, she knew, but it did. *It did*.

She turned and went to the window.

"Alf."

But she didn't feel like replying. She threw her leg over the sill, found a toehold below, and swarmed up the side of the house and onto the roof, without looking back.

It was dark already, the moon hidden by clouds, but she ran over the roof. Jumped down onto the next building and then climbed down to the ground. Saint House was by the river, and she stuck her hands into her pockets, bent her head, and headed north into London and back to St Giles. She wouldn't think about St. John. Wouldn't think about him in his warm house with his wife and baby.

She could take care of herself by herself, and that was all that mattered.

So. She'd think about business instead. She'd buy her supper at the One Horned Goat and nose about there. Maybe talk to Archer and the regulars and see if anyone knew who had hired the Scarlet Throat gang to attack Kyle last night. She was a bit wary of alerting the Scarlet Throats themselves, so she was going about her information gathering in a roundabout sort of way. She'd already talked to the pickpocket gang, to a couple of the shadier pawnbrokers, and to the linkboy who'd been with Kyle. She had a bit of news, but not enough to earn that second purse yet.

And some of her best sources came out only at night.

She was nearly to St Giles, the streets getting darker because the shopkeepers didn't bother putting lanterns outside their shops to light the way, when she twigged that she was being followed. The streets weren't empty—there were people going home to St Giles—so it wasn't obvious at first.

But then she noticed that the lanky fellow in the battered tricorne had been across the street, in step with her, since Covent Garden.

And he was wearing a red neckcloth.

Alf pretended to step in something nasty, and made a show of bending and scraping her shoe against the cobblestones as she took a quick look behind her. There were two men just steps away. They *might* not be following her.

And the sun *might* not come up in the east tomorrow.

She straightened and kept her stride the same, her shoulders still hunched against the cold, her head still bent as she hurried past more shops.

At the next alley she darted inside and legged it.

Footsteps pounded behind her, so close she could almost feel the hot breath on the back of her neck. If she could get a little bit of a lead she could go up and over the roofs and lose them in a trice.

But on the street . . .

This was how they'd caught Kyle last night, she thought as she ducked to the right into another lane. They'd herded him like a ram to slaughter.

Best not let herself be cornered, then.

She deliberately didn't take the next, smaller lane. Instead she headed west and back into the better parts of London.

Someone cursed behind her and then she felt fingers catch at her coat.

She staggered, off balance.

Shoved her hand into her coat pocket and palmed the dagger.

Whirled and stabbed blindly at the attacker. High, up under his face.

She didn't hit anything, but he swore and let go of her coat, raising his hands to protect his throat.

Alf turned and ran again, panting now, the dagger still clutched in her hand. The lane opened up into a bigger street, and she was so relieved she nearly didn't see the tough coming from the left.

He barreled right into her without stopping, knocking her clean off her feet, and slammed her to the ground. Her knife clattered away into the dark street as she felt the first blow to her back. The second to her thigh.

Curl into a ball. Cover your head and eyes, throat and belly. All the soft bits. All the parts that could be gouged and hurt the worst.

That was the first thing you learned in St Giles. It was practically a lullaby taught to the babes at their mothers' paps.

But if she curled up they wouldn't stop with a blow or two. They'd kick her until her ribs broke, until her skull caved, until she lost sense and uncurled and they could get at her soft bits.

And then they'd kill her.

So she kept moving. On hands and knees. Scrambling to right herself, though she knew it was near hopeless. Even as someone kicked her in the side, again and again. She got her hand into her waistcoat pocket as she crawled, and when the next kick came, she caught that leg and stuck it with her second dagger.

The man howled and fell against one of the others. And that was all she needed. Just a second's breath of time.

She was up and on her legs again, running. Limping, to be honest. Her arm and side were all afire, and something in the right side of her face was just numb, no pain or feeling at all.

But she jumped and caught the lower rail of a balcony. Swung and brought her legs up just before one of the toughs swiped at her feet. She clambered onto the balcony, scaled the window and the next and thence to the roof.

And once there? She took flight. Spreading her wings over the rooftops of London.

Running from the dark woods and the monsters.

Chapter Four

One day through bribery and blackmail the Black Warlock found a weakness in the White Sorceress's defenses. He did not hesitate. Why should he? Had the sorceress discovered one of his weaknesses, she would not have spared him or his.
So the warlock stormed Castle White and set it aflame with magical fire with all the White Sorceress's family trapped inside....
—From *The Black Prince and the Golden Falcon*

Hugh swallowed a mouthful of white wine and set the glass beside his plate at supper that night. He sat alone in the dining room, a fire blazing in the hearth at his back, the long, dark, polished dining table set for only one. The room was big. Huge, actually. Katherine had envisioned many convivial parties here early in their marriage.

Perhaps she'd thrown those dinner parties while he'd tramped all over the Continent and India.

He took a bite of his beefsteak. He should've had his supper served in the library. Various papers and maps were spread out on the table next to his place. Among them was a letter from the Duke of Montgomery, now the ambassador to the Ottoman Empire and living in Istanbul. Montgomery had written in his usual flowery and maddeningly cryptic style to say that the last leader of the Lords of Chaos had been the old Duke of Dyemore and that to his knowledge there was no successor to the leadership.

Hugh snorted, tossing aside the missive.

Why Montgomery hadn't thought to give him this information months ago when he'd set him after the leaders of the cabal, he didn't know, but it was just like the man. The Duke of Montgomery was a villain with obscure motives and nonexistent morals. Hugh suspected that the majority of his actions were undertaken purely for his own amusement, and the rest for reasons known only within the dark corners of the duke's own mind.

He sighed and pushed aside the remains of his beefsteak on his plate. He had the beginnings of a violent headache behind his right eye. Sometimes his headaches were accompanied by nausea. Best not to overindulge.

He drained his wineglass and set it down, rising from the table.

Dyemore had perished sometime last autumn—in somewhat mysterious circumstances. Had the Lords of Chaos truly been leaderless for months? From what little Hugh and his men had been able to gather about the society, it seemed unlikely that they were that unorganized. Surely by now someone was either in power or trying to gain the leadership position. If he had to guess, he'd point to Sir Aaron Crewe. Though neither the eldest, the richest, nor the most highly ranked of the four men on the list Montgomery had given him, Crewe had amassed a great deal of political power for a man not much past thirty. Hugh's investigations had revealed that Crewe had risen rapidly from an obscure country family. If—

The door to the dining room burst open and slammed against the wall, Bell running in. "Your Grace, Alf's been 'urt!"

"Show me," Hugh snapped.

Bell was out the door again, Hugh right on his heels.

The boy ran to the kitchens.

The room was crowded with people.

The cook, maids, butler, housekeeper, and footmen were grouped at one side. The long kitchen table was still set with half-eaten dishes. His household had obviously been eating their supper.

By the back door were his men.

Riley leaned, arms crossed, against the doorjamb as if bored. Talbot stood next to him, alert and frowning. Jenkins squatted close to, but not touching, Alf, and as Hugh neared he could see why.

Alf was sitting on the kitchen flagstones, curled into himself, his upper lip lifted like a feral dog's, his hat missing, his eyes glittering dangerously.

The lad held a bloodstained dagger in his right hand.

Hugh halted behind Jenkins and thrust out an arm to keep Bell from coming any closer.

Alf swung his gaze to meet Hugh's, something sparking in his eyes.

Without taking his eyes off the lad, Hugh said, "I'd like the house servants to leave, please."

Behind him he could hear the tromp of feet and the rustle of fabric as the town house servants left.

Then it was just his men and Alf.

The boy's breath was ragged. The dagger in his hand trembled.

"What happened?" Hugh asked.

"Burst in the kitchens like this, sir," Riley replied. "Won't let us help him."

"Jenkins?" Hugh asked softly.

"Ribs, sir," the former soldier said just as quietly. His black leather surgical case was on the kitchen floor by his side. "Wound on the head. Maybe stab in the leg. Blood on his coat from somewhere. Hard to tell from where."

"'M fine," Alf said, his voice cracking. There was a spreading bloodstain on the right leg of his breeches.

"No," Hugh said evenly, "you're not. You came here for help. Let me give it to you."

"Just let me rest 'ere awhile. I'll be fine."

"Don't be an idiot," Hugh snapped. "Jenkins here is one of the best men for fixing a body up after a scrape. He stitched my own wound last night."

Alf was already shaking his head. "No one touches me, guv. No one."

Hugh felt his jaw clench even as he felt a stab of pity. The boy reminded him of a hurt feral terrier, growling and snapping at the hand offered in help. But he couldn't let sympathy keep him from doing what must be done. "Be that as it may, I'm ordering you to let Jenkins doctor you."

"No."

"Talbot," Hugh said, giving a well-established order.

"Aye, sir." The former grenadier nodded.

Alf tensed, his eyes swiveling to Talbot.

Hugh took two steps forward, knocked the dagger from Alf's hand, and caught him in a bear hug, pinning his arms to his sides.

The boy arched his back. "Oi! Not fair!"

Hugh grunted, but Alf was lighter than he'd expected. He threw the boy over his shoulder and clamped an arm firmly over his wriggling legs.

"With me," he said to his men, and strode from the kitchens and into the servants' hall.

Bell lit the way with a candelabrum.

Hugh turned a corner, found the servants' stairs, and mounted them, climbing to the servants' quarters. The boy had gone limp on his shoulder. Perhaps he'd fainted.

"Is there an empty servants' room?" he asked Jenkins.

"This one, sir." Jenkins opened the fourth door on the right.

The room was under the eaves, the ceiling sloping down from the doorway to the casement window. There were two narrow single beds on either side of the window, a row of hooks on the wall, a stool, and a chest of drawers with a washbasin on top by the door.

He stooped to avoid hitting his head on the ceiling and gently dumped the boy onto one of the beds.

Alf stared solemn eyed up at him. "Not my master, guv."

He was such a tough little thing, even wounded and surrounded by bigger, older men.

Hugh brushed the boy's tangled hair off his delicate, bruised face. "I know I'm not your master, imp. But let Jenkins see to your leg as a favor to me, hmm?"

Alf didn't exactly agree, but his body visibly relaxed.

Jenkins pulled the stool over, sat, and opened his surgical case. He took out a large pair of scissors, bent over the boy's bloody breeches, and matter-of-factly cut the leg off from knee to hip, pulled off Alf's shoe, and then slit his bloody stocking away from the leg as well.

Underneath the filthy breeches the boy wore ragged smallclothes, stained with blood.

Jenkins set aside the scissors, found a rag in his bag, and used it to gently blot the blood from a sluggishly oozing stab wound just above the boy's knee.

Hugh eyed the cut. It looked deep and as if it would need stitches. He called to Talbot. "Bring some brandy."

Talbot nodded and ducked from the room.

Alf met Hugh's gaze, his own defiant. "Don't need none of that, guv."

Hugh rested his hand on the boy's ankle. "It'll help with the pain."

Jenkins threaded his needle.

"Who did this to you?" Hugh asked.

Talbot came back in and handed a bottle to Hugh. He uncorked it before tilting the bottle to Alf's lips.

The boy took a small sip, swallowed, and nodded. "Ta. They was waiting for me tonight. Big toughs, three of them. Between Covent Garden and St Giles."

Jenkins nodded to Dell, who brought the candelabrum closer, throwing bright light on the knife wound. The candlelight jumped and flickered as Bell trembled.

"Steady," Jenkins murmured. He pinched the edge of the cut together with his left hand and with a firm right hand thrust his needle into Alf's skin.

Alf didn't flinch, but his lips thinned as Jenkins placed another stitch.

Hugh held the boy's gaze. "Do you think the attack on you is linked to the attack on me last night?"

"Know it. Was making inquiries today." Alf's brown eyes flicked up to his, big with pain. "And they was wearing red neckcloths. That's the gang what tried to kill you last night. Call themselves the Scarlet Throat gang. On account of the neckcloths—and the way they like to kill their victims." He made a graphic gesture across his neck with his finger.

Bell's hand jerked at the gesture, the candlelight jumped again, and Jenkins growled under his breath.

Hugh balled his fist by his side. They'd attacked this boy

because he'd sent him into St Giles alone to make inquiries for him. He should've never sent Alf in alone.

The boy winced as Jenkins tied the knot on the second stitch.

Hugh offered the bottle of brandy again.

Alf sneered. "Nah, guv. Don't need any more of that."

"We won't think the less of you," Hugh said mildly.

"What makes you think I cares what you think of me at all?" The boy's lips twitched impudently.

Hugh raised his eyebrows. Was the boy fearful of losing his senses in front of his men? While he watched Jenkins set another careful stitch, he wondered what the boy's past must've been like to make him so skittish.

"Talked to your linkboy today," Alf whispered, interrupting his dark musings. "And some pickpockets."

Hugh looked at him. The boy's big brown eyes were hazed with pain, but a smile played around his pink lips. "And did you find out anything?"

"Not much," the lad admitted, exhaling slowly as Jenkins pulled the stitch tight. "There was a toff maybe asking about hiring toughs in St Giles a sennight ago. Maybe. Some say the man smelled of rotten eggs."

"Rotten eggs," Hugh repeated, flat.

Alf winked. "Told you wasn't much."

"No other description?"

The boy closed his eyes. "Guess 'e was a right common-looking cove. Neither tall nor short nor black nor fair nor old nor young. Just with a snooty accent and smelling of rotten eggs. 'Spect you'll be able to skip outside your grand 'ouse, sniff the air, and lay your 'and on 'is shoulder at once, right, guv?"

Talbot bowed his head and coughed into his sleeve, Bell's eyes grew wide as saucers, while Riley outright chuckled.

Alf opened his eyes and looked straight at Hugh, the boy's gaze full of laughter even through the pain.

Insubordinate whelp. Hugh narrowed his eyes at the lad, hiding his amusement.

Jenkins tied off the last stitch and snipped the thread neatly. Then he took linen strips from his bag and began bandaging the boy's leg.

Alf bit his lip.

Hugh patted the boy's ankle. Alf was brash to the point of cockiness, but his bones were delicate and small. The thought of his being set upon by three grown men, of having to run for his life across London, made something in Hugh clench in rage.

He jerked his chin to his men to leave the room as Jenkins finished tying off the bandage.

Bell lit a single candle, took it, and set down the candelabrum before all four tromped out.

Hugh glanced at Alf's drooping eyelids. "Sleep here tonight. We'll talk more in the morning."

"Can't keep me 'ere, guv," the boy slurred, sounding half-asleep already. "Told you. Not my master, 'member?"

Hugh squeezed that fragile ankle before letting it go. "I might not be your master, imp, but that doesn't mean you're not under my protection. Stay here. That's an order."

Alf's eyes widened, big and brown and heavily lashed. Hugh waited for the inevitable protest.

It never came.

Instead Alf smiled . . . and fell asleep.

Hugh stared at the boy a moment longer. He might be an independent urchin, used to having his own way and running free, but Hugh would be damned if he'd let the boy come to grief again while in his employ. Alf was one of his now.

To keep him safe he might have to clip the boy's wings.

He turned wearily to the door and realized only as he closed it softly behind him: his headache was entirely gone.

THE FIRST THOUGHT Alf had on waking was that she wasn't sleeping in her nest.

She wasn't safe.

And someone was whispering nearby.

She held herself still, keeping her breaths even and slow, her lips soft and parted.

"Maybe he's a new footman."

"Then why's he hurt?"

"Maybe Papa doesn't like him."

"Father wouldn't hurt a footman, Petey!" the first voice exclaimed, and then with less certainty, "Probably not, anyway."

The speakers had forgotten to whisper, and their voices were high. They were children.

Alf opened her eyes.

She lay curled on her side and her whole body hurt. Two faces bent over her, one with blue eyes, the other with black. Both jumped back when they saw that she was awake.

They were two boys. The black eyes belonged to the older one, maybe seven or eight years old, with black curling hair. The blue-eyed one was over a head shorter and had fair hair and pink-and-white skin like an angel. He looked to be about Hannah's age—five or six. They were both dressed like little gentlemen in brown waistcoats, breeches, and coats, tiny neckcloths tied properly at their throats.

Alf yawned and gingerly pushed herself up to sit against the wall, wincing as her ribs protested the movement. She made sure to throw the covers over her lap. She still wore only her smallclothes, shirt, and bindings. When she looked up again, the boys were staring at her as if she were an African tiger in a cage.

She smirked at them. "'Oo's your father, then?"

"The Duke of Kyle," the smaller one piped up, and Alf felt the shock go all the way through her.

She'd no idea Kyle was married.

"Hush, Petey," hissed his brother.

"But he is!" cried the younger boy, tears filling his big blue eyes.

"Where's your ma?" Alf asked, hoping to forestall the tears.

"She's dead," the older one said, and the younger one started screaming like a fishmonger with a new tray of mackerel to sell.

Her heart clenched. She wanted to pull the little boy into her arms, but she wasn't his mother. His mother was apparently dead and gone, and nothing in the world would change that.

So instead she reached down, pulled off her remaining shoe, and took out the tiny dagger.

The boy snapped his mouth shut.

She withdrew the dagger from the thin sheath and the razor-sharp edge glinted in the morning light from the window. "Want to 'ear 'ow I fought off three men trying to kill me last night?"

Little Blue Eyes gulped and nodded, and even his sour-faced older brother looked interested.

"'Ave a seat, then," Alf said, patting the bed. "What's your names?"

Blue Eyes was already climbing on the bed beside her. "'M Peter," he said. "*Lord* Peter."

She snorted at that because *Lord* Peter had just wiped his runny nose on his coat sleeve. "And you?"

The older boy was eyeing her with a watchful expression that reminded her of his father. "I'm Christopher."

"Kit," said Lord Peter bossily. "Ever'one calls him Kit. 'Cept Lady Jordan. But his *real* name is Staffin."

Alf blinked, confused. "Your name is Staffin?"

"No," the older boy said patiently as he finally gave in and climbed on the bed. "It's Christopher Fitzroy, the Earl of Staffin. I'm the heir. I'll be the duke when Father dies."

He sat beside her, gazing quite matter-of-factly at her as he told her of his titles and that someday he'd be a *duke*.

"What's your names?" Peter piped up from her other side.

She looked down into his pink-and-white angel face and had to laugh. "Alf. Just Alf. I 'aven't any other names. Only the one."

The little boy grinned back at her, and she saw that he was missing his two upper front teeth. "Tell us the story now."

"Know where St Giles is?" Alf asked them.

They both shook their heads.

"Just as well." She stared at them, her face grave. "It's only the meanest, dirtiest, *worst* part of London, where all the thieves and beggars and cutthroats go at night. It's where I live."

Kit's eyes were big, and Peter leaned into her arm.

"Last night, after dark, there I was a-walking 'ome all alone, just thinking on my supper, maybe some sausage and cheese—"

"*I* like sausage," Peter interrupted.

"Hush," Kit said.

"When I figured someone was following me." Alf paused. "*Clomp. Clomp. Clomp.* Right behind me. Someone big. And when I went to look, what d'you suppose I saw?"

"What?" Peter whispered.

By this time he was clutching her arm with both his hands, his grief over his mother momentarily forgotten. She felt a pang. This was nice, having two little bodies snuggling close to her, telling wild tales and watching the boys' awe.

"Three. Big. Blokes." She looked at one boy and then the other, her voice lowered to a hoarse whisper to heighten the drama. "They was as large as apes, their arms near dragging on the ground."

Peter shivered against her, his blue eyes wide.

"What did you do?" Kit whispered.

"Took to my 'eels," Alf told him. "Ran as fast as I could, I can tell ye. But they was right be'ind me. One grabbed me and I went down 'ard. Rolled and curled. Put my 'ands over my face and 'ead and my knees in front of my belly. 'Ad a dagger in my 'and—"

"That one?" Peter asked, pointing to the one she'd taken from her shoe.

"Nah." She winked at him. "I always like to 'ave a couple blades on me, see, just in case. So I lost the first when the bastard shoved me down. But the second—the *second*—I planted good and 'ard in one of them's leg."

"You *stabbed* a man?" Kit had gotten up on hands and knees in his excitement.

She narrowed her eyes, trying to look daring and fierce. "I did."

"Was there lots and lots of *blood*?" Peter gasped.

Which was when a deep voice interrupted from the doorway.

"What," Kyle said in slow, measured tones, "is going on here?"

Both boys' heads whipped around as they looked guiltily at their father.

Alf sighed silently. She'd have to show them how to work on that.

She leaned forward, slipping the dagger back into her

shoe with a pass of her hand, all the while smiling at Kyle. "Morning, guv."

"Good morning, Alf." He nodded. "I see that you're feeling better this morning."

"Wonderful what a good night's rest will do you." She winked.

"Hm." His black eyes slid from her and narrowed on the boys. "Your nursemaid is in tears. She's been searching for you both for the last half hour. You're late for your breakfast and for your morning walk. What have you to say for yourselves?"

Kit slipped off the bed and stood to attention like a little soldier. "I'm sorry, Father."

Peter's lower lip wobbled, a rainstorm threatening again. He hopped from the bed and slid behind his brother.

Kyle's lips thinned as he looked at his older son. "Take your brother and go straight to your nurse. Make your apologies to her."

For a moment black eyes glared up at black eyes and Alf caught her breath at the anger the little boy showed toward his father.

"Yes, sir," Kit said finally as he took the younger boy's hand and led him from the room.

Kyle stared after his sons.

Alf cleared her throat. "Well. I thank you for the bed and the doctoring, but I s'pose I ought to be on my way."

The duke turned back to her frowning. "Not without breakfast."

"Don't want to put you out, guv."

Her reply merely made him look irritated. "It's already made."

She raised an eyebrow. "Since you put it that way, I'll accept your gen'rous 'ospitality."

She *had* missed her supper last night, and her stomach was reminding her of that fact.

A corner of his mouth cocked up. "Good. Here." He held out a pair of boys' breeches, a coat, and some stockings. "Bell kindly offered something to wear to breakfast."

"Ta." Alf took the clothes and swallowed. Her small-clothes weren't particularly revealing, but he might still notice that she lacked a certain bulge.

She pulled on the stockings slowly, the blankets still covering her lap.

Kyle turned and eyed the pile of her ruined clothes in the corner.

Quickly she jumped up, turned her back, and pulled on the breeches and coat.

She looked up to find Kyle watching her like a hawk. "How is your leg?"

She smiled, ignoring the dull, throbbing pain. "It'll do."

He grunted and strode to stand in front of her. Before she could duck he had her chin in his broad fingers and was examining her face.

She held her breath at his touch, impersonal though it was.

"You've got the beginnings of an ugly bruise," he said at last, letting her go. "But it doesn't look like you'll have a black eye."

She shrugged. "I've 'ad worse and survived."

His black eyes stared at her a moment as if he was thinking of arguing, but then he just strode to the door.

She blew out a breath, refrained from sticking her tongue out at his back, and followed him.

He led her down several flights of stairs and into a formal dining room.

"There," Kyle said, and pointed to a fine long table, shining with wax and laid with the loveliest breakfast she'd ever seen.

There were plates of eggs, ham, sausages, and kippers, a basket of bread, little dishes of butter and jam, and a big pot of tea.

Alf blinked and looked at Kyle, who was looking back at her as if he served urchins from St Giles breakfast at his own dining table every day.

Of course aristocrats were a strange lot at the best of times—and she *was* very hungry.

Alf sat, poured herself some tea, and started filling her plate with everything.

Kyle pulled out a chair across from her. "I thought—"

The door burst open again and Alf looked up, a spoonful of eggs halfway to her plate. If she wasn't to eat this wonderful breakfast after having it spread in front of her, she might very well cry.

A swell cove slid into the room, already talking. "Hugh, it's imperative that you give me an advance on my allowance at once."

The man was tall, but not nearly as broad as Kyle. In fact he seemed a mere boy next to the duke, his face narrow and fine, his thin fingers dripping in lace. He was handsome, though, his skin pale and unblemished, his features regular and set in the unconscious arrogance of a man who'd had everything handed to him since birth.

"Good morning, David," Kyle said. "I'm busy." He inclined his head to her. "Perhaps we can discuss this later."

Alf took a bite of ham and chewed it, watching as David turned to her.

His blue eyes skimmed over her, past her, around the room, and back to Kyle. "An *urchin*? Never tell me you'd put off your own brother-in-law because of some filthy beggar you found on the street?"

Alf swallowed her ham and started buttering a piece of

bread. She added a generous spoonful of jam. The room was silent save for the clink of her spoon against the little jam dish, and finally she glanced up again.

Kyle's dark brows were lowered, his black eyes narrowed and glinting.

He'd looked like that the night before last—just before he'd run his sword through one of the footpads.

She caught his eye as she bit into her bread and jam and winked. Fact was, she'd been called much worse than *urchin* and *filthy beggar*. Names hardly bothered her.

But she was rather pleased that they seemed to bother *him*.

Kyle's lips pressed together at her wink, but his shoulders relaxed a bit.

He looked at David. "Why are you here?"

The younger man flung himself into a chair. "I've told you—I'm in need of funds. Just until the next quarter, then I shall repay you, my word. I've got tradesmen pounding at my door day and night, nipping at my heels like flea-bitten dogs. One even followed me to my coffeehouse, can you credit it?"

Kyle sighed. "You haven't repaid the last loan I made you."

David slapped the table. "Because I haven't the money."

"Exactly."

"You can't expect me to live on nothing!"

"I expect you to live within your means," Kyle snapped.

The younger man drew himself up proudly. "Katherine would've been horrified had she known that you would treat me so shabbily after her death. We were very close, my sister and I. For shame, Kyle, for *shame*."

Kyle sighed. "My wife chose to provide you with a steady source of funds from the money I gave her. That was her own charity. I have no reason to continue it. The allowance your father provides you is more than—"

"Why this odious judgmental tone?" The younger man's eyes narrowed nastily. "Do you seek to punish me for Katherine's transgressions against you? For Peter and—"

Kyle rose, his legs braced apart, his face like stone. "Get out of my house."

David stood as well, so fast his chair screeched against the floor. He skittered back like a gutter rat, but he was still talking as if he just couldn't stop his tongue. "You don't understand, the way you were raised, the peasant blood from your mother, how a true aristocrat lives. What is expected of us and what we should do for family and—"

"I understand that if you don't leave now I'll strip and whip you myself," Kyle said, still in that calm, deadly voice.

David tossed his head and stalked to the door—though it would've been a better exit if he hadn't been in such a hurry.

Alf watched the door slam behind him and then poured herself another cup of tea. It was nice and strong. She didn't often drink tea. The tea leaves found in St Giles had already been used at least once, bought out the back door from houses like this one to be resold to people like her. She tipped the little pitcher of white, creamy milk over her cup and filled it half-full of the stuff, and then added two lumps of the sugar.

She took a sip of the hot, sweet brew and caught Kyle's eye.

He cleared his throat. "I'm sorry about that."

"I don't guess you can pick your family." She set her cup carefully back down. "'E was your wife's brother?"

He grimaced, gesturing with contempt at the closed door. "David Townes, Viscount Childress. He's heir to the Earl of Barlowe, but his father is a canny old bastard and knows his son is a spendthrift. Barlowe keeps him on a very tight rein, hence that little piece of melodrama."

She nodded, surprised that he'd told her so much. So surprised, in fact, that she pushed for a bit more. "What did 'e mean? That your mother was a peasant?"

He frowned, sitting back down. "I'd rather discuss the attacks."

She looked down at her teacup, hiding her disappointment that he wouldn't answer her. How could a duke have a peasant for a mother?

But maybe it was just the viscount's way of insulting Kyle.

She slouched in her chair. "Told you just about everything I knew last night, guv."

"Humor me," he clipped out.

"Very well." She smirked. "Tell me 'oo you think might've 'ired the Scarlet Throat gang, guv. 'Oo wants you dead?"

Two lines appeared between his black brows. "That's none of your business."

"You're the one wanting to discuss things, guv, not I. Besides"—she picked up another piece of bread and began buttering it—"Gots a knife wound in this 'ere leg says otherwise."

He cursed under his breath as she scooped up a big spoonful of jam and smeared it on the bread. She'd always loved jam, and this was strawberry with lovely bits of the fruit in it.

He sighed. "The whole thing is quite complicated, and I'm not sure you'd understand."

She watched him in amusement as she took a bite of her jam and bread. If she were a highborn lady, she'd have jam and bread and tea *every* morning for her breakfast. "Try me."

"It's either political—in which case you should be watching for men with Russian or Prussian accents—or..." He rubbed his temple.

"Or...?" she prompted.

"There's a sort of club," he said at last, sounding reluctant. "I've been tasked with bringing them down. They're called the Lords of Chaos."

Alf swallowed the bite of bread and jam she'd taken and dusted off her hands. His words brought up all sorts of questions, but she asked only one. "Tasked by 'oo, guv?"

He stared at her intently for a moment, and then he stood. "Come with me and I'll show you."

Chapter Five

*The White Sorceress and her husband fought the flames,
but the fire was magical. It yielded to neither water
nor sand nor wind, but burned on relentlessly. She
watched as first her husband burned to death, then one
by one her four eldest children perished in the flames,
screaming for their mother. Finally only her youngest
child, a girl of six, remained, clutched in the White
Sorceress's arms....*
—From *The Black Prince and the Golden Falcon*

The problem, Hugh mused as he waited for the carriage to
be readied, was that Alf would be off like a shot if he let
him. The boy would stubbornly go back to St Giles—and
might be dead by nightfall. He wasn't used to taking orders
and apparently had an innate suspicion of those trying to
help him as well, if last night's argument was any indication.

Hence Hugh's decision to simply bring the boy with him on
his errand to see Shrugg this morning. This way he could keep
Alf by his side, where he could watch him and protect him.

The boy also seemed to enjoy flouting authority—Hugh
hadn't missed that Alf refused to address him properly as a

duke. Usually he didn't pay much attention to the nicety of people addressing him as *Your Grace*—his men often didn't, used as they were to his command position in the army. He knew that when his men addressed him as *sir* instead of *Your Grace*, no disrespect was intended.

Quite the opposite, in fact.

When Alf addressed Hugh in his cavalier manner as *guv*, Hugh was fairly certain that more than a touch of disrespect was intended. What was more troubling than the boy's mockery was Hugh's own reaction: he found he didn't mind.

Worse: he found Alf's teasing rather amusing.

"This 'er?"

He turned at the sound of the boy's voice.

They were in the entry hall—an opulent room, naturally, with gray-and-green-marbled floors and green fabric walls. Alf had been squinting at the chandelier above—a great, gaudy thing that Katherine had bought in the first year of their marriage—but now he saw the boy had wandered to the grand staircase. He stood staring up at Katherine's portrait.

Hugh had the urge to snap at him to mind his manners and get away from the painting, but that was rude. And the lad was merely curious.

He took a breath and walked over, glancing at Katherine. It was a full-length portrait and she stood in what looked like classical ruins, one arm leaning on a broken pillar. She'd chosen to be painted in a draped white dress, almost a chemise, with an ermine cape carelessly thrown over it. Her mahogany hair—her pride and joy—was undone, cascading down one shoulder, and her head was half turned away from the viewer, the better to reveal the long line of her white neck.

She was beautiful in the portrait as she had been in life, but Hugh had never thought the painting did her justice.

The pose was too static. The artist, however accomplished, hadn't captured Katherine's essential vivaciousness. She'd been able to walk into a room and instantly command it, drawing the attention of both men and women.

He looked at her now and felt nothing. "Yes, that's Katherine, my late wife."

"When did she ... ?"

"Last September." She'd been gone almost five months.

He felt the quick look Alf darted at him. "I'm sorry, guv."

There wasn't much he could say to that without appearing rude. He kept the portrait up only for his sons' sakes.

The boy tilted his head. "I can see Lord Peter in 'er. They 'ave the same eyes. Pretty and blue."

Hugh glanced at Alf in amusement. "You like blue eyes?"

The boy scuffed his shoes against the floor. "Doesn't everyone?"

"I don't know." He examined the boy, realizing he knew very little about Alf. "Do you have a sweetheart with blue eyes?"

"Me, guv?" Alf looked at him, wide eyed, and Hugh thought he must've hit on some truth. He'd never seen the boy so flustered.

He cocked an eyebrow. "Or a lass that you're interested in?"

Alf blinked and seemed to regain some of his customary aplomb. "Tell you what, guv, if'n I *did* 'ave a lass I fancied, it wouldn't be because of the color of 'er *eyes*. At least not that alone."

"No?" Hugh felt his lips twitch. He really oughtn't to tease the lad. "Tits or arse?"

Alf appeared to goggle for a moment. Then he glared. "Arse. Most definitely arse. But that's not what I'm talking about."

"Then what?"

"Other things." Alf waved his arms over his head in illustration. "*Bigger* things. If she laughs and what she laughs at. If babies and little children make 'er smile. If she takes care of 'er family even when they drive 'er wild. And if she likes looking at the stars at night." The boy set his hands on his hips and glared at him. "Those things are more important in a sweetheart than the color of 'er blasted *eyes*."

Looking at the stars at night? Hugh looked at Alf a little sadly. "Why, imp, you're a romantic."

A blush lit the boy's downy cheeks. He lifted his chin. "And that's not allowed, is it? That an urchin from St Giles should have romantic dreams? Is romance only for rich coves?"

"Oh, it's *allowed*," Hugh said. "Just be sure to take care with your romantic's soul. I have the feeling Fate doesn't give a fig where you hail from or what the state of your finances when she decides to crush your dreams."

Alf opened his mouth—and then closed it and looked from him to Katherine's painting and back again. He grimaced in what looked like sympathy. "I can understand why you might feel that way, guv, but—"

"Actually, you understand very little," Hugh replied crisply. He was tired of this ridiculous conversation. "Come, the carriage must be ready by now."

He strode to the front entrance to his town house, feeling unaccountably irritable.

Alf, however, made sure to keep up, and as Hugh made to open the front door, the boy leaned toward him.

"One thing you got wrong though, guv."

"What's that?" Hugh growled.

"I'm not that partial to blue eyes." He looked amused. "I like my lasses with dark eyes."

*   *   *

SEEING LONDON THROUGH a carriage window was very different from walking the streets, Alf reflected five minutes later. She was on the edge of the fine red leather seat, peering out the glass. Strange to see the streets from *inside* a carriage. There were the sweeper boys with their brooms ready to clear the way for a penny or two for those crossing the street—and to flick muck on the clothes of those who refused to pay. Here were two ladies, arm in arm, one in a dark-red dress, the other in a blue striped skirt and a jacket. They tilted their heads together as a young officer on horseback rode by.

Alf was higher inside the carriage, the street sounds muffled by glass. Apart. Not down in the noisy, mostly messy street. Even those ladies in their lovely dresses had to rub elbows with the milkmaids and charwomen they passed.

She sat back in the seat. Little wonder the rich sometimes seemed to have trouble thinking of everyone else as people.

She glanced across the carriage at Kyle.

He sat staring out the window, lost in his own dark thoughts. Was he in mourning for his beautiful, dead wife? She wanted to keep prying, to crack him open, and find out if he was hurt inside or indifferent to that regal, gorgeous creature draped in ermine in the portrait. But that strange moment between them in the hall had passed—the man who had teased her about having a sweetheart had disappeared.

Just as well, really. He was a duke, her employer, nothing else.

Except that when she'd been wounded last night she'd fled to him. Not her nest. Not St. John. *Him*.

True, the way into St Giles had been blocked and she'd been fearful of more Scarlet Throats waiting for her there, but that hadn't been the only reason she'd sought out Kyle for safety.

Even afraid and in pain, she'd instinctively known she could trust him, a man she hardly knew.

Maybe it was that kiss.

Alf snorted under her breath. She could just hear what Ned would have said to *that* thought. *Never trust anyone, especially not a bloody toff.* It had practically been her bedtime story when they'd lain together, curled tight against the cold. *They might talk pretty, but they're only after what you can do for them, or worse—what's between your legs. Best trust no one but yourself.*

Well, and Ned, of course, but he hadn't been around for a long, long time. She'd had to learn to figure out whom to trust and whom to run away from on her own.

And she trusted Kyle.

Across from her he sighed and sat up. "We must be nearly there."

Alf glanced out the window and realized that the carriage was pulling up in front of an enormous brick building fronted by two tall towers with a clock between them.

St James's Palace.

Which was where the *King* lived.

She darted an incredulous look at Kyle, but he was already preparing to get out of the carriage and didn't seem to notice. Surely he didn't mean for *her* to go in?

But he was looking at her impatiently now.

She took a deep breath and stood, moving carefully because her leg was still giving her pain.

Kyle stepped from the carriage and turned to watch her descend, poised as if he might offer help.

She shot him a glare.

His mouth quirked up at that, and then they were walking into the royal palace. Alf tried not to stare, but really there was no help for it. There were guards all in fancy costumes and finely dressed people standing about, the ladies in ridiculously wide panniers. The guards seemed to recognize Kyle. A liveried footman hurried over, bowed, and led them through the reception hall and into another corridor, this one less crowded.

Alf looked around curiously as they walked, wondering if the King himself had trod this hall. Well, he must've, mustn't he? This was where he and the Queen lived. The palace was grand, but not nearly as wonderful as she'd imagined a king's home would be. For one thing the rooms were smaller than those she'd seen in the few aristocratic houses she'd been in, and for another they were a bit fusty and old-fashioned. Still. It was a *palace*. Princes and princesses and kings and queens slept and ate and breathed here, almost like real people.

Eventually their corridor narrowed, and it looked as if they were in the servants' quarters, of all things.

Abruptly the footman stopped before a nondescript door, opened it, and said, "The Duke of Kyle to see you, sir."

They entered a cramped, crowded office.

Alf raised her eyebrows at the stout little man getting to his feet behind the enormous desk. He was well over fifty, with a jowly face and sad, lined eyes, and he wore a gray wig with tiny little curls across the front. If this was King George II, he looked nothing like his portraits.

"Kyle!" exclaimed the man, his cornflower-blue eyes bulging a bit. "What's this I hear about you nearly being killed the other night?"

"Your spies are as quick as ever, I see, Shrugg," the duke replied drily.

Definitely not the King, then. Alf fought not to feel disappointed.

"Yes, well, I shouldn't have to rely upon whispers and

rumors for information about your health." The other man frowned, causing his face to slump into a mass of lines. "I had to tell Him over luncheon and you know how delicate His digestion is."

Kyle arched a cynical-looking eyebrow as he took one of the chairs before the desk. "I'm surprised He had any reaction at all, frankly."

Shrugg's look was chiding. "You *are* his son, Your Grace."

And that was when Alf realized that they were talking about the *King*. Stunned, she sank into the other chair before the desk, looking between the two men. She had so *many* questions, but she knew better than to interrupt this *fascinating* conversation.

"One of several and a bastard to boot," Kyle was drawling.

"An *acknowledged* bastard, Your Grace," Shrugg retorted. "And therein lies all the difference."

Kyle waved away that point as if he'd grown tired of the debate—which Alf found *very* frustrating. "The attack is why I've come to consult with you."

"Oh?"

The duke nodded. "It wasn't a footpad who happened to cross my path. I was deliberately targeted and nearly assassinated by nearly a dozen men."

Shrugg sat back in his chair and was quiet for a moment. Then, for the first time, he glanced at Alf. "Who is this?"

"My informant, Alf, from St Giles. Alf, this is Copernicus Shrugg, the King's personal secretary. Amongst other things."

Alf nodded at the old man, who was examining her closely. "'Ow d'you do?"

"You trust him?" Shrugg asked without taking his gaze from her.

"I'd not have brought him otherwise," Kyle said mildly.

Shrugg nodded and at last looked at the duke again. "You think the attack was the Lords of Chaos."

Kyle nodded once. "Yes, I do." He sat forward in his chair, his elbows on his knees as he spoke. "I was returning from a dinner at the Habsburg ambassador's residence, where I overheard a Russian spy delivering probable secrets to a Prussian—"

Shrugg interrupted with an exclamation.

Kyle waved it aside. "I'll send you a report. The day after the attack I hired Alf to find out who sent the assassins after me, and he got a description, but not a very good one."

Shrugg turned his attention to her.

Alf lifted her eyebrows. "The cove stank of rotten eggs. Maybe." She glanced at Kyle pointedly. "Might not even be the one you're looking for, guv—I told you that."

"That's it?" Shrugg looked incredulous.

"Apparently." The duke didn't seem perturbed either by Shrugg's words or by her own caveat. "But mark: he didn't have a foreign accent."

"Pish!" Shrugg threw up pudgy hands. "That's hardly damning evidence of the Lords, Your Grace."

"No, but then Alf was followed and beaten last night," Kyle said coolly.

Alf winced and cleared her throat. Both gentlemen glanced at her.

"About that," she said. "See, the Scarlet Throats—those're the roughs what tried to kill the duke 'ere," she inserted for Shrugg's benefit. "Them and me sort of 'ave a 'istory, you might say."

"A history," Kyle repeated, flat.

She nodded. "They 'ate my guts. And I'm not too fond of 'em, truth be told."

"You never told me that," Kyle said.

"'Adn't 'ad the chance, 'ave I?" she retorted. "Between being stabbed last night and breakfast this morning and gallivanting off to see the King's secretary, right nice gentleman though 'e is." She smiled angelically at Shrugg.

Who cleared his throat and appeared to stifle a smile.

"Point is, they might've 'ad a reason *other* than me asking questions about your attack to beat on me," she finished.

Kyle grunted. "Be that as it may, I still think this the work of the Lords."

"I remain not entirely convinced, Your Grace," Shrugg said, shaking his head lugubriously.

"'Oo are these Lords, exactly?" Alf asked.

Kyle answered her. "A club or society of aristocrats. They meet in secret, wear masks, and have a tattoo of a dolphin or porpoise on their person. When one shows another the tattoo the second must do whatever the first asks."

"Like what?"

"They're powerful men. They're in the government, in the church, in the military, in society. One might ask another to back a bill in Parliament or to marry his daughter or to give his son a commission in the army." He glanced at her, his black eyes grave. "The members don't know each other, apparently. And if they try to leave the Lords or if they talk about the Lords to outsiders, they're killed."

"Huh," Alf said, sitting back in her chair. "'Cepting for that killing people if'n they talk, I don't see that much difference between these Lords and most of swell society."

"What do you mean?"

She shrugged. "You're always working together, ain't you? Making deals, deciding amongst yourselves 'ow you're gonna run the rest of us. These Lords 'ave just made themselves a smaller secret club within your whole *bigger* secret club."

Shrugg frowned. "You are a very cynical young man."

Kyle held up his hand to the older man without looking at him. He was watching her intently. "I suppose in an odd way you might be correct, though I think those in government might disagree."

Shrugg snorted.

"*However*," Kyle continued, "there's another matter to consider—one much darker."

Her eyes narrowed, unease trailing up her spine. "An' what's that, guv?"

"What these Lords of Chaos do at their meetings. They call them revels." He grimaced and studied his hands, clasped between his legs. "More like drunken parties in obscure country locations. Various victims are brought in for the night. Women. Girls. Boys. Some do not leave alive." Those black eyes flicked up to hers and for a moment they were unguarded. She saw anger, sorrow, and determination in his gaze, and it took her breath away. "Do you understand?"

She said slowly, "I've lived all my life in St Giles, guv. I knows well enough what men in their cups can do to women and girls and boys."

It was why she donned a mask and motley and went hunting in the dark woods at night, after all.

To bring down the monsters.

A muscle in his jaw flexed. "Then you know why the Lords of Chaos have to be destroyed."

She stared at him a moment, transfixed. Oh, she knew why these animals must be stopped, but the very fact that *he* knew—knew and cared enough to do something about it—gave her pause. In her experience, aristocrats looked the other way or simply didn't care when the poor, the weak, the less clean were hurt and exploited.

Any more than they'd care if a beetle were trampled underfoot.

Yet Kyle did seem to truly care.

"Alf?"

She blinked. He was waiting for her answer.

So she nodded once. "Aye, 'spect I do know why these Lords need to be destroyed."

"And yet," Shrugg sighed, "we still have not established that there is any link between the attack on you, Your Grace, and the Lords. Have you learned anything new from the information you already have?"

Alf frowned. "What information's that?"

Kyle grimaced impatiently. "The Duke of Montgomery, before he sailed off to Istanbul last fall, was kind enough to leave me with a list of the names of four men he implied were members of the Lords. Nothing else, mind you, just the names. And no"—he turned to Shrugg—"I haven't been able to find anything more on them, despite keeping them under watch. They all appear to be respectable members of London society. Very lucky members of society, mind—they've all improved their fortunes in the last ten or twenty years—but there's nothing illegal that I can find."

"Why can't you just arrest them?" Alf asked.

"Because," Kyle replied, sounding as if his patience was wearing thin, "they're all aristocrats, and powerful aristocrats at that. One of them is the Earl of Exley. If I bring them in with only the say-so of *Montgomery*, of all people, it'll do nothing but cause a great scandal, and they'll be released and gone to ground before I learn anything at all."

"But if they're out there right now..." Alf bit her lip. She hated to think of these men possibly hurting children at this very moment.

"They aren't the only ones," Kyle said gently. "Remember

it's a society. There are dozens, perhaps hundreds of members. Besides," he continued, "Montgomery was kind enough to send me another letter, which I received yesterday."

He took a letter out of the pocket of his coat and passed it across the desk to Shrugg.

The other man opened it and started reading, then grunted. "He's prattling about water pipes here. Tell me the pertinent part."

Kyle nodded. "He says that the old leader of the Lords was killed last fall and to his knowledge there wasn't a successor."

Shrugg threw the letter on the desk in apparent disgust. "That doesn't mean much. I respect Montgomery's sources of information—God knows the man has more spies than I do—but he's been out of the country for over a month now."

"Yes, but he goes on to say what I've always suspected: the leader had a list of names of the members," Kyle said, tapping his finger on the letter. "Someone still has that list of names—either the new leader or simply someone keeping it safe until the new leader is chosen. If we find that list we have everyone." He sat back in his chair. "And then we destroy the bastards."

Shrugg narrowed his eyes and inhaled for a long moment, then said, "Even presuming I take your line of reasoning, how do you go about finding this list?"

"At the moment?" Kyle held out his hands. "I'm not sure. I've had men inside both the Earl of Exley's and Lord Chase's town houses. My men have looked in the obvious places for anything damning and didn't find anything. Sir Aaron Crewe and Lord Dowling have proven harder to infiltrate." Kyle shook his head. "But if I *was* attacked by the Lords instead of foreign spies, then I think my best option is to go looking for the Scarlet Throat gang. I want to know who hired them to kill me."

Alf cleared her throat. "Erm…as to that…" She took a breath and made a decision. This was more important than her fear of the Scarlet Throats. "I knows a gin 'ouse in St Giles where we might find some of the gang. I can take you there tonight."

Kyle frowned. "Why didn't you tell me this last night?"

She gave him a hard smile. "I likes to keep my sources secret, guv. They're my bread an' butter."

"I'm paying you for your information."

"And I just gave you some." She lifted her chin, swallowing. "If'n you don't want to dirty yourself, I can do the investigating just fine on my own."

But Kyle shook his head and she couldn't help the relief that flooded her—that is, until he said his next words: "No. You need to heal that leg before you go into St Giles again. You'll stay at Kyle House while I take my men tonight."

She felt her mouth drop open. "Stay abed? What do you take me for, guv? A lily-livered coward?"

"I take you for a *boy*." He stood, big and broad and cocksure. Well, he was a duke, after all, wasn't he? "One that has been hurt in my service. I'll not let it happen again. You're under my protection now. Until this matter is resolved, you'll do as I say."

IRIS WATCHED IN her dressing table mirror as Parks, her lady's maid, brushed her hair in preparation for bed. Parks had been with her for nearly two years now. She was efficient, neat, and quite taciturn. She also never pulled Iris's hair when brushing it, so Iris supposed she should be grateful. Parks might not be as fashionable as a French lady's maid, but she wasn't as expensive, either.

Which rather mattered, since James had left her a tidy but not extravagant income. Enough to live very comfortably on.

Not enough to establish an independent household. As a result she made her home with her brother, Henry, and his wife, Harriet. Fortunately, she was fond of them both, but there were small inconveniences in living in someone else's house, even a relative's. For instance, lately she'd been thinking that she'd rather like to have a small dog, just to keep her company. But of course she couldn't purchase one. Harriet loathed both dogs and cats. And sometimes Iris thought how nice it would be to paint her bedroom walls a soothing light blue. Right now they were a dark green—Harriet's favorite color.

She supposed that when she married Hugh, things would be very different. She could have a dog or even two. Redecorate the house, if she so wished. Spend without worrying over the expense at all—though she really wasn't the sort to be extravagant.

That was, *if* she married him.

Parks lifted the brush from her hair, cleaned it, and replaced it on her dressing table. "Will there be anything else, my lady?"

"No, thank you. Good night, Parks," Iris murmured.

The lady's maid curtsied and silently left the room.

Iris picked up the lit candle on her dresser and carried it to the bed. It was quite a nice bed, with emerald-green hangings and a lovely soft mattress, and now she felt guilty for even thinking unkind thoughts about living under Harriet's roof.

She set the candle on her little bedside table and climbed into bed. She didn't lie down, though. She liked to read a bit before falling asleep at night.

Iris reached over and picked up the slim red leather book lying on her bedside table—Katherine's diary. She'd been reading it for the past several nights, in bits and pieces, because of course it was hard and she often ended in tears.

But it was also lovely.

She could hear Katherine's voice when she described a new gown she was having made. Or when she wrote scathingly about a soiree where all the refreshments ran out before eleven of the clock. Or when she laughed at a gentleman she'd seen with an odd manner of snorting snuff.

It was a way of remembering her friend again.

Had it been anyone but Katherine, Iris might've hesitated to read the diary with its sometimes *very* frank details of her lovers. But Katherine had enjoyed the attention of others, loved it when both men and women stood waiting on her every word with bated breath.

She would've laughed to know that Iris was reading her diary now.

So Iris opened the book to the page where she'd left off—Katherine had just taken a new lover—and started reading.

Five minutes later Iris felt her entire body go cold at the words on the page.

The diary fell from her hands.

Chapter Six

The White Sorceress looked straight up and saw a small
spot of blue sky. She knew she would burn and follow
her husband and her four elder children soon,
but she could not bear that her youngest child
should also perish.
The Sorceress whispered a spell in the girl's ear, and as
she did so she opened her arms and a golden falcon flew
up into the sky.
Then the flames consumed the White Sorceress with a
curse upon her dying lips....
—From *The Black Prince and the Golden Falcon*

That night Hugh walked down a narrow lane in St Giles, his men at his back. He'd had to use all his persuasive skills to talk Alf into giving up the location of the nameless gin house the gang that called itself the Scarlet Throats was sometimes known to frequent. The boy was as stubborn and as headstrong as any army mule he'd ever encountered in his years of service. Hugh had been forced to put Talbot on guard duty at Alf's servants' room door for most of the day, just to make sure the boy would *stay* and rest. When they'd left, he'd assigned two footmen in Talbot's place. He hadn't trusted only one against the imp's native cunning and charm.

And that was the thing: Alf had a quick wit and the ability to make connections in trains of thought almost as well as Hugh himself. There was *potential* there. If he could but school some discipline into the boy, he might take Alf under his own command as one of his men.

But that was a consideration for later.

Right now he was on the hunt for the men who'd attacked him and Alf.

The gin house Alf had directed them to was off a small courtyard, in the cellar of a tenement.

Hugh glanced at Jenkins, Talbot, and Riley. "Ready?"

"Aye, sir," Riley said with a white-toothed grin. He had two pistols strapped across his chest and a sword at his hip, and looked like nothing so much as a pirate.

Jenkins and Talbot merely nodded.

Hugh stepped carefully down the cellar steps and opened the door to the gin house, ducking to enter.

The room was as dark as a cave and as low. Stone steps led down into a room lit only by a fire, a few flickering lanterns, and the sullen glow of smoking pipes. Hugh moved slowly, letting his eyes adjust to the dark. Men sat in hunched groups over barrels or makeshift tables made from boards and crates. A few were even slumped against the wall. Most held tin cups of gin. The place stank of smoke, urine, and alcohol.

No one looked up at their entrance, but Hugh would bet his right hand every man there had an eye on their movements.

Alf had intended to come here on his own, and the thought boggled Hugh's mind. One scrawny lad unarmed, save for his bravado and a few knives, walking into this den of danger. Probably Alf's plan had been to insinuate his way into this place, asking careful questions without raising an alarm.

Hugh had an entirely different strategy. There was no way he could come in here and not be known as an outsider.

Besides. They'd attacked and wounded Alf last night. They'd already proven that they knew he'd been asking questions about them and their attempt on Hugh. There was no need for pretense here.

And every need for bloody reprisal.

He walked deliberately through the low, smoky room, aware of Riley, Talbot, and Jenkins at his back. Heads ducked as he prowled past. By the fire, though, was a group of six men who sat unnaturally still. Two of them wore red neckcloths.

Hugh halted by the table. "I'm looking for the men who tried to kill the boy Alf last night."

The man sitting to Hugh's right had a drooping left eyelid and was one of the two wearing a red neckcloth. He leaned over slowly, hawked, and spit. A gob of spittle hit Hugh's boot.

Hugh grabbed the back of the man's head and slammed him face-first into the tabletop.

Behind him there was a shout, and one of Riley's pistols went off with a boom.

Hugh blocked a blow from the man to his left and then knocked him down, chair and all, with a fist to his jaw.

"Watch it, sir!" Talbot used one of his clubs to deflect a descending knife meant for Hugh's back.

The man holding the knife launched himself at the grenadier.

Talbot almost casually smashed him on the side of the head, laying him flat.

Hugh drew his sword and slashed at another ruffian aiming a stool at Talbot's back. Talbot grinned at the man and caught the stool, then wrested it from the ruffian's hands and broke it over his head. Talbot pivoted and kicked another man in the legs as he started to charge.

Hugh turned.

Jenkins stood straight, a razor-sharp knife in each hand. Before him was a much larger man with a thin line of blood oozing from a cut along the side of his face. He held a knife in his own hand but didn't seem entirely sure whether he wanted to engage Jenkins again. Smart man. Jenkins was proficient with his knives—both on his patients and on his enemies.

Riley was grinning and weaving like a madman, a pistol in one hand, his long knife in the other. He was fighting two toughs, and all the while he was insulting their heritage in the most filthy terms possible.

A movement near the door caught Hugh's eye. The second man with the red neckcloth was creeping toward the door.

Hugh shoved aside a table, elbowed away two men fighting, and dashed up the stairs and to the door. Outside, the small courtyard was dark, lit only by the half moon high above. He glanced around, but didn't see the Scarlet Throat. There were two narrow alleys leading from the courtyard, and several doors. Damn it! If the man got away—

A low whistle came from above.

He looked up.

The Ghost of St Giles crouched on the rooftop, and his pulse jolted at the sight. She pointed, straight-armed, at the nearest alley entrance.

Hugh grinned ferociously and ran down the alley the Ghost had indicated. Ahead he could just make out a movement in the shadows. The fleeing Scarlet Throat, it must be.

He glanced overhead.

The Ghost leaped, graceful and lithe, between buildings, and he felt a lightning bolt of something pure and wonderful in his chest, expanding like a small explosion. Something almost like joy. Here, in a stinking St Giles alley, late at night, his legs stretching, his lungs gulping icy winter air as he ran down the ruffian ahead.

He hadn't felt like this in years. The last time—

He ran out of the alley and into a courtyard. Even before Hugh could wonder which way his quarry had turned, there was another whistle, and he saw the Ghost darting over the roofs, making for a lane across the courtyard. She obviously had the Scarlet Throat still in sight.

He slid on cobblestones as he ran to the lane. Someone yelled from behind him. And then he was in another narrow passage. There was an abrupt right-angle turn, and he took it, ignoring the yowl of a cat as he raced by, and then he burst into a courtyard.

The Ghost was there.

On the ground, her half cape a black whirl as she danced with her swords, their prey cornered. Something caught his attention about her movements—something not quite right—but as he watched, she knocked aside the man's knife and placed her long sword against his throat and the thought died.

She smiled.

And he was amazed that anyone thought her a man.

Even under a half mask and wide-brimmed hat, in a man's doublet, leggings, and boots, she stood so gracefully. Pert chin tilted up, right arm thrust out straight before her, she held the deadly sword tip against the Scarlet Throat's Adam's apple. Her left arm was to the side in counterbalance, her short sword in her left hand. She was slim and small, but so quick and ruthless. A man would have to be constantly on his toes with her around.

She turned her head slightly and cocked it toward him as if to ask, *What's taking so long?*

Of course she knew he was there.

Hugh strode to stand beside her, looking at the ruffian.

The whites of the man's eyes shone in the moonlight as his gaze darted from the Ghost to Hugh.

"Who hired you to kill me?"

"I...I don't—"

The man's stutter was cut off with a small cry when the Ghost pressed her sword tip slightly into his skin. Blood began trailing down his neck.

"'E didn't give 'is name!" the man said. "Honest! 'E'd be a fool to."

"What did he look like?"

The Scarlet Throat's eyes rolled to look at the Ghost.

She jerked her chin at him, her sword pressing into his neck. Fresh blood oozed out.

The ruffian gulped. "'E were a bit shorter than you"— he nodded at Hugh—"wore a black coat and breeches and an acorn-brown waistcoat, nicely embroidered, that. Black greatcoat. White wig. Talked like a bloody duke."

"He was titled?" Hugh interrupted.

The man shrugged. "Dunno."

"What else? Did you see the color of his eyes? How old he was?"

"Don't know what color 'is eyes were." The man screwed up his face as if thinking. "He might've been thirty. Or forty."

Hugh bit back a curse. "Had you ever seen him before?"

"No."

"Bloody hell," Hugh spit. "Is there *anything* you can tell me about him?"

"Stank of rotten eggs," the Scarlet Throat said promptly.

Beside him the Ghost chuckled under her breath.

"And 'e 'ad a queer sort of mark on the back of 'is wrist," the man said. "A fish or a whale or a—"

"Dolphin," Hugh said, triumph flooding his chest.

The Scarlet Throat looked confused. "Don't rightly know what a dolphin looks like."

"Doesn't matter." Hugh looked at the Ghost. "Let him go."

The Ghost lifted her sword and the tough was running away almost before she'd cleared his neck.

Hugh watched her sheathe her swords. He touched his finger to her chin, feeling soft skin, and tipped up her face. He couldn't tell the color of her eyes in the dark and behind the ugly half mask, but he saw the glint of moonlight in their depths.

"Who are you?" he whispered, that strange wildness still in his veins.

She didn't answer.

So he did what he'd wanted to do since he'd first seen her tonight, there on the rooftops of St Giles: he bent and covered her mouth with his. Her lips were soft, so soft, and she tasted of wine and honey. He angled his head, drawing her slim body closer, sliding his tongue along her bottom lip until she opened her mouth beneath his. He dipped inside. Once. Twice. Slowly. A seduction. Because he could tell she wasn't experienced in this. And then she caught his tongue with hers, meeting him as an equal, and a groan rumbled in his chest.

She was so sweet. So *right*.

She laid her palms flat against his chest and pushed. Reluctantly he raised his head and stepped back, watching her. She stood panting, her lips parted, gleaming wet in the moonlight.

She closed her mouth, swallowed, and rose on tiptoes

against him. Fast and hot she kissed him once more, and then she was gone, slipping away into the night shadows.

Favoring her right leg ever so slightly.

Hugh narrowed his eyes as he stared after her and finally remembered when last he'd felt the wild, mad joy she provoked in him.

When he'd believed himself in love with Katherine.

ALF MADE A face as she turned over carefully in the narrow bed later that night. She hadn't pulled out the stitches fighting in St Giles, but the stab wound had bled through the bandages by the time she'd made it back to Kyle House. Her leg ached like holy hell. It probably served her right for being so pigheaded, slipping out the window and going into St Giles after Kyle had ordered her not to. But the man wasn't her master, no matter what he seemed to think. The Scarlet Throats were as much her enemies as his—maybe more so, since they'd been after her for years now. She'd wanted to be there when he'd invaded the gang's territory.

And besides, if she hadn't gone tonight, he wouldn't have kissed her again.

She closed her eyes, remembering the press of his hard lips and the thrust of his tongue. He'd been hot and demanding, tasting of the strong drink he must've had at his supper. He'd smelled of sweat from running and brawling, but it wasn't a bad smell. He was a clean man, Kyle. He was warm and big and—

A scream, shrill and high, pierced her dreamy thoughts.

Alf tumbled from the bed and was out in the hallway before she'd even considered the matter.

Another scream.

She was on the servants' floor, and a few doors opened, maids and footmen peeking out in nightclothes with lit candles.

The scream hadn't come from this floor, though.

She ran to the end of the hall and down a set of stairs to the floor below—the nursery floor—her bare feet slapping against the wooden boards. A door was open, spilling light into the hallway, and she could hear someone crying and an adult murmur.

Alf hesitated.

Should she return to bed? She'd come all this way, though, and Ned had always said curiosity was her failing.

She tiptoed down the hall and peeked inside the open door.

It was a bedroom—a child's bedroom. A banked fire was the only light. Kit was curled tight as a snail in his bed, his arms wrapped over his head. Kyle was pacing, barefoot and bareheaded and wearing only a nightshirt, before the fireplace.

He must've sprinted to get here before her.

In his arms was Peter. The little boy was weeping still as his father walked slowly from one end of the room to the other. The little boy's fist was clutching the placket of Kyle's nightshirt, pulling it open so that black curls of chest hair poked out the top.

Alf caught her breath at the sight.

Peter rubbed his small, red face against his father's big chest as he sobbed, getting the nightshirt wet with snot and tears, and yet Kyle didn't seem to mind. He simply turned at the end of his trek and paced back again. And now she could make out that he was humming, or maybe crooning, low under his breath, some sort of song. She'd never seen a man do such a thing. She'd witnessed women comforting babies and children often, of course. Women always had babes and children around them in St Giles—at their breasts or bound to their backs or slung at their sides. Women worked and walked and slept with their children close by, but men hardly ever did.

It should've made Kyle seem less manly to be doing what was considered women's work.

But it didn't.

The boy was so small in his arms, pink feet dangling and vulnerable. He looked scared and sad. Kyle's arms were big and strong and holding him gently against his broad chest.

The sight made her catch her breath. Made something inside her squeeze, deep in the pit of her belly.

She *yearned*.

Maybe to be that little boy, held so securely. Maybe to touch that broad chest and those black curls, peeping out of the man's nightshirt.

Maybe just to *be* with this man.

She must've made some sound then, for Kyle glanced up and saw her, standing there in the doorway like some beggar before a grand feast.

And if she'd been dressed as a woman, if she'd been wearing a white dress embroidered with blue and yellow posies, she might've swanned into that room. Walked right up to him and laid a hand on his shoulder, just to feel his male strength under her fingertips.

But she wasn't a woman tonight.

She was a boy.

So she did the only thing she could. She turned and fled back to her room.

HUGH WOKE LATE the next morning with an aching head and a stiff cock. He squinted at the bright sun streaming in the windows opposite his bed, cursing under his breath. He liked to rise early, but Peter's nightmare in the early hours had made that all but impossible.

Now he stretched and winced, wondering if he should call for a hot bath. Sometimes that helped to calm the pain in his temples. Or...

He closed his eyes and rubbed his right hand lazily across his chest, brushing his nipples, breathing deeply as he felt them tighten. Felt the answering pull in his sac. He flattened his hand and ran his palm down his stomach, across coarse hair to his cock, heavy and hot between his legs. He thought about the Ghost last night, standing so proud and graceful. In tight leggings and boots, her legs outlined for all to see. Her mouth had been sweet and wet beneath his, and he'd made her pant when he'd thrust his tongue between her lips. Had he made her wet in those men's clothes? Had she gone home and touched herself thinking of him? Stroked her little pussy until she arched and trembled?

He fingered the head of his cock. His foreskin was drawn back, exposing the sensitive flesh, and he thumbed across the wet slit, rubbing around it, then stroked firmly down and then up.

Thinking of her, that wild fey woman he'd met only twice.

She'd been unbound and free beneath her motley. Had her nipples been tight against the inside of her tunic? If he'd opened her tunic, spread the edges wide, would he have found her breasts pale and naked in the moonlight? Her nipples small, dark buds against white skin, waiting to be ravished?

Would she have smiled so cockily at him as he pinched her tits?

He groaned softly, spreading his legs so that he could roll his balls in his other hand. Found a good, fast pull on his cock as he thought of her, the ache building deep in his balls.

He'd've bent his head to her, taken a nipple in his mouth, and sucked on it hard. Made her squirm with the same need he had. Thrust a hand down those leggings and found her cunt. She'd be soft and wet for him. Soft and swollen. Moaning with want. He'd rip the damned leggings off and pick her up and thrust into that hot, wet—

The pain in his head burst white as his spunk overspilled his hand.

Hugh gasped, opening his eyes, staring at the ceiling blindly as two more spurts sullied his stomach and hand. His heart was thudding, his breath coming in quick pants, and his headache had receded to a dull throb.

He lay, inhaling deeply as he caught his breath.

Who was she, the Ghost of St Giles? Who had taught a woman how to fight like a man? Swords weren't inexpensive. She or someone else had bought her weapons. Had made that costume that fit her far, far too well. Did she have a lover? A husband?

He grimaced at the thought and rolled off the bed, then padded naked to the dresser. He found a cloth there and wiped his spend from his body. If she had a husband, the man was a fool to let her wander the streets of St Giles alone. To let other men fight with her.

To let other men kiss her.

The water on his dresser was cold, but Hugh had been used as a soldier to washing under less-than-luxurious conditions. He hurriedly made his ablutions and was in the process of dressing when Jenkins entered the room with a jug of steaming water.

"Morning, sir."

When not serving as an amateur physician or as part of a raiding party, Jenkins was his valet.

"Good morning," Hugh replied. "How are Talbot and Riley?"

"Talbot has a bit of a sore head, a result of having a chair smashed over his crown," Jenkins replied gravely. "Riley reports no injury at all."

"And yourself?" Hugh looked the older man in the eye.

"I am well, thank you for inquiring, sir." A trace of a smile graced Jenkins's face.

"I'm glad to hear it," Hugh replied. "Though do examine Talbot again this evening. I wouldn't want to lose him due to pride."

"Of course, sir."

Jenkins shaved Hugh as he contemplated what little they'd learned from the raid on the gin house the night before. The man who had hired his attackers was a member of the Lords of Chaos, but beyond that they had very little. Why would a man stink of rotten eggs anyway?

"There, sir," Jenkins said, wiping the last of the soap from his face.

"Thank you." Hugh nodded and shrugged on his coat before leaving Jenkins to his valeting.

He headed up the stairs to the nursery.

It had taken over an hour for Peter to fall back asleep after his nightmare. His face had been puffy from weeping, his blond hair stuck to his forehead in sweaty strands. Kit had been balled up, facing the wall in his cot, either asleep or studiously ignoring them both.

Hugh stopped at the top of the stairs on the nursery floor and sagged against the hallway wall. Sometimes it seemed as if Peter's nightmares were getting worse, that Kit's anger was growing, that the whole damned mess since Katherine's death was insurmountable and he, an army officer, leader of men, behind-the-scenes operator, and bloody *duke*, should be able to do something more for two little boys, his own *sons*.

Goddamn Katherine. Goddamn her for forcing him to make the choice to leave not only his home but the bloody country. And goddamn her for dying and devastating their sons.

Hugh pushed himself off the wall and strode to the nursery.

He could hear the boys' voices as he neared, and then another's. His footsteps slowed.

"...But I don't *like* mathematics," Kit said. "I don't see why I should have to do it."

Hugh grimaced. Both boys had a tutor, but since Katherine's death Kit had been rebelling against his studies and Peter—though he had fewer studies to begin with since he was only five—was following his lead.

"'Spect it's because your tutor's told you to." That was Alf's voice. What was he doing in the nursery of all places? And where was the blasted nursemaid?

"Do *you* have to study?"

"No, course not."

"Then I don't see why I should, either," Kit said, his voice sounding flat and final.

Hugh frowned and took a step, about to burst in and give his son a lecture, but Alf spoke instead.

"'Cause your mother loved you, didn't she." Alf's inflection sounded more like a statement than a question.

Kit answered it anyway, his voice small and sad. "Yes."

"Course she did. And your mother—'oo loved you, mind—would've wanted you to study," Alf said. "Otherwise she wouldn't 'ave got that tutor in the first place. 'Sides, you're gonna be swells when you grow up, you and Lord Peter 'ere. Fat lot of good as a duke you'll be if'n you don't know your numbers. You'll 'ave to get your butler to do your sums for you and then all the other swells will 'ave a good laugh at you and you'll end up with your face red as a beet and your tail between your legs."

Alf's blunt statement took Hugh's breath away. No one had spoken to the boys thusly since their mother had died.

"How come you don't have to study?" Peter piped up.

"'Cause my mother didn't love me," Alf said.

The nursery was so quiet Hugh could hear the boys breathing.

Finally Alf spoke again. "One day, long ago, my mother left me on a corner in St Giles. I remember she said she 'adn't the money to feed me anymore. She told me to stay there and not to run after 'er because she'd slap me 'ard if I did. So I stood on that corner and watched 'er walk away. I wasn't but five years old, more or less. Same age as Peter."

Hugh closed his eyes. *Jesus.* He was well aware that there were orphans and abandoned children in London, but the thought of someone he *knew* having lived through such loss was terrible. More, the thought of *Peter* all alone and having to survive in London—in *St Giles*—was incomprehensible. Five years of age was so young—so close to being a babe in so many ways.

Alf had been a babe. How had he lived?

"But where did you sleep?" Peter sounded anxious.

"I got lucky," the older boy replied. "I 'ad a friend by the name of Whistling Ned on account of 'ow 'e 'ad a tooth missing and 'e made a whistling sound when 'e talked."

Hugh heard a muffled giggle from one of his sons.

Alf continued, "Ned took me in with the gang 'e ran with. Fed me. Took care of me. Made sure I was warm and no one 'armed me. And in return I 'elped out with the gang's business."

"What business?" Peter wanted to know.

"Robbing 'ouses."

It sounded as if both boys gasped, and Hugh blinked.

"Robbing is a sin," Kit said, sounding serious.

"Oh, I know," Alf replied. "A very bad sin indeed. But you must remember as I was only a wee child. 'Ow was I to know it was such an evil thing, 'elping my friends and feeding my aching belly? The bigger boys would lift me up and I'd crawl in a window and unlatch a door or window for them, and then Bob's your uncle, they'd be in."

The boys were making admiring sounds at this detailed description of Alf's criminal past. Hugh might be worried at their clear hero worship were it not for the fact that he'd seen Alf's face last night, peeking in the nursery. The boy had obviously heard Peter's terrified nightmare scream and come to see if he was well.

Alf might try to hide it, but he had a soft heart under his cocky bluster.

Hugh was distracted at that moment by the nursemaid, Annie, appearing at the top of the stairs, a tray of tea in her arms.

"Oh, Your Grace." Annie stopped, looking apprehensive. No doubt she had his dismissal of the other nursemaid fresh in her mind. "I...that is, I only left the boys because that lad Alf said he'd look after them while I popped down for their tea."

Hugh sighed. Obviously he needed to tell the butler to hire a replacement nursemaid for the one he'd thrown from the house. A single nursemaid wasn't enough to mind two active boys.

He nodded. "That's fine."

Annie looked much relieved, and he entered the nursery on her heels.

Alf was sitting on the bed with the boys. They were on either side of the older lad, exactly as they had been yesterday morning when he'd found Alf telling them gory tales.

All three looked up at his entrance. Peter's blue eyes wide

and innocent and looking as if he was entirely recovered from last night, Kit's black eyes immediately going sullen and wary, and Alf's looking cocky as if he was hiding a secret.

For some reason it was the last that provoked Hugh into speech. "What are you doing here?"

"Thought I'd pay a visit to Peter and Kit 'ere. See what 'appens on the floor below me." The boy got to his feet and shot Hugh a mocking glance. "Wasn't a footman sitting outside my door this morning so I thought it was all right to come out. I can go back of course if that don't please you, guv."

"Naturally you may have the run of my house—"

Alf's eyes widened. "Oh, guv, that's right *generous* of you, truly!"

"—within *reason*." Hugh glared. "And I prefer you stay *in* the house for the time being." He glanced at the boys, who were watching their exchange avidly. "We can discuss this later."

"We certainly can," Alf muttered under his breath.

Hugh turned to his sons. "Peter. Are you feeling better this morning?"

His younger son immediately straightened. "Yes, Papa."

"And you, Kit?"

But his heir was scowling down at his toes.

Alf turned and poked the older boy in the side. "Your father's speaking to you, Kit."

Kit glanced up, blinked, and then said, "I'm well, Father."

"Good." Hugh pressed his lips together. "I'll leave you to your tea and your lessons, then."

He turned to the door. And found that Alf was by his side.

"Thought I'd come with you, if'n you don't mind." The boy smirked up at him. "'Aven't 'ad my breakfast yet and I'm right peckish."

"Ah." Hugh strode to the stairs. "Then you may join me and I'll tell you what we found at the gin house last night— though I warn you it wasn't much."

The boy shook his head. "Told you you should've taken me, guv. They weren't like to talk to toffs."

He grunted as he descended the stairs. "I've a mind that they weren't like to talk to anyone."

Alf shrugged. "Maybe so. Maybe so. But 'twas *my* information and 'twasn't fair to leave me behind."

"You made your opinion on the subject more than plain last night," Hugh replied, amused at the boy's brashness.

They made the dining room and Hugh called for tea and breakfast before he started telling Alf what had happened at the gin house—omitting mention of the Ghost of St Giles since he didn't see how her appearance figured in any way into the investigation of the Lords of Chaos.

The footmen had just finished leaving tea, eggs, fried kidneys, kippered herring, and toast when Cox the butler showed Iris in.

Hugh rose, frowning. "You're very early this morning."

Her face was white, and she didn't even seem to notice that he wasn't alone.

"Hugh," she said, her voice trembling. "Katherine's death may not have been an accident."

"What do you mean?" he asked slowly.

Iris looked up at him, and he saw her gray-blue eyes were tear filled. "I think she may have been murdered."

Chapter Seven

*The Golden Falcon flew high up into the blue sky, afraid
and grieving and confused. She flew over hills and
forests and lakes until her weary wings could hold her
small body aloft no more.
And then she plummeted from the sky and landed on
the terrace of a castle—the home of her family's enemy:
Castle Black....*
—From *The Black Prince and the Golden Falcon*

Iris halted and blinked as she realized that Hugh was not the
only one in the dining room.

But he was already advancing on her, a dark look on his
face. "What are you saying?"

She glanced out of the corner of her eye at the ragged
boy—really more of a youth—boldly staring at her over a
plate of eggs. "Perhaps we ought to discuss this in private."

"What?" He scowled as if she had suddenly lapsed into
Chinese and then followed her gaze to the boy. "This is Alf.
One of mine. You may speak in front of him. Alf, Iris Dan-
iels, Lady Jordan."

The youth nodded at her.

Hugh turned his full attention back to Iris, which was rather disconcerting, actually, what with his rough voice and intense gaze. "Now. What in hell did you mean that Katherine was *murdered*?"

"I..." Iris swallowed and pulled out a chair and sat without waiting for him to offer. Sometimes he didn't. Perhaps it was a result of his rough upbringing or his years in the army. Oh, her mind was wandering from the point! "I said she *may* have been murdered."

"Iris!"

She inhaled and closed her eyes to order her thoughts. It helped that she didn't have to see his dark eyes staring at her so...so *threateningly*, almost. "When I came to visit the boys the other day I discovered a diary under Christopher's bed—Katherine's diary. I think he must have found it and hid it. I can't imagine otherwise why it would be hidden there. I know I shouldn't've taken it, but I missed her so, and..." She opened her eyes and looked at him apologetically. "She did things that she should not have done as your wife. Things that hurt you. I feared that she might have written them in the diary."

He nodded curtly, waving an impatient hand at her delicacy.

Iris sighed. She'd never understood him. He'd not acted as she thought most husbands would on realizing they'd been cuckolded. As far as she could tell, he'd simply up and left for the Continent. Quite a cold reaction, really, considering that he and Katherine had initially married for love—and a blazing, passionate love at that.

She shook her head and continued. "Katherine did write about"—she darted a look at Alf—"*those* things."

Hugh nodded. "As I said, you may speak in front of him."

Had he no heart? No male pride?

She took a deep breath and decided to be frank. If *he* wasn't embarrassed, why should she be? "She wrote of a particular lover last summer. A man she was initially enthralled with. Katherine thought she loved him. But then, in September, she discovered a book of terrible illustrations hidden in his bedrooms. They depicted grown men with small children." She felt her face heat, but she forced herself to go on. "The men having intimate relations with the children, you understand."

Alf made some sort of movement, and his fork clattered to the table.

Hugh never even blinked, though his gaze grew savage. "What did Katherine do?"

"That's just it," Iris whispered. "In the last entry in the diary, Katherine vows to confront her lover—and to expose him to society."

And at last Hugh closed his eyes, looking pained. "Oh, Kate."

Iris felt the tears start. She'd cried late last night after she'd read the passage and realized what it meant.

Impulsively she leaned forward and covered his hand. "You understand, don't you? She must've gone to him. She was so brave. So determined in her convictions. If she thought that this man could hurt a child, she would've gone in like an avenging angel."

He nodded.

"'Ow did she die, your lady wife?" Alf asked.

Iris sniffed, straightening and fumbling for her handkerchief. It seemed so odd to have this intimate conversation in front of the boy, but if Hugh trusted him . . .

It was he who answered Alf. "She fell from her horse. She was found in Hyde Park, her neck broken, by her groom. The horse was grazing nearby. The groom said that she had told him to wait while she met someone. When she did not return after an hour, he went in search of her."

"She was never a very good rider," Iris said quietly. "And the horse was a high-strung black gelding." She smiled painfully at the memory. "She insisted on riding him because of how striking she looked."

"When I received your letter telling me how she'd died, I never questioned it," Hugh said, looking at Iris. His lips drew back from his teeth. "But if she met him alone that day—if she went in, all righteous anger and threats..."

Iris shivered. "She was so fierce and...and *wonderful*, sometimes one forgot how delicate she was. Her neck was quite swanlike." She wrapped her arms around herself, trying to chase away the image of Katherine, her beautiful neck deliberately broken. Her body left to lie on the ground like so much debris in Hyde Park.

"Did she give the name of this lover?"

Her gaze jerked up at Hugh's harsh words. His face was quite cold now. Calm, collected, and cold.

She shook her head. "She referred to him only by initials: A.C."

"Did you meet him?" he asked. "You must've seen him with Katherine at some point. At a ball or an afternoon tea, perhaps? She confided in you I know."

Iris shrugged helplessly. "She could be quite secretive, especially when she took a new lover." She felt her face heat again in embarrassment at discussing this with him. "She thought it made the affair more romantic."

He made a low impatient sound in his throat. "There was nothing else to describe him in the diary? The way he spoke or moved or what he wore?"

"Oh," she said, suddenly remembering. "There was one

thing. He had a tattoo. On his wrist. Of a dolphin, of all things. But I don't see how that . . ."

Her voice trailed away, for Alf had straightened in his seat and was staring at Hugh now. Almost as if they shared some sort of secret.

"The Lords of Chaos," the boy said. "'Er lover must've been a member!"

"That's why he killed Katherine," Hugh said grimly, staring at the boy. "And that's why he tried to kill me the other night."

"I DON'T UNDERSTAND," Lady Jordan said, but Alf wasn't paying any attention to her.

She was too busy watching Kyle, seeing his mind work behind those black eyes, those curling, almost pretty eyelashes. It was a bit like the feeling she had when flying over the rooftops. For a second she wished—oh, how she wished!—that he could see her as she truly was—as a *woman*.

But that was folly, and dangerous to boot, so she'd take what she could in this moment instead.

She leaned forward, holding his black eyes, holding his attention, all for herself.

Just her, plain Alf from St Giles. "You couldn't figure out why they'd attacked you *now*. Well, maybe one of the men you're investigating as part of the Lords of Chaos was *also* your wife's lover. Maybe 'e started sweating and worrying over why you 'ad men following 'im. Why you were so set on finding out about 'im. Maybe 'e thought *you* thought 'e 'ad something to do with poor Katherine's death."

Kyle's savage black eyes narrowed. "Sir Aaron Crewe."

Alf held his gaze. "And 'oo might 'e be, guv?"

"One of the four men on my list," he said, his beautiful lips curling with grim satisfaction.

She was smiling at him now, her heart soaring at having made this discovery with him—sharing in matching wits and putting together the pieces.

"What are you two talking about?" Lady Jordan said sharply, and Alf fell suddenly to earth.

Kyle turned his attention to her, and Alf only just kept from scowling.

She watched, a little amazed, as he told the lady about the Lords and the dolphin tattoos and tried to skip over the parts about rape and children, but Lady Jordan turned out to be surprisingly stubborn and in the end had gone bone white when he'd finished.

"Dear God," she said softly. "That such a society should exist, should operate in secret in England and none of us be aware..." She shuddered and then looked with determination at Kyle. "You must stop it, Hugh. You must."

"And so I shall," Kyle said with utter certainty. "Now think: did you ever see Sir Aaron Crewe in Katherine's company?"

"If I did I was not aware of it," Lady Jordan said. "I'm afraid I don't know the gentleman."

Kyle rose from his seat. "Crewe has a town house in London. I'll start there. You return home, Iris, and I'll send word when I have news."

"What will you do?" Lady Jordan stared at him.

"I'm going to arrest Crewe," Kyle replied impatiently.

The lady's eyes widened. "But... Hugh, darling, we have only the diary and speculation. This is hardly evidence of a man's guilt."

Kyle turned and stared down at Lady Jordan, his face a hard mask, his black eyes glittering. "Iris, I believe that a member of the Lords of Chaos murdered the mother of my sons. I'm going to arrest him and then I'm going to search his house until I find the evidence of his disgusting love for small children. With that I can blackmail him into telling me everything he knows about the Lords of Chaos. And after that? I'll make him regret ever having drawn breath in this world. Now please go home."

For a moment Alf thought Lady Jordan would refuse his instructions—she got an almost mulish look on her face. Today she was wearing pink silk, delicate and pretty, and the contrast between her ladylike appearance and her expression almost made Alf laugh aloud.

But then Lady Jordan composed herself and nodded. "Very well."

She stood and took a step toward Kyle so that now they were quite close and then...

And then she leaned forward and kissed him on the cheek. "Be careful, please."

Alf stared. Somehow she hadn't thought, hadn't *considered*, what Lady Jordan was to Kyle. She looked between them, Kyle so big and manly, Lady Jordan so delicate in that pretty pink gown.

She had to duck her head. Hide her face. For she knew it burned with jealousy. They were like two halves that, put together, made a whole.

They *fit*.

The reminder filled her with black boiling bitterness, heaving in her chest, prickling in her eyes. She was nothing. Just a guttersnipe from St Giles, dirty and stinking, without education, women's clothes, elegant ways, or the knowledge of how to flirt with a man.

Oh, it wasn't fair, it wasn't.

But then most in life wasn't, she knew that well enough from scavenging in St Giles as a child.

She'd survived that and she'd survive this.

Alf raised her head and threw back her shoulders—and only just in time, for Kyle was striding to the dining room doors.

"I'm coming with you, guv," she called.

He glanced at her over his shoulder, his face dark and irritated. "I've no need of you."

"I'm still in your employ, ain't I?" she demanded. "This here's my investigation as well."

She could tell he was about to deny her.

She smiled sweetly. "Or I can just go back to St Giles."

He swore under his breath and pointed a finger in her face. "Don't get in the way. Don't try anything that'll get you hurt."

He pivoted toward the door again before she could voice her indignant protest.

At least he was letting her come along this time. She hurried after him.

He was already snapping out orders to the haughty butler when she caught up with him.

He turned to her as she made his side. "We'll take my men to Crewe's house and I'll question him there."

"Will you take 'im before the magistrates?" Alf asked as they clattered down the staircase.

He grimaced. "It depends on what he says."

"But the diary, guv!"

"Aye, we have that," he said with satisfaction. "But it's what Katherine wrote about the illustrations of children and men that Crewe kept that are most important there. He'll not want that to get out, and I can use that fact in questioning him."

They'd made the lower level now, and she laid a hand on his arm to stay him. "But if 'e *murdered* 'er."

He turned at her touch, his black eyes stormy. "I know

well enough what the stakes are, but Iris is right: the diary is tenuous at best as evidence. We'll use it only as a last resort."

She opened her mouth to argue further, but at that moment Talbot, Jenkins, and Riley tromped into the entryway.

"Sir?" Riley tilted his head in inquiry.

"We're to Sir Aaron Crewe's town house," Kyle said. "I've information that he may be behind the attacks on me and Alf. He also might've been involved in my wife's death."

Talbot's eyes widened while the other two men exchanged grim glances.

"Yes, sir," Riley said soberly, appearing to speak for them all.

Kyle nodded curtly and led them outside to where his carriage was already waiting. Talbot took a seat beside the driver. Kyle climbed in the carriage and Alf followed with the other two men. She sat beside the duke and looked out the window as the carriage lurched into motion.

Alf glanced at Kyle out of the corner of her eye. What was he thinking? Had he known his wife had had lovers? Had he cared?

Had he loved her?

Did he love Lady Jordan?

She scowled and glanced out the window again. A woman carrying oysters in a great basket on her head bawled her wares. A beggar sat on a corner, his hand outstretched, his swollen and deformed feet in rags. Soldiers swaggered past in a group, one calling something to a pretty serving girl in a mobcap, who tossed her head at him.

Inside the carriage no one spoke. Everyone was still and tense.

Outside, London Town whirled by in constant, hurrying, yammering movement.

Alf sighed silently. What did she care if Kyle loved or

didn't love? He was like a star in the night sky above and she but a sparrow. No matter how high she might try to fly, she'd never reach him.

She told her mind this. She told her heart this. And yet she still felt a pull. He'd hunted with her in the dark woods of St Giles. He knew the thrill of the chase. He'd kissed her—*her*, not Lady Jordan—twice after their victories. He and Lady Jordan might match on the outside—their clothes, their accent, their ranks—but there was something wild that lived inside both her and Kyle.

The carriage jerked to a halt and Alf blinked, looking up. They were in front of a town house, not half as nice as Kyle's, but rich enough.

"We're here," the duke said, and looked at her. "He's dangerous. Stay close to me."

HE SHOULDN'T HAVE brought the boy, Hugh thought as he descended from his carriage. Shouldn't have let Alf wheedle his way into what very well might be a dangerous situation. But the shock of finding out that Katherine's death might not have been accidental, of *finally* having a trail to follow, had made him soft.

Well, what was done was done, and besides, they were already standing outside Crewe's town house. He shot a look at Talbot and then gave a pointed nod to Alf. The boy was still limping from his wounds, though he was trying hard to hide it.

The grenadier nodded. Good. Talbot was a smart man. He'd know to keep Alf safe.

Hugh leaped up the front steps of the white stone town house and knocked.

The door opened almost immediately to reveal a frowning butler. "Yes?"

"I'm the Duke of Kyle," Hugh said. "I wish to speak to your master at once."

"Sir Crewe hasn't yet risen, Your Grace," the butler replied in conciliatory tones. "I will inform him that you called, of course, and—"

Hugh didn't wait for the end of the sentence. He simply shoved past the man.

Inside was a small entryway and a hall that led straight back to a dark wooden staircase. Ignoring the butler's sputtered protestations, he made for the stairs. Crewe's bedroom would no doubt be on the floor above.

He took the treads two at a time, his men at his back, and when he made the upper floor nearly ran down a maid standing in the hall.

The girl squeaked in alarm.

"Where is your master's bedroom?" Hugh demanded.

"Second door on the right, sir," she said, pointing.

He was at the door in half a dozen strides. It was unlocked and he flung it open.

And then stopped short.

The curtains were still drawn, the room shadowed, but even so the hanging shape in the center was unmistakable.

Behind him the maid screamed.

"Bloody 'ell," Alf whispered beside him. "Is that Crewe?"

Almost at the same time, the maid sobbed, "Oh no, the master!"

"Guess that answers that question," Riley muttered.

Hugh crossed to the windows and drew the curtains. Sunlight immediately flooded the room. He looked up at the corpse hanging from the chandelier. The man might've once been handsome, but the face was bloated and discolored now.

In the hall the maid was weeping loudly, and he could hear other servants coming, summoned by the commotion.

Hugh jerked his chin at Talbot. "Shut the door."

The big grenadier did as he ordered.

Hugh glanced at Jenkins. "Suicide?"

The one-eyed man was pacing in a circle around the hanged man. "Certainly looks that way, doesn't it, sir?"

"What was 'e standing on?" Alf asked abruptly.

Hugh looked at the boy.

Alf gestured at the floor, and then up at the corpse. It was several feet off the ground. "Must've 'ad to stand on something to get up there, right? A chair or a stool. Then 'e would've kicked it away to 'ang. 'Cept there's nothing close enough, is there."

He was right.

The bedroom was relatively small for an aristocrat's town house, holding only an ancient curtained bed, a chest of drawers, a desk, and two chairs—both properly upright and set against the walls.

"Could he have stood on the bed?" Riley wondered.

"Not and put his head in that noose," Talbot said with finality. "Too far away."

Hugh looked between the bed and the corpse, measuring the distance with his eyes, and nodded. "Cut him down."

Riley grimaced.

Talbot simply went and got both chairs, placing one on either side of the body. He stood on one chair, and Riley climbed on the other. Riley held the body while Talbot sawed at the rope—a short but laborious process. The rope gave suddenly, making Riley grunt as the weight fell against him, but then Talbot caught it as well, and they both lowered the corpse to the floor.

Jenkins knelt to examine the body.

"'E stinks," Alf said, wrinkling his nose.

Jenkins glanced up at the boy. "He wasn't dead long

enough to stink, but you're right. He smells of rotten eggs. This is why." The corpse was wearing only breeches and a shirt and Jenkins carefully pushed back one of the sleeves. The arm underneath was smeared with a yellow paste. "He used an ointment with sulfur in it for his skin. You see? Here. And here." He pointed to where the skin was mottled red and patchy, even with the pallor of death. "He was suffering from some sort of skin affliction and used the ointment to soothe it."

Alf looked up, his brown eyes bright. "Then 'e was the one to 'ire the men what attacked you in St Giles, guv."

"It would seem so." Hugh grimaced.

So damned close. If he'd been here last night, would he have found Crewe still alive? Of course he'd not known about the connection to Katherine last night. Hadn't narrowed his suspects down to Crewe last night.

Jenkins pushed the other sleeve up, and there was the dolphin on the back of the wrist.

Hugh balled his fists, feeling his shoulders tense, feeling a headache forming. This *thing* on the floor had in all probability taken his sons' mother, had left Peter crying in the night, Kit looking at him with angry eyes. And beyond that, beyond his personal grief and thirst for revenge for a woman he'd once loved, this was the end of a once-promising trail to the Lords of Chaos.

Hugh wanted to smash his fist into the wall.

The door opened.

He pivoted to face the intruder. The man standing there was tall, thin, and pale, a walking skeleton. Of middling age, he wore his graying mouse-brown hair clubbed back, his suit a discreet dusty gray. One might mistake him for a banker or lawyer.

He was neither.

Daniel Kendrick, the Earl of Exley, was a powerful member of Parliament, a wealthy landowner, and a shrewd businessman. He was also almost impossible to investigate. As far as Hugh had been able to determine, the man led the life of a slightly boring monk.

Exley's light-blue eyes widened fractionally at the sight of him. "Your Grace. Is it true what the servants are saying? That Sir Aaron Crewe has hanged himself?"

"That is certainly what it looks like." Hugh gestured to the body on the floor.

The earl took a step forward and peered around Riley. He caught sight of the body and grimaced. "Dear God. Poor Crewe. He was in debt, but I had no idea it was so dire."

"Indeed?" Hugh drawled. "What, may I ask, are you doing here, my lord?"

Exley frowned. "I'm not sure it's any of your concern, but I was to meet with Crewe about a business matter this morning. Naturally when I found the household in a state of uproar I came up at once. And your reason for being here with so many men?" His eyes lingered on Jenkins, who had finished his examination and was rising.

Hugh waited until Exley had returned his gaze to him. "I wished to speak to Crewe."

"Ah." The earl shook his head. "Then it was simply your misfortune to find him."

"Was it?"

Exley's forehead wrinkled as if in confusion. "What else?" He sighed. "In any case, you and your entourage may go. I shall notify his solicitors and the authorities and see that his affairs are properly taken care of until such time as his heirs can arrive."

Hugh raised his eyebrows. "How very kind of you to put yourself to such trouble."

"No trouble for a friend."

Hugh stared at him a moment longer, but Exley's expression was perfectly blank. Hugh bowed curtly. "My lord."

The earl returned his bow. "Your Grace."

Hugh pivoted and exited the room. He'd hardly stepped into the hall when Alf was by his side. "Oi! Don't you want to search the room?"

Hugh shook his head. "No point. If Crewe was killed, as we suspect, then no doubt anything of use to our investigation was already taken by the murderer."

"Bloody 'ell," Alf swore under his breath.

And Hugh couldn't help but agree.

Chapter Eight

The Black Warlock's son was only a boy of twelve—too young to go to war. While his father was destroying the White Family, the Black Prince was at home studying. He happened to be in his room by the terrace window when he saw something fall upon the stones outside. And when he went to look, he found a young falcon with feathers of purest gold, wounded and afraid....
—From *The Black Prince and the Golden Falcon*

It was well past midnight that night when Alf leaped lightly down from the stable rooftop into the mews behind Kyle House. She paused in the shadows and glanced up and down the mews, but all she saw was a cat darting into the stable. She was still in her Ghost of St Giles costume, and it wouldn't do to be seen by anyone.

When darkness had fallen she'd needed to dance on roof-tops, feel the night wind at her back, find a rogue or two to bring down. Find a way to be *free*, or go insane.

After Kyle and she and his men had found Crewe's body, they'd retreated in defeat from his house. The carriage ride back had been awful. The men not talking, Kyle obviously in pain from what looked like a headache—he seemed to get them regularly, from what she could see—and she...

Well, she really didn't belong here, did she? She wasn't even the boy they all thought her—the boy *he* thought her.

So she'd gone out as the Ghost to St Giles, looking for trouble, and she'd found some right enough. Except now, hours later, even after giving a sound drubbing to a footpad trying to rob a moll, she still felt itchy and out of sorts.

The rooftops and the moon hadn't calmed her. She wasn't sure she even knew *what* she wanted anymore. To return to St Giles and her life as a boy? To stay here under Kyle's thumb, aware all the time of his broad shoulders and black, glinting eyes?

She was stuck. She couldn't *move* either way.

She went over the gate and into the gardens behind Kyle House and made her way silently up the gravel path. The house was all in darkness.

Save for a single light on the first floor, coming from a tall glass door.

Alf halted and stared, her breath, quick and light, fogging the night air. Was it he? Was he still awake at this hour? Perhaps still sitting up with an aching head? Jenkins, the quiet one-eyed man who'd sewn her up with gentle hands, had given Kyle a wineglass of something when they'd gotten back from Crewe's house. Kyle had downed the contents in one gulp—almost like medicine.

She frowned. It shouldn't matter to her if his head hurt or if he had regular headaches.

But it did.

The garden path led to a series of steps and a short walkway. She approached the lit glass door cautiously. It was the library—the same one she'd been brought to the first time she'd entered Kyle House. She peered in the room and at first it seemed deserted, and she felt a bit disappointed.

Then she saw his leg, sticking straight out from the chair before the dying fire, and her breath caught. His leg wasn't moving.

Her eyebrows rose. Was Kyle *asleep*?

She crept closer, her mask almost against the glass.

He sat in a wing chair before the hearth, a candle guttering on the table beside him. He had a book on his lap, splayed facedown, and his head was thrown back, his eyes closed, his mouth a little open.

Oh yes. *Asleep*.

She really ought to creep away again. To find the safety of her bed and go to sleep herself. It was far, *far* too dangerous to stay and risk the possibility of discovery.

But she'd always been attracted to danger.

She tried the handle of the glass door and found it unlocked. She smirked as she turned it and let herself into the room.

He didn't move as she tiptoed closer and bent over him, feeling bold. Feeling as if she were a wicked thief. She bit her lip and studied him, all unawares.

He'd taken off both wig and coat and sat in only rumpled shirtsleeves and waistcoat, his jaw shadowed by his dark stubble. Thick black eyelashes lay against his cheeks, his forehead marred by the spider legs of the stitches and the bruising around them, now turned yellowy green.

Her gaze fell to his mouth. That mouth. His plush pretty lips were parted as he slept, and she was tempted.

Oh, she was tempted.

He belonged to another, but it was night and the night was *hers*. What happened by the light of a guttering candle surely didn't count, did it? She'd never had many things, and what she'd had had mostly been stolen or scavenged.

Why not this?

She leaned a little closer and pressed her mouth to those pretty, pretty lips and inhaled his breath.

For a moment he was still beneath her, and then he moved, his hands rising slowly to grasp her arms.

She drew a little back, watching him.

His eyes opened, black and drowsy, staring into hers. He seemed entirely unsurprised to find her in his library, kissing him.

She smiled and for the first time that night felt herself settle. She placed her hands on his shoulders and straddled his lap. Knelt on the chair and bent her head to his again, opening her mouth over his, her palms on either side of his face.

The book tumbled to the floor.

She skimmed over his upper lip, feeling the odd prickle of his stubble. Caught his lower lip between her teeth.

An ember fell on the hearth.

Something sparked, and he took charge of the embrace. He opened his mouth beneath hers, angling his head, kissing her slowly, lazily, lushly, as if he had all the time in the world. She could feel her heart beating fast, could hear his breathing in the quiet room. He found the laces of her tunic and pulled at them, parting the edges. Beneath she wore a plain man's shirt, and he parted that as well. And under that?

Nothing at all, not even her bindings.

She could feel the chill of the air against the damp skin on her throat and between her breasts. He picked her up, never taking his mouth from hers, and rearranged her so that she lay across his lap, her head on one shoulder. He thrust his hand into her gaping clothes and she felt it, hot and large, against her bare breast.

She gasped into his mouth.

His palm was rough with calluses, but his touch was gentle—so gentle—as he brushed against her skin. Back and forth, lightly, teasing her nipples, until she arched under him, pushing herself into his hand.

He curled his fingers around one breast, so large that he entirely covered her, warm and heavy, and then he flicked her nipple with his thumb, sending a spark through her.

She moaned.

He bit her bottom lip, sharp and fleeting, and then licked it as he pinched her nipple.

She squirmed under him, clutching at his shoulders. She'd never done this with anyone. Never been this close to a man. It made her feel so wild, so free, and she wanted more. Wanted to tear the shirt from his body, to feel his arms and his chest, to run her hands over his bare skin as well.

She growled in her throat at the thought.

He chuckled softly.

His hand was suddenly gone from her breast, and she groaned in disappointment, but then she felt it again.

At the fall of her breeches.

Her breath caught as she felt him open the buttons one by one.

He lifted his head and watched her, saying nothing, but one eyebrow rose in question.

She inhaled and let her hands fall to her sides, a silent assent.

The corner of his mouth curled in a male smile that was not quite kind.

She kept her gaze locked with his as she felt first her breeches loosen, and then the buttons of the boys' small-clothes beneath.

His fingers slid against the skin above her curls, making her belly tremble. She felt his hand slowly move over her hair, down into that secret, warm place between her thighs.

That part that made her a woman. Not a boy.

His eyes glittered black and triumphant in the candlelight as his fingers parted her slick folds.

She gasped, her eyelids fluttering, trying to close against her will.

Holding his gaze was harder than leaping a five-story tenement. Harder than dueling three armed toughs at once.

Harder than hiding, every moment of her life, who she truly was.

But she kept her eyes open, for she was no coward. She was the Ghost of St Giles and she'd look Kyle in the eye even when he found that special nub at the top of her slit and touched it just like *that* with one of his thick fingers.

His beautiful upper lip lifted in a sneer then, but he nodded at her in approval. As if she'd passed a test of endurance. As if she'd done something brave and noble.

He bent and kissed her again, his finger working against her faster, more strongly. She lifted her hands, feeling his hair, short, but softer than she'd thought it would be. Her breath coming in gasps into his mouth. She wanted to spread her legs, but she couldn't, not really, not while still wearing the breeches. And she could feel the warmth, the wetness building in her quim.

She squirmed against his hand, moaning into his mouth.

He was going to make her...make her...

She touched his cheek, the bristles of his beard prickly under her palm, his face warm and intimate, and arched into his hand, his fingers curved through her wet flesh, possessing her, holding her as if she were his.

As if maybe he might be hers as well, impossible though that was.

And on that thought she felt the stars fall from the sky

and she flew up and up and up over rooftops, over London, maybe to the moon itself.

Oh, it was lovely.

Better even with him than when she did it herself.

She felt so warm and limp and melty, her eyes closed, her chest heaving.

Her mouth was curving into a smile.

She felt so wonderful in fact that she didn't realize he was taking the mask from her face until it was too late.

HUGH PULLED THE mask from the woman in his lap and for a moment the world tilted on its axis.

The face revealed was . . . a *boy's*. Was *Alf's*.

But he'd felt the small, perfectly tipped breasts.

The evidence of her wet *cunt* still glistened on his fingers.

He blinked and the world righted itself.

This was Alf on his lap, her sweet, round arse against his hard cock.

The delicate features re-formed—still the same as before—but now he saw the tilt of her chin, the slim little nose, the pink lips, the winged eyebrows above big brown eyes. The jaw was too fine for a boy, the neck too elegant. She was so obviously female that she could nevermore look like a male to him.

Alf was most definitely a *girl*, not a boy.

And as he knew the truth, she leaped to her feet.

She snatched the mask from his lax hand and was out the French doors while he was still rising.

"Wait!" He scrambled after her, feeling like a bull chasing a deer. "Goddamn it, wait!"

But by the time he was through the open door, the garden was deserted. He squinted into the dark night. Had she hidden herself? Surely she couldn't have disappeared so quickly?

He went out onto the terrace and called softer, trying not to frighten her, "Alf."

He could see no movement.

Then he remembered how nimbly she climbed buildings.

He whirled to scan the facade of Kyle House.

She wasn't there, either.

God*damn* it.

He went back inside the house because he simply didn't know what else to do—and then stood staring at the fire. It was tempting to dismiss the entire episode as some sort of wine-induced dream.

Except he knew bloody well it wasn't.

He could still smell her on his fingers. He brought them to his face and inhaled, closing his eyes, and his still hard cock jerked. He'd woken to her kiss, so tentative and shy, but mischievous as well. And he'd responded without thought, without hesitation, dragging her into his lap, plundering that sweet mouth, exploring those pretty little breasts. He'd never stopped to wonder *why* she had sought him out in his library, *why* she'd kissed him.

Why had she run? Was her disguise so important to her? Was her name truly Alf, or was that some sort of disguise as well?

Bloody hell, had she been playing him for a fool this entire time?

"Christ!" He thrust both hands into his shorn hair at a new realization.

How *old* was she? When he'd thought Alf a boy he'd estimated her to be no more than sixteen or seventeen. Of course if she'd truly been living in St Giles all this time then it was highly unlikely she was still an innocent, much less a virgin. Except...

Except her lips had trembled under his. She'd seemed surprised and excited when he'd touched her.

Dear God, had he just debauched a *child*?

ALF LEAPED FROM one roof to another only minutes later, catching the toe of her trailing boot on the eave. She fell hard, shingles clattering to the alley below, her hands scrabbling for purchase as she slid on the slanted roof. Her legs overshot the edge and dangled into space before she could stop her slide.

For a moment she hung there, her ribs aching, her leg throbbing, a sob catching at her throat.

Stupid, stupid idiot.

She'd well and truly buggered it this time. She could hear Ned's voice inside her head, chiding her as she grunted, painfully reaching up the roof to search for a fingerhold. There. She could feel a hole where a shingle had broken off. She dug her fingers into the wood and pulled, gasping. Flung her other arm as far as she could up the roof and grasped whatever she could, ignoring splinters cutting into her palms, and crawled like a panting, broken creature onto the safety of the roof.

She turned and lay on her back, catching her breath, her face wet with tears, and stared at the moon, gauzed over with clouds. She didn't even have her mask on—she'd shoved it inside her still-open tunic. Slowly she began buttoning her shirt and then her tunic.

Her fingers were shaking.

He'd seen her.

He knew.

No one alive knew except for St. John, and even he never discussed it with her. He'd tried a time or two, but she'd either changed the subject or left until he'd stopped trying to pry into her life and her past and why she was the way she was.

Hiding all the time.

But *Kyle*. Kyle had had his hand on her quim when he'd bared her face. He knew her as Alf and the Ghost and a woman.

She was revealed.

She didn't know what to do.

Maybe she should flee. Run back to St Giles and her hidey-hole nest. Stay away from Kyle and his black eyes and big hands.

Never let anyone know, Ned had said. *Never let them close. Never reveal yourself. Hide yourself away, Alf. Don't let anyone in to hurt you. Better to go it alone than to expose yourself to danger.*

She stood, trembling, and looked around. She wasn't even sure where her feet had taken her, but she soon realized.

She wasn't far from Saint House—St. John's home. She could . . . maybe she could ask him what to do.

She tied her mask back on her face, pointed herself in the direction of Saint House, and, moving more cautiously than she had in years, loped across the roof. The moon guided her through the cold winter night. When she was very little, Ned used to say the moon was a round, fat lady watching out for them.

Saint House came into view. It was a great old building, with two shorter wings extending from either side to form a courtyard between them. She ran and leaped to the roof of the right-hand wing. From here she could see that there was a light on in the upper floor of the main building.

The light was below the practice fencing room—where the nursery was.

Alf crouched low and tiptoed closer until she could see into the room. Perhaps one of the nursemaids was up with the baby. St. John's little girl. But when a figure crossed the lit window, it wasn't a nursemaid she saw.

It was Lady Margaret. *Megs*. That was what he called her. Her heavily pregnant form wrapped in brightly printed silk, her hair down about her shoulders, she cradled the baby in her arms and paced.

Alf caught her breath. She was so close she could see the other woman's smile as she looked down at her beautiful baby. And then St. John was there beside her. He said something. Megs looked up and he bent and kissed her over the sleeping baby, and Alf...

Alf turned away. She couldn't look anymore. It wasn't right seeing something so private, but that wasn't the reason there were fresh tears in her eyes. That wasn't the reason she blindly fled back over the rooftops.

She would never have that. Not as she was. Not dressed as a boy, not dressed as the Ghost. She had nothing and nowhere to go, did she? Not when she came right down to it. She either had to go back into St Giles and return to being Alf, with the constant threat from the Scarlet Throats and others like them, or return to Kyle.

And she couldn't do that, could she?

Except.

She'd done nothing *wrong*, had she?

She paused, leaning against a chimney, trying to think, the moon calm and serene above her. Dressing as a boy wasn't *wrong*, was it?

She wiped her nose and her eyes. Besides. She and Kyle weren't done yet—not by a long shot. They hadn't brought down the Lords of Chaos. Of course she wasn't sure that he would want to work with her anymore. But he *needed* her, he did. She was the one with the connections in St Giles. She knew how to worm out information.

And there was that kiss tonight. Maybe he wouldn't want to kiss her again—not now that he'd found out that the Ghost and Alf were one and the same—but if she didn't go back, she'd never know, would she?

She had nothing to lose. Nothing at all.

And when this was all done? Well, then she could go back to her life in St Giles. If he told no one what he knew about her, why, none would be the wiser. She'd go back to being Alf the boy.

Back to hiding day and night.

Her breathing was calmer now. Alf pushed away from the chimney and ran back the way she'd come.

Ten minutes later she swung down from the eaves of Kyle House to her room in the servants' quarters. She'd left the window open hours before when she'd first gone out as the Ghost, and now she slithered in, easy as you please.

She took off her swords and Ghost costume and hid them under the bed. Washed herself in the cold water left in a jug on the dresser. Bound her breasts and put on her boys' clothes, and then went to bed, determined not to worry about what she'd say to Kyle on the morrow.

But as she fell asleep, her mind drifted to beautiful lips curled in male satisfaction and knowing hands that had touched her as no one else ever had, and she wondered: could she ever truly return to what she'd been before?

Chapter Nine

※

*Now the Black Warlock was not a loving father. He
ruled his kingdom and his son with violence and fear.
The Black Prince had never had a pet, though he'd often
longed for one. Carefully the boy picked up the golden
falcon and took her into his room. He lined a wooden
box with a soft cloth and carefully placed the falcon
inside. Thereafter the boy secretly nursed the bird
himself, feeding her with meat from his own plate....*
—From *The Black Prince and the Golden Falcon*

Hugh woke the next morning to a hard cock and the vague
memory of dreams involving masked boys who turned into
wanton women.

He groaned and sat up, rubbing at his aching head. Jesus,
he did not need this in his life. The Ghost had been tantaliz-
ing as a nameless, faceless will-o'-the-wisp. A woman who
fought and danced and taunted him.

As Alf she was dangerous.

He didn't want to *know* her. Didn't want to care about her,
didn't want to worry about her, didn't want to long for her.

Didn't want any part of this madness. What he'd felt for

Katherine had led to ruin. What he felt with the Ghost—with *Alf*—was far too close to that same feeling.

He had other, more important, matters to mind.

He had to find another trail to follow on the Lords of Chaos.

On that thought he rose and hastily washed and dressed. He ought to call his men to gather and plot a new course, but he found his footsteps heading up the stairs instead. Something impelled him toward her room, even though he knew she wouldn't be there. Perhaps she'd left something, some indication of where he might find her. If nothing else he'd send Bell back to the One Horned Goat to ask after her.

But if she wanted to hide...

He scowled as he mounted the last flight of stairs, his head pounding harder. An urchin like her in the warren of lanes and alleys and hidden rooms of St Giles? He might never see her again.

Dear God, how had she survived all these years? She'd said that the Scarlet Throats were after her—more so now that he'd sent her on their trail. They'd already beaten her once. What would they do if they found her again? Had she run straight back into their arms?

The thought twisted something deep inside him, and he felt a shard of pain in his right eye.

He strode down the hall to her room and threw open the door, bracing himself for the emptiness.

And then stood struck dumb by the sight that met his eyes.

She was there.

Alf lay curled in her bed, fine brown hair spread around her face on the pillow, and she wasn't alone. His sons were snuggled close on either side of her. Alf wore her boy's shirt and Peter lay with his fist clutched in the loose fabric over her breast, his head butted under her chin. Kit was wrapped around her back, his arm thrown over her side. They lay so close to her there was no way she could move even in sleep, as if she were essential to their slumbers, essential to their life in some way.

He stared, relieved that she was here, puzzled as to why she'd chosen to come back. How had his children come to be here? Had they sneaked upstairs in the middle of the night? Was the nursemaid not aware of their absence?

Why?

What comfort did they find in Alf that they couldn't find in him, their father? Or even in Iris, a woman they'd known all their lives?

What had this slight, fey creature done to them all?

At that moment Alf opened her eyes, and he inhaled silently.

Her eyes were sleepy and a little dazed. Her cheeks flushed from sleep and, no doubt, the warmth of his sons, snuggled so close to her. She looked at him and seemed to become aware almost at once, her brown gaze sharpening. There was the mocking amusement he'd seen from the lad, Alf, the biting wit.

But now it was in feminine form.

She stared at him, and her soft pink lips—*God*, he'd been a blind *fool* to ever have thought that the mouth of a boy—smiled. Full and warm. Like sunshine. Like joy and hope.

The smile of a woman. Lethal as a spear to the chest.

Dangerous. *Seductive.*

He realized his headache was gone as his cock stiffened to life again. He stared at her, this boy, this woman-girl, this Ghost, this comfort to his children, this maddening enigma that caught and ensnared him when he needed his attention, his *sanity* elsewhere.

He glanced away, angry at himself and his weakness.

"Get up and meet me downstairs. We need to figure out what next to do about the Lords of Chaos."

"Right you are, guv," she whispered. Her tone sounded mocking.

But perhaps that was just his imagination.

ALF WATCHED KYLE leave the room and her smile died.

He'd said nothing at all about last night. Nothing about discovering she was a woman.

Everything was back to normal.

Why then did her heart ache? This was what she wanted, wasn't it? She could resume her life as Alf the boy. Could still wield her swords at night as the Ghost of St Giles. Could forget everything that had happened last night

Except that wasn't likely to happen, now was it?

Even if he could forget so easily, she found she could not.

She sighed and sat up.

Peter made a fretful sound and rolled against her, kicking his legs, while Kit yawned hugely.

Alf looked down at the boys fondly. "Best be up, you two."

They'd sneaked into her room in the early hours of the morning, and she'd been too tired to bother chasing them away.

"Don't wanna," said Peter.

"But you must," she said briskly. She couldn't prepare for the day until after they left. "Your nursemaid will find you gone if you're not back in your beds soon."

"Come on, Petey," Kit said, slipping from the bed. "Annie won't let us have pudding tonight for supper if she finds us gone."

The smaller boy whined, but he rolled over to his hands and knees and crawled off the bed backward and then stood unsteadily.

His blond hair stuck up all over his head and was quite adorable.

Alf smoothed it back from his face. "All right there, Peter?"

The little boy nodded sleepily. He'd been sniffling, his face wet with tears, when he'd stumbled into her room last night, led by Kit. She hadn't said anything. Simply made room for them both, one on each side of her, and sang a little song Ned had taught her as they'd fallen back to sleep.

Peter looked up at her, his blue eyes big. "Will you come to visit us later?"

She winked at him. "Course."

"And sing the moon song again?" he asked anxiously.

She had a sudden urge to kiss him—but that wouldn't be quite right for Alf the boy. Instead she smiled. "Aye, I will."

"Come *on*, Peter!" Kit called by the door.

Peter ran to him. "Don't forget," he called to Alf before both boys disappeared.

Alf sighed. She missed Hannah. She hadn't been able to visit the little girl while she'd been at Kyle House. She wished she could somehow bring Hannah and Mary Hope here. See Peter and Kit and the girls all together, perhaps playing in the nursery. She smiled a little sadly. If that ever happened Peter and Hannah would quarrel over who was in charge.

She shook her head fiercely. Wishes wouldn't accomplish anything.

She got up and set about getting herself ready for the day. First she checked her stitches—they were reddened, but still in place—and then she swiftly washed herself before dressing again.

Half an hour later she started down the stairs.

All the servants were gone from this floor by this time of the day, of course, already about their duties long before the sun rose. It made her glad she wasn't in service, for it had always seemed a hard, thankless job, working for the swells.

She meant to turn toward the kitchens, to see if she could find a bit of bread and tea to break her fast, but as she made the first floor she heard men yelling.

And truth be told, she'd ever had a curious turn of mind.

So she crept along the grand hallway toward Kyle's library, where she'd kissed him last night.

Where he'd put his hot hands on her body so frankly, as if he had every right, and reminded her what she was beneath her layers of disguise.

As she neared she could hear what the yelling was about.

"Your own flesh and blood!" one man was saying in a working man's London accent. "We're only asking for what your ma would've wanted you to give us were she still alive."

"Now don't bellow so at 'Is Grace," another voice said, this one slower and with a cringing tone to it. "'E's a good lad, 'e is. Won't let 'is poor old Uncle Jack starve without roof nor food for the winter, will 'e?"

"I've given both you and my cousins ample funds in the past year, Uncle," Kyle replied in a clipped voice.

"Do you see, Da?" the first voice scoffed. "'E's forgotten where 'is ma came from. I'll not grovel for pennies thrown in the muck."

A burly man with black hair and wide shoulders burst from the library, nearly knocking Alf down as he brushed roughly past her.

Alf stared after him. The man's gait and size reminded her of Kyle... save for the fact that he was dressed in worn brown breeches and coat and a wide-brimmed black hat.

She turned back to the library door and peered inside.

Kyle was standing by the fireplace in a white wig. He wore dark-blue breeches and coat over a dove-gray waistcoat, his shirt a snowy white. In front of him was a gray-haired man, almost as tall as he, but standing with his shoulders bowed, his head submissively bent. Beside the older man was another black-haired man, as large as the one who'd brushed past her in the hallway. He was staring rather vacantly into the fireplace, a carved dog clutched in both hands.

The older man leaned closer to Kyle. "I'm that sorry, Your Grace, that sorry indeed. You know Thaddeus 'as a temper on 'im and 'e's right proud—prouder than a butcher should be, truth be told. But if'n you could just see yer way to providing me and the boys with a *small* loan—a pound or two only. Why, I'd be that grateful. Just enough to patch the roof on the shop." He ducked his head again, his eyes a tiny bit too innocent as they swept the room. "Why, you'd hardly miss it, rich as you are."

There was a short silence, and then Alf saw Kyle's gaze move to the big, silent man. "How are you, Billy?"

Billy smiled at his name and lifted his toy without meeting Kyle's eyes. "Dog."

Kyle stared a moment longer at him and then glanced back at his uncle. "He seems well fed at least."

The older man straightened, looking indignant. "Of course 'e's well fed. Clothed well, too. 'E's my son."

Kyle nodded. "I'll make you a gift of one hundred pounds to put a new roof on the shop and to do whatever else you might need."

Alf inhaled. A hundred pounds was a lot of money—a fortune for people like her.

For people like these relatives of Kyle's.

But Kyle was already shaking his uncle's hand while the older man thanked him profusely.

Kyle turned toward his fireplace as his uncle went to the door. She wasn't surprised that the gray-haired man hurried away with Billy as soon as he could, now that he'd gotten what he'd come for.

That left her standing in the doorway, staring at Kyle with her lips pursed.

He was gazing into the flames, his face expressionless now. "Have you eaten yet?"

He must be aware that she'd overheard at least the last part of the conversation.

"How did you become a duke?" she asked.

He looked up at that, surprised. "I thought you knew. I'm the son of the King."

"Oh, I understand that," she said softly as she entered the library, "but 'oo was your mother?"

He chuckled.

She raised her eyebrows.

He shook his head. "I'm sorry. You're such a strange little thing. You seem to know so much, and then you tell me you don't know who my mother was when I thought all of London knew—certainly those who read the scandal sheets."

"You've caught me out, then, guv," she said. "I don't read 'em."

"Don't you?" he cocked his head, examining her as if he truly did think her a strange little thing. What did he mean by that anyway? Was it because she dressed as a boy? She supposed that would seem odd to such as he. Still, she couldn't help a twinge of hurt at the comment. "Do you know how to read?"

"Of course," she said, feeling vaguely insulted. "I couldn't do my work otherwise—a lot of it is in notes and letters."

"I'd like to know how you learned someday." He nodded. "As to your question: my mother was an actress, born into a family of butchers, as you heard. Her name was Judith Dwyer. She caught the eye of His Majesty, and I was born as a result."

She frowned. "But 'ow ... that is, 'ow are you a duke?"

"Ah." He shrugged. "The King formally acknowledged me, created the title the Duke of Kyle, and granted it to me along with quite a lot of land and money. I was given tutors and sent to an expensive school. Brought up to be a duke, in fact." His lips twisted. "Such is the way aristocrats are made. Of course my mother never changed. Her accent was very similar to yours when she was tired or forgetful." He smiled humorlessly. "My uncle and cousin have followed the family trade. She ran away at twelve and joined a theater. Apparently she was an accomplished actress, though I doubt that was why she caught the King's eye. She was also, unfortunately, very beautiful. My mother never had another lover after the King—though many offered. It seems she made the rather naive mistake of falling in love with him. So while I benefited from her liaison, she, *she* was crushed." He glanced up at her, his black eyes pained. "She died when I was seventeen. Of a fever. I was away at school."

"I'm sorry," she whispered.

"Why should you be?" he asked, his beautiful mouth twisting down. "It happened years ago. Besides, I have the title, the lands, the money. Is that not a fair exchange for a woman's affections?"

She didn't dare answer that. "And the men who just left?"

"Her brother and his sons," he replied. "I only see them when they want money."

"You shouldn't give in to beggars," she said abruptly, her voice sounding loud in the quiet library. "They'll just be back for more."

He turned, looking at her curiously. "I thought you'd be sympathetic to their cause. I have a lot of money and they do not. And they *are* my blood relations."

She lifted her chin, her eyes narrowed, her words heated, though she wasn't entirely sure why. "Why should I sympathize with those men? I don't know them. Besides, it's the way of the world that some are born with money and some are not. Their pleading and your guilt won't change that. You could give all your money to them, bit by bit, and they'd not be satisfied until they'd 'ad your last penny."

His eyebrows rose. "Then you don't think I should help those in need?"

She shook her head, her lips curving at the clear trap. "Didn't say that, guv. 'Elp all you want. But keep your eyes open to those 'oo will drain you dry and walk away without a second thought. They don't deserve your pity or 'elp, no matter their blood or your money."

For a moment his black eyes watched her without expression, and then he said, "You're very cynical for one so young, Alf."

"I'm not cynical, I'm *practical*." She frowned, feeling insulted. "And 'ow old do you 'ave to be to become cynical in your world anyway, guv? I'm one and twenty. In my world that's plenty." She looked him in the eye. "I was born and bred in St Giles, after all. Comes with the air we breathe there."

"I suppose, then," he said slowly, his voice deepening, "that the wonder is that you have a spark of innocence about you at all."

Her breath caught as he held her gaze. She'd been innocent last night before he'd touched her. Had he known? Was that what he was talking about now?

He took a step toward her, and she was poised, waiting. He looked every inch the duke today—despite the story of his mother's origins. He was dark and imposing, his black eyes heavy lidded, and she wanted...she wanted...

The air moved behind her, and Alf turned to see Lady Jordan in the hallway, peering into the library.

Looking between her and Kyle with a tiny line knit into her brow.

"Well?" Lady Jordan said. "What happened with Sir Aaron?"

"SIR AARON CREWE is dead," Hugh said, and for a moment Iris actually felt her heart freeze in horror.

Her hand covered her mouth as she stared at him. He looked very stern and unapproachable standing before the fire in his library. And once again he was with that odd lad, Alf. "You didn't..."

"No," he snapped. "He was dead when we found him at his house."

"'Ung 'imself, 'e did," Alf elaborated, belatedly adding, "my lady," when Iris looked at him, wide eyed. "At least that's what it was meant to look like."

"My God." She glanced back at Hugh. "What does he mean?"

Hugh sighed as if her questions—perhaps her mere presence—was an imposition, and for a moment she was hurt.

Then she drew herself up. Katherine had been her most intimate friend from childhood. She'd loved Katherine— more than anyone in this room. Certainly more than Hugh had at the end. She owed it to Katherine to make sure that her death was properly investigated.

So she looked Hugh Fitzroy, the Duke of Kyle in the eye and said, "*Tell me.*"

"Come," he said. "Let us go into the red sitting room where you can be more comfortable, and I'll have tea sent in."

He held out his arm to her and escorted her to the sitting room down the hall, and Alf followed.

The boy always seemed to be about these days.

The red sitting room had been Katherine's favorite place to take afternoon tea and gossip—when she wasn't shopping or attending salons and the like. Iris felt a pang in her chest as she entered the room with Hugh. She'd spent so many happy afternoons lazing here with Katherine.

She glanced at him, wondering if he had any idea how Katherine had spent months picking out the crimson fabric that lined the walls or that she'd changed her mind three times over the legs of the pink silk chairs she'd had specially made.

No, she thought, as he ushered her to the dark gold settee Katherine had talked about having replaced just before she'd died, he had no idea. He'd left before Katherine had decorated this room. And at the end she wouldn't be surprised if Hugh hated his wife.

He'd certainly had cause.

Iris frowned sadly.

Hugh was murmuring to a footman now, no doubt ordering the tea. Alf took a seat opposite her on one of Katherine's pink silk chairs, and Iris surreptitiously studied him. The boy was wearing an old, worn coat, much too big for him, his hair pulled back in a messy tail. He turned his head to watch Hugh as he finished with the footman and strode over. Iris caught her breath as she saw the boy's profile.

Because that *wasn't* a boy's profile.

She knew it all at once. The neck was too tender, there was no Adam's apple; the movement of Alf's hips, even her gait that had seemed oddly *off*, was explained. Oh, she was very, *very* good in her male disguise, but now that Iris could see, it was impossible to miss.

She watched as Hugh sat down in a chair next to Alf's, the both of them across from Iris.

Almost as if they were in league together.

Her eyes narrowed. Did he know of Alf's deception?

But he began speaking, and her mind was immediately diverted to other matters. "We think that Crewe was murdered."

"We?" she couldn't help asking, her voice sharper than she'd have liked.

He looked a little surprised. "I went with my men and Alf, as you know. Jenkins examined the body. There were indications that the death wasn't a suicide."

"What indications?" she asked.

He frowned, and she could tell he was trying to find a way to delicately tell her without offending her sensibilities. She was a lady, after all, and needed protecting.

Alf obviously felt no such worry. "There was no chair under Crewe where 'e was 'anging. 'E couldn't 'ave gotten strung up without someone *putting* 'im up there."

Hugh winced. "Yes. Also, Jenkins informed us later, after we'd left, that he'd observed bruising on the body—bruising that wasn't from the hanging."

She cocked her head, her mouth opening on a question just as the maids entered with the trays of tea. They'd also brought fresh scones—still hot from the oven—with butter and jam, and it was several minutes before they were done setting up everything on a low table.

She waited until the servants had closed the doors behind them before she leaned forward. "Why didn't Jenkins tell you about the bruising while you were at Crewe's house?"

Hugh scowled. "Because a friend of Crewe's, the Earl of Exley, arrived at the house before he could."

"Exley? I don't—"

"He's a member of the Lords of Chaos." Hugh shrugged. "One of the men on the list the Duke of Montgomery gave me. Perhaps it was a coincidence that he showed up so soon after Crewe's death, but I don't think so."

She blinked at that. "You think the *earl* killed him?"

"Or had him killed."

"Good Lord," she said slowly, truly shocked. "What shall you do next?"

He looked away. "I'll have to begin anew. Investigate the remaining names on the list—especially Exley."

She frowned and poured them all tea as she thought the matter over. "Can you not simply have Exley and the others arrested? After all, you know that they are members of this society."

He accepted a teacup from her. "On what charges, exactly? That his name is on a list given me by the Duke of Montgomery? That we suspect him of being part of a secret society? No one has agreed to talk about what they've seen at any of the Lords gatherings, nor about what the Lords do to influence the government. We have no witnesses. The victims of the revels—those who have survived and whom I've discovered—are far too fearful to speak, and besides, the Lords wear masks." He set the tea down abruptly, looking frustrated. "I don't think most of the members even know who the other members are."

"But some do." Alf had taken a cup of tea and was busy munching on a scone, careless of the crumbs falling to her lap. She gestured with the half-eaten pastry. "Montgomery told you so in that letter."

Iris frowned. "What letter?"

"The Duke of Montgomery has been corresponding with me," Hugh said. "Most of his letters are filled with either gossip, tall tales, or riddles, but once in a while he lets slip a real bit of information. In his last letter he said that he had heard that the Lords of Chaos kept a list of its members. If we can find that list, or one of the leaders who knows the other members, then we may be able to break the society open."

"I see." Iris sipped her tea. "So Crewe and Exley were two of the names you received from Montgomery?"

"Yes."

"And the other names?"

"Lord Chase and Viscount Dowling," he replied.

"Oh." Her eyes widened.

His brows drew together. "What is it?"

"Viscount Dowling," she said, excitement rising in her breast. "He's a business acquaintance of Henry's." She glanced at Alf. "My elder brother, Henry Radcliffe. I live with him and his wife, Harriet." She looked at Hugh again. "I've even met Lord Dowling. He often attends Harriet's dinners."

"How long have Henry and Lord Dowling known each other?" Hugh asked, his voice calm.

"Why, years, I think." She frowned, trying to remember when she'd first heard Henry mention the viscount, but shook her head in frustration. "I don't know exactly. Before my husband died, at least—Henry has socialized with Lord Dowling ever since I've lived with him."

"Over five years, then," Hugh said, his eyes half-hooded.

Her fingers clenched around the delicate handle of the teacup in her hand on a sudden terrible thought. "You don't think *Henry* is..."

"Does 'e 'ave a dolphin tattoo?" Alf asked, and Iris might've felt resentful at the interruption except that the other woman was so pragmatic.

She exhaled. "Not to my knowledge."

"Just because 'e knows this viscount don't mean your brother is one o' them, does it?" Alf asked earnestly.

Iris nodded, taking another fortifying sip of her tea. "Of course. You're right."

Hugh was tapping a finger against his knee. "Iris, do you think it possible that you could arrange a dinner with Harriet? One to which both I and Dowling were invited?"

"I could," she replied slowly. "But I think there may be a more useful way for you to meet him. We received an invitation to Lord Dowling's masquerade ball in a fortnight." She bit her lip and leaned forward, a rush of excitement in her breast at her daring thought. "Both my brother and his wife are leaving for a trip to the country tomorrow. They'll be gone for at least three weeks' time, but since the ball is masked..."

Hugh's lips slowly curved into a triumphant smile. "I could go in your brother's stead."

Chapter Ten

*When the Golden Falcon was at last well, the Black
Prince hooded her and put jesses on her legs. Tiny
jeweled bells were sewn to the jesses, and they sang
when the bird moved. The boy put on a cloak and hid the
Golden Falcon beneath it. He rode with her away from
Castle Black until they were quite alone and no prying
eyes could see them.*
*He uncovered the bird then and whispered in her ear,
"I shall call you Longing."* . . .
—From *The Black Prince and the Golden Falcon*

Hugh felt his muscles tighten as he caught the scent of the
hunt. He leaned forward in the delicate sitting room chair
and placed his elbows on his knees. "If we can get into
Dowling's house, I can search it during the ball."

"They know 'oo you are, guv," Alf said, drinking the
rest of her tea, her pretty pink lips pursed. "Don't you think
they'd notice a big bloke like yourself poking about the
'ouse?"

He narrowed his eyes at her . . . and realized: she was

the bloody *Ghost of St Giles*. She knew how to fight—he'd fought alongside her—and she made her bread by searching out information. He'd be a fool not to use her. Why the hell hadn't he thought of it sooner?

She was a huntress—*his* huntress.

He smiled and watched as her eyes widened suspiciously. "Then *you'll* do the searching. We'll take you in as our footman."

Iris's eyebrows rose nearly to her hairline. "Alf's rather short for a footman, don't you think?"

He waved the problem aside without breaking eye contact with Alf. Her big brown eyes held no fear. In fact her lips were slightly parted, her face beginning to flush. Was this how she looked when she was aroused? He felt a responsive pull, low in his gut. A need to reach for her, to draw her into his lap and ravage her mouth.

He answered Iris, but his words were spoken to Alf. "They won't be looking very closely at the footmen."

Iris had her brows knit and was peering between him and Alf. "But—"

"It's Alf or me," Hugh said as gently as he could.

The girl smiled faintly, but the blush had traveled down her soft neck. How low did it reach? he wondered. Was she wet right now, thinking of the plans they were making?

"Very well," Iris said, her voice clear and abrupt, cutting into the thick silence of the room.

Alf cleared her throat, breaking their eye contact. She glanced swiftly at Iris and away again before asking him, "'Ow do you plan to go about it?"

"Carefully." He sat back. "We'll need to discuss this, plan how to get in and out of Dowling's house—and what to do if anything goes wrong. But first we need that information on the house. Can you get it?"

"Of course."

She stood and he was reminded of how petite she was. No wonder she'd been able to pass as a boy for so many years. Both hips and breasts were slight, her frame as slim and delicate as a bird's. She spent so much time arguing with him and bluntly speaking her mind that it was easy to forget how physically *small* she was.

She might be able to fight, but in the end she was a woman.

Hugh frowned and hesitated for a moment. A gentleman certainly shouldn't even consider placing a woman in such danger. A gentleman should send her away and tell her he couldn't use her now that her sex was revealed.

But she wasn't a lady, was she? She'd grown up in the worst area of London. More, she'd been doing this work for years before he'd ever met her—and done it quite capably, too.

And besides. He wasn't the usual sort of gentleman. That was part of the reason he was good at the behind-the-scenes work the King had him do: he was willing to do whatever it took to get the job done.

Including using a deviously skilled woman as an agent.

"I'll need to know where Dowling keeps his most important papers," he told her now, having made his decision. "Is it in his bedroom? A study? We'll need to know the layout of the house as well."

"I knows what you need, never fear, guv." She gave him a far too confident smile as she sauntered to the door. "I'll start by seeing if Dowling 'as let go of any staff recently. It's the footman what's lost 'is job and is feeling ill used that's the most liable to spill the information we want."

She saluted and closed the door of the sitting room behind her, as cocky as ever.

He just caught himself before calling out to be careful as

she left. Instead he took a mouthful of tea. God, he hated the stuff.

When he looked up again, Iris was sitting straight, her hands folded calmly in her lap. "Alf is a girl, you realize."

It was a very good thing he'd already swallowed the tea. "Yes."

She raised her brows fractionally. "And yet you send her out to do such dangerous work?"

He set the tiny china cup down overly hard, avoiding breaking it only by a miracle. "I didn't know she was a girl when I hired her. Besides, it's her job. Would you take it from her?"

Iris pressed her lips together, but she didn't answer. She was an intelligent woman. She must know that other means of employment in St Giles for a female were more harrowing—and dangerous—than intelligence gathering.

She leaned forward and refilled her teacup. "Have you thought that she could simply attend the ball as a woman?"

"I . . ." He blinked, staring at her.

Actually he *hadn't* thought of Alf in a dress. She'd always been in breeches—both as the Ghost and as a boy.

Calmly she sipped her tea, eyebrows raised again. "It makes much more sense than trying to pass her off as a footman. Besides, the invitation is for a gentleman and two *ladies*."

He leaned forward, elbows on knees again. "But how can she search a room in a dress?"

She widened her eyes in a look that reminded him oddly of Alf's mockery. "How, pray, would a dress hamper her? In fact, a lady wandering the back rooms of the viscount's residence is less likely to cause suspicion than a footman. She can simply say that she's looking for the ladies' withdrawing room. Generally gentlemen don't question a lady."

"But she's *not* a lady," he said softly. "You've heard her accent."

"She's a brilliant actress," Iris said seriously. "You must admit. If she's been posing as a boy for years, she's had to be. And she's obviously intelligent and quick-witted. What makes you think she *couldn't* act like a lady if she put her mind to it?"

Could she, though? He realized suddenly that there'd been no discussion between him and Alf, no acknowledgment that she was a girl.

Wasn't that odd?

"I'm not sure," he said slowly. It felt a bit dangerous, letting this out in the open. Acknowledging what Alf truly was to the world.

Or perhaps it was simply dangerous to *him* to acknowledge that she was female. It made her more real somehow— not just a seductive Ghost he dreamed about at night. Not just a cocky boy who teased him during the day.

A woman who was *both*.

A woman who he *knew*.

Who was quick-witted and could hunt with him—he'd never in his wildest dreams conceived of such a creature. She made his heart beat fast. Freed all those wild emotions he thought he'd safely locked away when he'd left England three years ago.

The mere thought caused sweat to bead at his back.

He pushed all that to the back of his mind as Iris asked, "What do you mean?"

"I've never seen her dressed as a woman," he answered curtly.

She nodded impatiently. "Because she disguises herself as a boy." Iris paused and looked at him more closely. She'd always been an intuitive female. "That's *not* what you mean. You think she considers herself a boy?"

"No." His answer was instinctive, but he knew it was correct. After all, she'd made no effort to stop his touching her breasts or her cunny, had reveled in it, in fact. "I know she's aware she's a woman. I just have the feeling she might balk at dressing as a woman."

She stared at him oddly. "How . . . ?" She shook her head. "Never mind. You'll just have to ask her, won't you, and find out?"

Damn it, he didn't want to ask it of her. It was too much temptation for him, and he knew Alf herself wouldn't want to do it.

And at the same time a part of him—that same part he'd kept so long in shackles—yearned to see her in feminine garb. And Iris was right: Alf was the most qualified of them to search Dowling's house during the ball.

Dressed as a lady.

This was madness.

Hugh clenched his jaw. "Yes, you're right."

"Then if that's settled?" She placed her teacup on the table at his nod. "I must be going home so that I can find that invitation."

He stood as she did. "Thank you, Iris."

"There's no need for you to thank me." She shook her head. "You know that Katherine meant a great deal to me."

"I do know, but you mean a great deal to me as well. Your friendship is important to me, never forget that." He took her hands in his and raised them to his lips, kissing the back of each fondly. This was the woman he meant to make his wife. She was a good friend—both to his late wife with all her many faults—and to him. He needed to regain his balance. To remember that this was what he wanted: friendship, suitability, peaceful contentment. He straightened. "Humor me, then, if I find the need to thank you again."

She shook her head affectionately. "You're positively lethal when you decide to be charming, darling Hugh."

He smiled and held out his arm. She took it and he walked with her to the front door and watched as she climbed gracefully into her waiting carriage.

His smile died as he turned and walked back into the house.

He'd felt wholly alive last night with Alf—sight, sound, touch, and even smell heightened; he'd been nearly drunk with her in his arms. Thoughtless. Intent only on the moment.

He was a man used to being in control. To analyzing every movement, every situation. His mind was his sharpest weapon. To be thus disarmed—and so easily—by her was near frightening. He'd chased that heady lust without thought, a visceral reaction—and something he hadn't done since Katherine. The whole thing made very little sense. His late wife had been a sophisticated, elegant lady, even as a nineteen-year-old maiden. Alf hid her femininity like the most desperate of secrets. She was brash and bold, and seemed to enjoy challenging him in an almost masculine way.

The two women couldn't be more dissimilar.

Yet they provoked a very similar reaction in him: unthinking desire.

Hugh halted at the bottom of the stairs and took a deep breath.

He needed to find and defeat the Lords of Chaos with Alf's help. And when that task was completed, he would send her away—safely out of his life.

Where she could do neither one of them harm.

THAT NIGHT ALF sat on the roof of Kyle House and stared at the stars twinkling high above. There were no clouds tonight, just the moon, almost full now, and all those prickling points of light in a vast black velvet sky.

Beside her the dormer window opened, and she wrinkled her nose, hating that someone had found her special place.

Then his deep, raspy voice spoke. "Aren't you cold out here?"

She turned her head—just enough to see Kyle's profile. "Nah. Pinched one of the blankets from the bed."

"I see." He cleared his throat. "I understand from Talbot that you were able to collect information on Lord Dowling's town house."

"Aye." She'd spent the entire day talking to various contacts. "Got a map of the 'ouse, too, from a footman who used to work there."

"Well done."

His praise made warmth spread through her chest. "'Spect I'll be able to find 'is study well enough from it. That's where Dowling keeps most of 'is important papers."

"That's what I wanted to talk to you about," he said. "I want you to accompany me and Lady Jordan to the ball."

She squinted, trying to see his expression in the dark, but it was impossible. "Thought that was the plan already, guv."

"It was, but we have a slight change. I want you to go as a woman."

Her breath caught in her breast, and for a moment it seemed as if she couldn't inhale. When she was finally able to draw breath, her voice came out hoarsely. "Can't."

"Why not?"

"I…" Thoughts, feelings beat against her chest and her stomach, and she had an urge to simply jump up and fly away across the rooftops. Find a place of safety and *hide*. "Ain't ever been a woman, guv."

Her voice came out a gruff whisper, and she wondered if he could hear her.

But he did. "How long has it been?"

"What?"

"How many years have you dressed as a boy?"

She turned her head to stare back up at the stars. She swallowed. "Always."

"Your mother dressed you as a boy?"

Her lips curled inward for a moment as she pressed them together. "My ma put a shirt on me. She didn't call it a boy shirt or a girl shirt, far as I can remember, but then I was very small when she abandoned me." Sometimes if you stared at the stars long enough you could fool yourself into thinking you could touch them. "After she left me I was in a gang of boys with my friend Ned, 'oo took care of me—taught me to read later on. 'E was the one to put me in boys' breeches. To protect me. To keep me safe." She smiled, remembering the scattering of freckles on Ned's white face, the gap between his front teeth, his shrewd blue eyes. "'E was a smart one, was Ned."

"What happened to him?"

Her smile died.

"Alf?"

"'E got to making 'is money other ways when 'e grew older," she said softly. "Selling 'imself to men paid more than the gang did. 'E'd go out nights and come back in the morning to wherever we was sleeping. One morning 'e just didn't come back. I was maybe twelve by then. Old enough to take care of myself. So I did." She freed an arm from the blanket and reached her hand out to the stars, pretending to catch one. "Maybe Ned met a rich bloke to keep 'im permanently. Or maybe 'e found a better way to make 'is way in the world. 'E knew well enough that 'e could leave me and I'd get along all right. Always looking out for me, was Ned."

He made a sound, a sort of cut-off word, but then didn't say anything.

It was quiet on the rooftop for a bit, just the two of them and the stars and the moon.

She tucked her arm back in the blanket, drawing it close. "They're so far away, ain't they, the stars? But they're always there, no matter where you might be in the world. You might be miles apart from someone, maybe in a different town or city, even, but if'n they look up, they'll see the stars, just the same as you. If you think about it, it's almost as if you're never really apart, ain't it?"

He cleared his throat. "My mother used to show me the stars when I was a boy."

She turned her head toward him though she still couldn't see him. "Really?"

"Mm, yes." His voice was almost a purr, it was so soft. "She was an actress in the theater, so her hours were late. I learned to wake myself up when I heard her climbing the stairs. If she was alone, she would let me sit with her as she ate her supper, and if it was a warm night we would sit on her balcony. After she ate and had prepared herself for bed, she would douse the candles and we would look at the stars. I would lean on her shoulder and she would point to the constellations."

"Which ones?" Alf whispered. "I never learned 'em."

"Never?"

She shook her head.

He shoved the window open wider, and then his broad shoulders were squeezing through. He climbed out on the roof, walking gingerly over to where she sat.

"Careful," she couldn't help saying. "You're bigger than me, guv. You don't want to go tumbling over your own roof."

He snorted and moved behind her to sit down, his legs on either side of her.

She stiffened. She hadn't expected him to sit so close. Just last night this big man had held her in his arms. Had touched her as a man does a woman, for the first time in her life. A faint tremor went through her body, almost as if her muscles and skin were reacting to him.

As if she somehow knew him on an animal level now.

He pulled himself closer still, so that his broad chest was right up against her back, his big arms surrounding her, a thousand times warmer than any blanket, and she felt her body go all limp, leaning back against him.

She felt safe. Protected.

His right arm came around beside her head, pointing straight and a little up. "Do you see that bright star there a bit above the rooftops?"

His breath ghosted across her ear, warm and humid in the night air, and she shivered a little. "Yes?"

"That's Sirius, the Dog Star."

"Dog Star?" She wrinkled her nose at the queer name. "Why's it called that?"

"Because it's part of a larger constellation, Canis Major. That means 'large dog.' Sirius is his heart. He's running upwards, into the sky. To the left of his heart are three small stars in a triangle—his head—behind, his body made of six stars in a rough rectangle, his running legs, and his tail." He drew each line in the air with his finger.

She looked and nodded, though she really wasn't sure how a dog could be made from all those stars. It just looked like a jumble to her. But she liked his voice, so close to her ear. The heat of his body and his words, slow and confident as he taught her.

"And here," he continued. "If you look at Sirius and draw a line almost straight up, you'll see three stars in a row."

She leaned a little forward. "Where?"

"Give me your hand."

She wriggled it free from the blanket and put it in his larger hand. He molded her fingers, making her forefinger into a point and wrapping his hand solidly around hers.

"Now," he said, his cheek next to hers, so close she could feel the prickle of his stubble. "Follow your hand as I show you. From Sirius, straight up"—he moved both their hands slowly across the night sky—"to the three bright stars in a row."

"I see them," Alf whispered. "Oh, I see them!"

She felt him grin against her cheek. "That's Orion the hunter's belt. He's the dog's master. From his belt there are three smaller stars hanging down. Do you see them?"

"Yes."

"That's his dagger. Around Orion's belt are four stars in a rectangle. Here." He moved her hand as he pointed to each. "Here. Here. And here. The upper ones are his shoulders, the lower are his knees or his tunic. Do you see?"

"Mmm," she murmured. She did, but she was mostly simply listening to his voice again.

"Now, in front of him he holds his bow." He traced a curve with her hand.

If she squinted, she thought she could see that...maybe.

"And his other arm is above his head, holding the arrow."

Well, that she didn't see at all.

She smiled anyway, turning to look at him. "What 'ead?"

His face was so close that they were almost kissing. She looked at his mouth—that mouth that had claimed hers—and then up into his eyes, black as the night.

"There's another star above the body," he said without turning away. He slowly lowered their arms, though he kept her hand in his. "I suppose that might be considered his head."

Her lips curved as she whispered. "'E 'as a dagger, a bow and arrow, *and* a dog, but no bleeding 'ead?"

"Perhaps the ancients considered a man's head inconsequential," he muttered against her lips, and then he was kissing her, there on the roof, beneath the wide night sky, his arms enclosing her in heat and security. It was very nearly like flying. Like jumping into the open air, not quite sure if she'd make the leap or not, her heart beating hard and fast in her throat, thrills in her veins, her muscles quivering hard in excitement.

Alive. She felt alive when Kyle kissed her.

She raised her hand to his cheek as she opened her mouth beneath his, feeling the cool skin of his jaw and the heat of his tongue, flying, falling, sailing into air.

He drew back.

She blinked.

"I must go in," he said, and his voice was clipped and even, as if they hadn't just been kissing.

As if she hadn't just been soaring.

He stood and the cold came rushing back. "Think on what I've asked you to do, Alf."

And he left her alone on the rooftop.

For a moment she couldn't think what he'd wanted her to do, and then she remembered: he wanted her to become a woman.

She shivered.

HUGH WOKE THE next morning to the slam of his bedroom door.

"I can't do it, guv," Alf's husky voice exclaimed. "Thought on it near all night and I just can't and that's all there is to it."

Hugh yawned and opened his eyes.

Alf was dressed in her usual boys' attire and standing beside his bed. He could see from the little light peeking through the part in the still-drawn curtains that it wasn't much past dawn.

The imp was pacing back and forth, worrying her bottom lip with her teeth, apparently oblivious both to the fact that she'd woken him and to the fact that he slept in the nude.

Bloody hell.

"What can't you do?" he asked, keeping his voice calm. Even.

"Be a lady!" She threw her hands straight up in the air. "Guv, I just ain't right for it. I can't wear a dress, can't swan about in one. Can't curtsy and do all those lady things. That Lady Jordan'll 'ave to do it for you—she's a real lady, after all."

"Which is precisely why she *can't* do it."

Hugh braced his hands on the bed and levered himself up into a sitting position against the headboard. The maneuver made the sheets slip to his waist.

She stopped in midstride, only inches from the bed, her gaze fixed on his bare chest.

"Alf?" he prompted.

"Hmm?" Her eyelashes lifted as her big brown eyes looked at him, a little dazed. Had she any idea what her gaze did to him? He was already hard beneath the thin sheets— she must see it—and he was holding on to his control by the barest thread.

"Lady Jordan can't search Dowling's house," he said. "She hasn't the experience and the skills you have. She also wouldn't know what to do if she ran into trouble."

Her pink mouth crimped mutinously. "But—"

He arched an eyebrow. "Can you defend yourself, say against a footman?"

She rolled those big brown eyes, snorting. "Of course."

"Lady Jordan *can't*." In truth he didn't believe that it would come to that. A footman would have to be a fool to attack a lady at a ball. But he wanted to be prepared for all eventualities. "She doesn't know how to handle a knife. She's never been in a fight. *You* are our only choice."

She stared at him, and her fierce little face crumpled, and for the first time he saw an emotion he'd thought he'd never see there: fear. "I *can't*."

"Why?"

She shook her head mutely.

"I've seen you leap and run about the rooftops," he said. "I've seen you fight multiple armed men with swords—men who are stronger and bigger than you. *Why?* Just tell me, why can you face them without fear while the thought of wearing a dress for one night renders you speechless?"

She blinked hard and he saw actual tears in her eyes, his fierce little warrior. "I'm not..."

Perhaps he should let her go. Perhaps he should show some gentleness—*compassion*—and find some other way to search Dowling's study.

Except that he had a mission to accomplish: to bring down the Lords.

To avenge his dead wife and orphaned sons.

To stop the corruption in the heart of England.

And if the most expedient way to do that was to force a small, fierce warrior urchin to face her own fears, then by God he'd do it.

He held her fast with his gaze and demanded, "You're not *what*, Alf?"

Her pointed chin jerked up and she glared at him. "I'm not *female*. Not anymore. It's been too long. I've been a boy too long."

"My cock would beg to differ."

Her mouth dropped open. "Wha—?"

He grabbed her wrist and dragged her over the bed, and thrust her hand crudely against the sheet covering his crotch. "Do you feel me? I'm hard for you." He ground his cock up into her captive palm. "And I assure you I'm not at all interested in boys or men. Only women."

Only you, a treacherous part of his mind whispered, but he ignored it. He was doing this for a mission, just that. It had nothing to do with the two of them. With the desire to see her bloom into the woman he wanted deep in his conflicted soul.

She stared down at her hand over his cock and her fingers flexed once.

He bit back a groan, and the thing within him, the thing locked away, rattled its chains.

Her wide eyes slid to his, and she suddenly started struggling.

He let her go before she could injure herself or him.

She scrambled back, falling off the bed, and to the floor on her arse. "I can't. *I can't*."

"You *can*."

He flung aside the sheets and rose, stalking toward her, naked. He bent and picked her up by one arm, still walking, dragging her along with him, his anger out of control, his desire unleashed, and pushed her against the door.

He leaned down, shoving his face into hers, and growled, "You *can* because I need a *woman*, Alf. Not a boy, not a girl disguised as a boy. Not a vigilante Ghost. Not an urchin informant. A woman. *You*. I need you. Become the woman you already are, Alf. Do it for me."

He opened the door and pushed her out of the room before he did something he would regret later.

And then he leaned his sweating forehead against the door, his fists braced on either side.

His cock was hard and his heart beat too fast with turbulent emotion—emotion *she'd* engendered.

He slammed his fist into the door, making it shake.

He could not—*could not*—go down this road again.

Chapter Eleven

> *The Black Prince tied a long cord to the Golden Falcon's
> leg and let her go. She flew up into the air, but when she
> reached the end of the tether he whistled shrilly and she
> perforce had to return to his gauntleted arm. He fed her
> scraps of meat then and whispered words of praise in her
> ear. Again and again he did this, telling her how wonderful
> she was, how beautiful, until at last the sun began to set.
> Then he placed the bird back under his cloak and
> returned to the castle....*
> —From *The Black Prince and the Golden Falcon*

Alf landed on her arse—again—in the hall outside Kyle's
bedroom. She shuddered, feeling tears spurt from her eyes.
She couldn't.

She *couldn't.*

But Kyle had said he needed her.

He needed her to be a woman.

Something slammed against Kyle's door.

She sat up, gasping, swiping at the tears on her face with
the sleeves of her boy's coat. She didn't know how to be a
woman. How to dress. How to move. How to *be.*

She closed her eyes, wrapping her arms around her legs, remembering the jump of his big cock under her hand. Remembering his broad chest, naked and hairy, as he'd risen from his bed and stalked toward her. The angry gleam in those black, black eyes as he'd pinned her to the door and told her what he needed from her.

Oh, she wanted him, this aristocrat, this duke, this rich cove built like a prizefighter. She wanted him with every breath she drew, a painful longing inside her lungs, until it felt as if she'd break apart and shatter into tiny pieces of glass if she could not touch him.

Even for a little while.

She knew—she wasn't stupid, no, far from it, so she *knew* well enough that when he said he *needed her* it wasn't the same need she had for him. But it was a sort of need. And if that was all she could give him—a stunted, half-formed, ill-gotten shadow of the thing she carried within herself... well, she'd do it and be glad.

Alf drew in a deep, shuddering breath. Wiped her face one more time. And got up off the bloody floor.

She wasn't a coward. She'd grown up in the dark woods of St Giles. Learned how to hide as a child. Learned how to fight and defend those weaker than she as an adult.

Now maybe it was time to let herself be vulnerable once more. If that wasn't courage, she didn't know what was.

She ran down the stairs, passing the stuck-up butler, who shouted something after her. She didn't even bother giving him the finger, just kept going. No point in halting and thinking, because if she did, she might turn around and stop herself, and she couldn't do that.

She mustn't do that.

She ran out the front door and down the front steps. She

hadn't even bothered to use the servants' entrance, that was how upset she was.

It was early morning and the day was clear, but it was cold outside and the wind was blowing. She hadn't time to go back for a hat, though. She merely bundled her hands under her arms and broke into a jog along the sidewalk, dodging the other passersby. It was a good thing she knew her job so well—she'd found the address of the place she was headed days before, just as a matter of curiosity. She never knew when a bit of information would come in handy.

Ten minutes later she ran up the steps of an elegantly sedate town house and knocked.

A maid answered the door. "Yes?"

"'Ave a message for Lady Jordan," Alf said. "From 'Is Grace, the Duke of Kyle."

The housemaid raised an eyebrow. "At this hour? My lady isn't risen."

"Right important, 'e says 'tis. And I 'as to give it in person."

The maid sighed and let her in, then showed her to a receiving room.

"Wait here while I fetch my lady," the maid said, giving a suspicious glance at Alf's outfit before closing the door behind her.

Alf bit her lip and paced to the window overlooking the street. Outside, carriages were rumbling past. It was a nice room. Pink and blue fabric lined the walls. No gold, though. This wasn't a duke's house, after all. The Radcliffes were from an old aristocratic family, even though they weren't titled, not particularly rich, as far as Alf could tell. Henry Radcliffe, Lady Jordan's older brother, had married an heiress, which had improved the family's fortunes. He was a good businessman, though—or at least he'd managed not to lose his wife's dowry on bad investments, as so many aristocratic husbands seemed to do.

A china clock chimed on the mantelpiece over the fireplace, and she drummed her fingers against the windowsill. Toffs took so bloody *long* to dress in the morning.

The door opened and Lady Jordan floated in. She was wearing white again today—maybe it was a favorite color. This dress was striped—the barest contrast, white on white, running up and down the sleeves and the bodice and the skirts— and edged in white lace. It was lovely and elegant and *ladylike*.

And reminded Alf why she was here.

Alf almost hated her.

"Yes?" Lady Jordan asked, her slender brows drawing together. "The maid said you had a message from Hugh."

"No, I don't. I lied." Alf lifted her chin, staring at the lady. Staring at the woman who was everything she wasn't. "I needs your 'elp, see, 'cause I ain't really a boy. I'm a woman. And I wants to know 'ow to become a lady."

"Ah," Iris murmured.

Alf was staring at her with the most belligerent expression Iris had ever seen on another woman's face. As if the younger woman wanted to hit her. Or expected to be summarily thrown out.

She was suddenly rather glad that both Henry and Harriet had already left for the country. If there was to be some sort of contretemps, then at least Harriet wouldn't be here to hear it.

Her sister-in-law was something of a stickler for the social niceties, even at the best of times, and a possible row with a female urchin posing as a boy in the sitting room?

No, Harriet would *not* approve.

Iris cleared her throat. "Would you like some tea?"

Alf blinked and then said, sounding cautious, "Yes?"

Iris smiled. "Lovely."

She went to the door and called for a maid, ordered tea and something to eat as well, then turned back to her unexpected guest.

Alf was looking a bit cornered. It struck Iris how much courage it must have taken the girl to have come here, to a woman she hardly knew, and lay herself bare. She doubted that she had that sort of courage herself.

Once, as a girl, Iris had tried to make friends with one of the cats that lived in the stables on the country estate where she'd grown up. Weeks of trips to the stables with chicken livers provided by a sympathetic cook had resulted only in scratched arms and hisses in the end.

Now she thought she might do a little better.

"Come, won't you sit down?" She gestured to one of the dainty ice-blue chairs.

The other woman eyed the chair distrustfully but sat down with a decided thump.

Iris suppressed a wince. At least the chair hadn't cracked under the rough treatment. She sat as well, and then the maids returned with the tea—thank goodness. The next several minutes were taken up with laying out the tea things, which was a relief. When the maids finally curtsied and left, Iris was gladly occupied with the familiar task of pouring tea.

"Do you like milk?" she asked.

"And sugar," Alf said gruffly.

"Of course," Iris murmured. She handed the other woman the cup and sat back with her own tea, watching Alf from under her eyelashes.

Alf held the dish of tea between her hands. They were delicate, those hands, even with ragged nails. "Will you 'elp me, then?"

"Yes." Iris took a sip of her own tea.

It occurred to her that in doing this she might be arming her competitor for Hugh's affections—she hadn't missed how he watched Alf. Perhaps he meant to take her as his lover. Perhaps he didn't even know himself what he wanted from Alf. She glanced down into the lovely red-brown swirl of her tea. But then Iris had never really had Hugh's affection to begin with, had she? And if she hadn't, then this woman really wasn't her competitor.

Perhaps it was past time to make that clear to herself... and to Hugh.

Iris looked up and straightened her shoulders. "Yes, I will. I think we'll have to make a list, don't you? Oh, and you really must call me Iris."

She set down her dish of tea and rose to find a bit of paper and a pencil in Harriet's writing table by the window.

"Now then," she said as she sat down again. "I'll need to contact my dressmaker today if we're to have any hope at all of having a gown made in time for the ball. In the meantime you'll need to practice walking in a dress, panniers, and heels. A day dress to wear so that you become used to stays—I think one of my lady's maids will have a dress you can borrow. Dancing lessons, of course, but I think I can show you those myself. Elementary dining lessons. Comportment. Oh, how to curtsy and be introduced to someone above and below you in rank." She narrowed her eyes at Alf speculatively. "How are you at accents?"

"Do you mean speaking like a gentlewoman, my lady?" Alf asked. "I confess I have been studying the accents of the upper crust since I was but a small wayward child. You would not credit how useful a nob accent can be in my line of business."

Iris was startled into laughter. "Yes, exactly." The accent was overpronounced, a little *too* enunciated, especially on the *h*'s, but they could certainly work on it.

Alf smiled, casting her eyes down demurely. "I think I can get by."

Iris returned her grin. "I do believe you're correct, but we haven't much time. Best we start right away."

BY EVENING HUGH was in a foul mood. Alf had fled the house directly after their confrontation, and he'd had no word since that she'd returned. He should've put a damned guard on the woman. Locked her in her room until she'd calmed down. At the very least ensured she was *safe*.

Instead she was out God knew where, and it was entirely his own bloody fault.

He swore under his breath, hunching his shoulders against the chilly night wind. He was in a darkened doorway, keeping an eye on Exley's town house. The damned man didn't look as if he was going to move tonight, which meant Hugh was wasting his time.

A fact that hardly improved his mood.

Perhaps he ought to have his men out searching for Alf, as useless an endeavor as that would be. At least it would give him the feeling he was doing *something*.

Riley slipped into the doorway beside him, and only years of training kept Hugh from starting. The Irishman could move like a ghost when he wanted to.

"What do you have for me?" Hugh asked.

"Lord Chase is dead," Riley said, and blew on his cupped hands. "Found late tonight with his brains blown out. Supposedly was cleaning his fowling piece, but..." The slight man shrugged to indicate what he thought of that conclusion.

"What in hell?" Hugh murmured under his breath. Chase was one of the members of the Lords of Chaos on the list Montgomery had given him. That left only Dowling and Exley alive. "Are they killing each other?"

"Talbot thinks they might be, sir," Riley said. "He's got Bell watching the Chase house, and he's following Dyemore himself."

That got Hugh's attention. "Dyemore's gone out?"

After learning that the old Duke of Dyemore had been the last known leader of the Lords of Chaos, Hugh had investigated the new Duke of Dyemore. He'd discovered that Dyemore had landed in London only weeks before. On disembarking the duke had apparently promptly holed himself up in his town house because few had actually seen him in London. Hugh had had a man watching Dyemore for the past several days, but the duke had barely left his house.

He shook himself now and glanced back at Exley's front door, which was still quiet. "Stay here. I'll send someone to relieve you for the night. I'm going back to Kyle House to receive word from Talbot. It can't be coincidence that Dyemore has decided to finally show his face on the day Chase dies."

"Yes, sir."

He left poor Riley stamping his feet against the cold and headed into the wind. What was going on in the inner workings of the Lords? It almost seemed as if they were fighting among themselves.

The old Duke of Dyemore had died suddenly and apparently without anyone in line to succeed him in the leadership of the Lords. Perhaps there was no one at the top.

Perhaps they were battling like rats to take possession of the dung heap.

Hugh frowned and glanced across the street to make sure he wasn't being followed. He wished he could talk the matter over with Alf. She might drive him half-mad with her cheek, but she was also sharp as a tack and able to make the kinds of logical connections that made discussing strategy like riding a galloping horse: exhilarating.

Except he'd driven her away.

On that morose thought he looked up and saw the lights of his town house. He leaped up the steps and knocked, nodding to his butler as the door was opened.

"Good evening, Your Grace," Cox said, taking his hat and cloak. "Would you like supper served in the dining room?"

"Later, thank you." Hugh made for the stairs, mindful that it was close to the boys' bedtime.

He hadn't seen them since this morning right after breakfast, when he'd introduced the new nursemaid Cox had found. Peter had seemed to like the new nursemaid, a motherly older woman named Milly. He'd chattered to Hugh about Milly and his lessons for the day while Kit still kept to monosyllabic answers. Annie, their established nursemaid, had reported that Peter had slept through the previous night without any nightmares.

Hugh sighed as he made the nursery floor. It hadn't escaped his notice that the boys were improving with Alf around. If she decided to stay away because of him, would Peter's nightmares return?

His steps slowed as he neared the nursery and heard voices.

"But *why* are you not a boy?" Peter asked, sounding quite worried.

Hugh stopped dead, holding his breath.

"Because I'm a woman," Alf said.

Her voice was matter-of-fact, and Hugh closed his eyes in relief. Oh, thank God, she'd returned. She was safe and sound.

"But you were a boy before—"

"Silly!" That was Kit, his voice both scornful and a bit uncertain. "She's always been a girl. She was just *disguised* as a boy."

"But *why*?" Peter's voice was stubborn and held a hint of tears. "I don't want you to be a girl. I want you to be *Alf*."

"I am Alf," she said, her words careful and precise. "I'm always Alf. I always *have* been. I always will be. I'm just telling you that I've been wearing boys' clothes but that I'm really a woman. I didn't want you to be upset when you saw me in a dress."

"But you talk different, too," Peter objected.

"Are you a princess?" Kit asked cautiously, but with an undercurrent of excitement in his voice. "Like in a fairy tale? Were you stolen when you were a baby and *forced* to wear boys' clothes?"

"Oh!" Peter exclaimed. "A princess!"

Alf laughed. "No, I'm sorry, I'm not a princess. I'm just Alf."

"Aw," said Peter, probably voicing the disappointment of both boys.

"Then why are you telling us now?" Kit asked, still sounding suspicious.

Hugh cleared his voice and stepped into the nursery. "Because I asked Alf to do so."

They were sitting on the floor, Alf, Kit, and Peter. Alf wore her boys' clothes as usual, but something was different about her, perhaps in the way she held herself. Perhaps in the way her hair was neatly clubbed back instead of half-falling in her face. Already she looked more feminine. Peter sat in her lap and Kit was perched beside her, leaning against her side.

He caught his breath. They looked...very like a young mother with her children.

Like a family.

He had to glance away for a moment and compose himself.

"*You* made Alf into a girl?" Kit sounded accusing.

He stared at his eldest son. "I didn't *make* her into anything. I merely asked her to learn to dress as the sex she already was."

"Didn't you like her as she was?" Kit asked rather belligerently.

"Yes," he replied, looking at her. "But I like her better when she doesn't have to hide who she truly is."

"I like Alf *all* the time," Peter declared, and turned to hug her.

The woman wrapped her arms around his son and hugged him back. She watched Hugh over the blond head, though, and he couldn't help but see a challenge in those big brown eyes.

He'd asked for this. He'd pushed her to do this.

And she had.

Something inside him rose at the knowledge, at the challenge in those brown eyes. He wanted to take her, pull her from this room, prove to her that he was the male to her female.

Instead he held himself carefully rigid.

"I'm so glad," Alf was saying to Peter, smoothing his hair back from his forehead. "I like you, too." She placed a kiss on his forehead and then one on Kit's forehead as well. "And I like Kit."

"Do you like Papa?" Peter asked.

"Petey!" Kit hissed.

"What?" the younger boy asked, bewildered.

Alf smirked—the same cocky smile she'd given Hugh as a lad. It had an entirely different effect now that he knew she was a woman. "Sometimes I do."

"Really?" Kit didn't sound particularly convinced, and Hugh blinked, feeling hurt. There'd been a time when his older son used to run to him, grinning, on fat little legs, and hold his arms up, begging to be held.

But that had been before he'd abandoned the boy.

Perhaps such hurts could never truly be healed.

"Yes, really," Alf replied firmly, interrupting his dark thoughts. "Sometimes, of course, your papa is quite stern and abrupt and won't listen to me and I want to throw potatoes at him"—Peter giggled at this—"but most of the time..." She looked up at him, meeting his gaze again, her brown eyes wide and soft. "*Most* of the time, I find I quite like him."

His heart seemed to stop for a moment as he looked at her. He'd understood the huntress, the cocky boy, the wily informant, and, since the night before last, the sensual woman. All of that he'd been braced to defend himself against.

He hadn't expected simple acceptance, though.

She'd laid him bare.

Peter squirmed in her lap, breaking the spell. "I'm hungry."

She glanced down at him. "I came up to have supper with Peter and Kit." She looked back up at him, her gaze cautious. "Would you like to join us?"

He blinked. The boys were watching him, Peter expectantly, Kit with his face shuttered. He didn't usually eat with the boys—it wasn't something adults did in aristocratic households.

He inhaled. "Yes, but why not come downstairs? I'm expecting news from Talbot."

She smiled at him as Peter gave a whoop, and even Kit looked pleased.

The boys ran ahead down the hall as he held out his elbow to Alf.

She took it with a shy look, and as they followed his sons he wondered if he'd made a mistake in asking her to arm herself with skirts.

Chapter Twelve

Day after day the Black Prince brought the Golden
Falcon out to train her, always handling her gently,
always whispering words of encouragement and praise,
until one day he untied the long tether and threw her
into the air. The Golden Falcon flew high into the sky,
until she was but a dot in the blue. The boy whistled.
The bird wheeled and swooped from the sky, landing on
his arm of her own accord.
And the Black Prince smiled at her....
—From *The Black Prince and the Golden Falcon*

"*Slow*-ly," Iris said several days later as Alf was trying—unsuccessfully—to rise gracefully from a curtsy. "You must perform it as slowly and as steadily as possible. Oh, and do keep your back straight. Pretend as if you had your back against a brick wall."

They were in the red sitting room in Kyle House today for Alf's Lady Practice—as she privately called it. Most mornings she'd been practicing at Iris's house, but today Iris had wanted to see the boys, and as a result Alf had a bit of an audience for her lessons.

Spread on a low table were a steaming pot of tea, along with a pitcher of chocolate, and several plates of tempting refreshments. Peter giggled as he watched her, while Kit was more interested in his cup of chocolate.

Alf blew a lock of hair out of her eyes. She felt like a fool. She didn't like feeling the fool. "A man must've invented the curtsy. It's the most awkward thing I've ever done. I don't know how anyone can do it gracefully."

"With lots of practice," Iris said pragmatically, and took another biscuit. She, of course, was sitting on one of the settees with the boys.

There was a plate of biscuits, one of muffins, and one of sliced cake, and Alf eyed them rather longingly.

"Once more," Iris said, sounding far too cheerful.

Alf bent her knees, remembering to keep her back ramrod straight. Her stays did help in this, since she was laced so tightly it would have been a bit hard to bend at the waist in any case. The problem was sinking down without wobbling.

A snort from Peter as she began to rise alerted her to the fact that she'd failed yet again.

"Beg your pardon, my lady, but might we be of service?"

The voice was from the doorway, and Alf straightened gratefully to see that Riley, Bell, and Talbot were standing there.

She raised her eyebrows. Although she'd exchanged a few words with Kyle's men, she wasn't entirely sure what they thought of her.

Especially now that she'd suddenly transformed into a woman.

But neither Riley, Bell, nor Talbot looked as if he were laughing at her. In fact they seemed genuinely interested in helping with the proceedings.

Alf glanced at Iris.

Iris raised her brows back at her and, on receiving a

shrug from Alf, nodded. "We'd be grateful for your help, gentlemen."

Riley drifted in, followed by the boy and the larger man. Bell was blushing and having a hard time meeting Alf's eyes. She wondered in amusement if it was because she was a woman now.

"What can we do, my lady?" Riley asked.

"Do you know how to make a bow?" Iris asked.

The Irishman grinned and made a sweeping formal bow.

Iris nodded in approval. "Very good. I'm teaching Alf about introductions. Why don't you be the gentleman at a ball and Alf will be the lady?"

Riley nodded and turned to her. "Miss Alf?"

She curtsied as he bowed, and then they did it again with Iris making comments about where Alf's hand should be and to keep her chin lowered just a little longer and smile, but never smile *too* widely, and certainly not with teeth.

Teeth were apparently not ladylike.

The whole thing was more exhausting than spending the night running over rooftops and dueling footpads.

At the end of half an hour Alf finally was allowed to sit down and have a biscuit and some fresh tea. She was laughing at one of Riley's stories when she glanced up and saw Kyle standing in the doorway, watching them.

Well. Watching *her*, anyway.

She felt her face heat as she saw the glint in his black eyes.

He jerked his chin at her in a sort of command, and she said, "Excuse me," as Iris had been teaching her, and calmly got up and went to the door.

He was waiting for her in the hall.

She walked toward him, aware of her skirts brushing against her legs and of her hair, pulled back and exposing her face. "It seems like we should trade jobs, guv."

He frowned, those black eyes intent on her. "What do you mean?"

She shrugged. "Just that you're spending more time watching these days than I am."

He stepped toward her. "Oughtn't I be? I asked a lot of you."

"You asked me to put on a dress."

"You yourself said it was much more than that."

He glanced up irritably as boyish giggles came from the sitting room. It seemed to remind him that they were standing in the hall. He took her hand and pulled her without comment across the floor and into the dining room.

He closed the door behind them.

She looked up at him, this powerful man. "What do you want from me, guv?"

"I don't know," he muttered, sounding angry—whether at her or himself, she couldn't guess—and his hands pulled her against his hard body.

He bent and took her mouth, sliding his tongue against her lips until she parted them. Until she let him in with a relieved sigh. She'd missed this. Missed *him*. She'd wondered if he'd decided he was done with her.

Apparently not.

His fingers brushed over her bare neck, ticklish and sweet, even as he thrust his tongue inside her mouth again and again.

"Alf?" The call came from outside the room.

For a second more he continued to ravage her mouth as if he couldn't tear himself away from her, and then Kyle lifted his head. His lips were reddened, his eyes dark.

Carefully he tucked a lock of her hair back inside her cap. "I don't know what the hell I want from you."

"BUT WHERE DID she *go*?" Peter asked several days later with that whine particular to five-year-old boys.

The headache Hugh had woken with seemed to tighten into a knot behind his right eye. He'd thought that spending a morning with his sons in the library might help them understand each other, but he was beginning to doubt his wisdom. Thus far Peter had been petulant and Kit still hostile. Perhaps he should double the pay to their nursemaids.

"Alf has her own life," Hugh said wearily.

The truth was that he hadn't seen or heard from her in almost a week now. Part of that time he knew had been spent with Iris, learning everything she would need to know for the ball, but the rest he had no idea about. For all he knew, she was still risking her life at night as the Ghost of St Giles. He had no hold on her, did he? She could do whatever she pleased. She'd made very sure to flaunt that fact to him by slipping out of her room and past his guards whenever she wanted.

And that was all his own choice. Because after his loss of control, after he'd kissed her in the dining room despite telling himself he wasn't going to touch her again, he'd decided to avoid Alf.

Which he had.

Hugh sat in his wing chair and rubbed at his aching eye as he watched the boys on the floor before the fire. He'd been attempting to interest them in a large book of maps, but that, like all his other plans of late, seemed to have failed.

"But—" Peter had begun when his elder brother interrupted.

"Quit asking, Petey." Kit sighed, sounding far too cynical for a seven-year-old. "She's just *gone* and there's nothing we can do about it."

"Alf's not coming back?" Peter asked, wide eyed. He looked from his brother to his father, his blue eyes filling with tears.

"I'm sure—" Hugh said helplessly.

"But I want Alf to come back," the little boy whimpered.

So did he. "Come here." He bent and lifted his son to his lap, the warm weight a comfort. Hugh looked at Kit, still scowling on the floor. "You, too."

The older boy slowly got up and dragged himself over, and Hugh pulled him close as well.

He closed his eyes, laying his cheek against his angry son's dark head. At least the boy let him do that.

He sighed, remembering when Kit was born. The red, wet bundle thrust into his arms, traces of birthing blood still caught in the whorls of his tiny ears. Hugh had unwrapped the baby's swaddling against the protests of the midwives. Had traced the wrinkled armpits, touched the curling toes, wondered at the perfect penis. Placed his palm over the delicate, round belly, his fingertips curling over the baby's shoulder, and known: he loved this tiny thing. Loved him mindlessly and forever.

Paternal love didn't die simply because a boy glared at his father. It merely watched and grieved.

Hugh swallowed. His damned eye felt as if it would burst from the socket. He wondered idly if it was possible for a man to die from a headache.

Peter gave a wiggle. "Alf."

"I know." He kissed the small forehead.

"No, Alf is here, Father!" Kit exclaimed.

Hugh's head jerked up as he opened his eyes. She stood there in her boys' clothes, grinning at him, cocky as ever, a covered basket at her feet. She must've come in by the French doors again, and it occurred to him that he really ought to put a better lock on the door.

The boys scrambled from his lap and ran to her, and the sight made him breathless. He stood watching as she knelt, laughing, and they hugged her. Peter's tears had dried and Kit's anger seemed to have evaporated.

How had she worked such magic?

She glanced up over their heads, her brown eyes glowing at him. "Miss me, guv?"

He had, oh, he had. "Where have you been, Alf?"

His tone was rougher than he'd intended.

"Oh, here and there." Her smile didn't dim. "I've things to see to. Doesn't interfere with learning to be a lady."

"I know that." He cleared his throat. "What things have you seen to?"

She looked down at the boys. "I have a friend I visit sometimes. A little girl named Hannah. She lives in the Home for Unfortunate Infants and Foundling Children in St Giles."

Peter's eyes widened. "How old is she?"

"About your age." Alf brushed back his hair. "She's got red hair and a friend called Mary who's only four."

Peter's nose wrinkled. "That's a *baby*."

Alf laughed. "That's what Hannah says, too."

She had her own life, out there in St Giles. Hugh stared. Someone had taught her to use those swords. He'd never asked who.

"And did you see anyone else?" he asked abruptly. *A friend? A lover?*

"Oh, a fair number of people, guv," she said, gently mocking. "There's many who live in St Giles. But mostly I went to see Hannah and to check on my rooms."

"Ah." He realized his headache had eased. Jenkins had commented just yesterday while giving him his draught that he hadn't had to make the concoction as often when Alf was about. Hugh had near bitten the poor man's head off. "How are your lessons progressing?"

She winced. "Fairly well except for dancing. I—"

Something squeaked from inside the covered basket.

Both boys were immediately on the alert.

"What's that?" Peter crawled over to the basket and peered at it without touching. Kit came to stand watching over his brother's shoulder.

"Something I found in St Giles." Alf glanced at Hugh, her eyes mischievous, and he was immediately suspicious. "You can open it if you'd like."

Hugh's eyes narrowed. "What—?"

But he was too late. Peter had already unlatched the basket and flipped back the lid.

"Oh!" Kit said, sounding so young, so sweet—sweeter than he'd sounded since Hugh had returned from the Continent.

Both boys were crowded close to the basket, so Hugh couldn't see what was within, and Peter was making high cooing noises.

This did not sound good.

Then Kit abruptly sat down on his bottom with a struggling puppy in his arms. The animal was wriggling and licking the boy's face, and Kit...

Kit, his always-angry son, was giggling.

"Let me hold him, Kit, please, please, *please*!" Peter said impatiently, and Hugh waited for the explosion and the argument.

Instead the older boy smiled at his brother. "Sit down, then, Petey, so you don't drop her."

"Her?" Peter asked, sounding confused.

"She's a girl dog, silly," Kit replied with elder-brother wisdom, but not unkindly.

He waited until Peter was sitting next to him and then placed the puppy in his brother's lap. "Hold her around her tummy, but not too tight. Don't want to squish her."

"I won't," Peter promised fervently.

He grinned down at the puppy now gnawing on his thumb. It was a small thing, most likely some sort of terrier, with soft-looking, medium-length, caramel-colored fur, darker around the muzzle and on the back.

"What's her name?" Kit asked Alf.

"I don't know." Alf shrugged. "I thought you could figure that out for yourselves." She glanced at Hugh, a wicked gleam in her eye. "That is, if your father lets you keep her."

Oh, the little *imp*. What he wouldn't give for two minutes alone with her right now to show her what he thought of this subversion.

He cleared his throat and watched as both boys turned pleading gazes toward him. Kit's face, he noticed, had lost its previous gaiety. Why was he always the presumed wrongdoer? "You may keep the dog."

His announcement brought forth exclamations of great joy from both boys, making the dog yip.

Hugh eyed the excitable trio. "Perhaps we should take her out into the garden."

The boys were out the French doors with the puppy before he'd finished the sentence.

He sighed and levered himself out of the chair, eyeing Alf as he rose. "So you've been in St Giles all this time?"

Her cocky smile had died. "No. Part of the time I was at Iris's house at lessons. As I told you."

"I've hardly seen you," he said moodily.

"I thought that was what you wanted," she replied, her small expressive face closed. "You kissed me and then said you didn't know what to do with me. You avoided me."

"That hardly matters." He flung up a hand irritably. "I didn't know where you were."

She lifted her chin. "I didn't know I was supposed to be telling you everywhere I go, guv. You never mentioned."

"Didn't I?" he growled, taking that chin in hand.

He glanced at the windows. The boys were chasing the puppy down the graveled path. He bent and took her mouth, hard and fast and not nearly enough.

Not nearly enough.

When he raised his head again it was to breathe words across her parted lips. Words he didn't stop to think about. Words that came straight from that part of himself he'd thought he'd locked away deep inside: "I'll say it now, then. You tell me where you are and what you're doing until such time as I'm done with you, do you understand?"

"Oh, I think I understand, guv," she whispered, and though her words were a concession, her tone was not.

She turned and walked out the French doors.

Damn it.

He wished for a wild moment that she'd hit him instead. That she'd yelled and raged so he could yell and rage in return. So he could unloose everything that he held so tightly inside. Everything animal and uncivilized that wanted to simply take her and damn the consequences and all that he *knew* would be the result.

Except he wasn't an animal. He wasn't uncivilized. He was a man in control of his emotions. A man led by his mind not his cock.

But as he followed Alf out into the garden, watching the sway of her hips as she descended the steps, he wondered if he was simply fooling himself.

For he wasn't sure he'd ever be done with Alf.

A WEEK LATER Alf lifted her arms as two of Iris's lady's maids helped her into the outer robe of her gown.

They were in a guest room of Kyle House. Iris sat on a gilded chair, her own cream-and-pink skirts pooled around her, having dressed hours before. She was directing Alf's toilet, and Alf was ever so glad to have her there.

Tonight she'd either turn a bare fortnight's lessons in being a lady into success, or make a right ass out of herself.

Alf stood in the middle of the room, already dressed in silk stockings, garters, heeled shoes, linen chemise, stays, small panniers tied at her waist, and embroidered petticoats. The outer robe was a bloody gorgeous deep violety-purple silk that seemed to shimmer in the candlelight. A flat ruffle of the same material was sewn all down the edges of the front and the hem of the skirt of the outer gown.

The maids placed the V of the embroidered stomacher between the edges of the outer gown and began pinning the two together.

Alf stared at the painted molding on the ceiling. This was the hardest part—standing still while the maids worked on dressing her as if she were a prize mare at a fair. The first time she'd done it, she'd spent the entire time torn between apologizing to the poor maids for having to work on her and wanting to make a run for it.

Standing still like this while others plucked and poked at her was like having bedbugs crawling all over her skin, never knowing where they might bite.

She shivered at the thought and met Iris's eyes.

The older woman gave her an encouraging smile. "Not much longer now."

Alf nodded and firmed her lips. The stomacher was almost pinned in place. She held her arms out to the sides so a third lady's maid could start sewing the lace falls onto her sleeves. The sleeves came just to her elbows, and there were *three* layers of lace. They were so pretty, they made her feel like a swan. She wished Ned could see her in this grand dress.

Ned would've *loved* this dress. They used to dream of

pretty clothes, huddled together in a shared bed at night in St Giles. They'd dreamed of fine food and heated rooms, too.

She blinked hard, for her face was already painted and she mustn't ruin the white rice powder.

The maid finished the lace falls and stepped back to pinch and fuss with her skirts.

Iris stood examining her carefully. "I think you'll—"

The door to the room burst open, and Peter came running in, followed by the puppy and his older brother. "Alf! Alf!"

The boy caught sight of her and stopped so suddenly he nearly toppled over.

Kit stumbled to a halt and frowned, staring at her.

The puppy was the only one who kept going, sniffing around the floor in interest.

"Alf?" Peter asked, sounding very unsure. His blue eyes were wide and wondering.

She smiled down at him. "How are you, my lord?"

He burst into tears. "You're not Alf!"

For a second she could only stare between the boys, Peter sobbing as if his little heart was broken and Kit looking suspicious and almost betrayed.

She swallowed, feeling shattered. Maybe he was right, something inside her whispered, maybe she wasn't Alf anymore all painted and primped. Maybe she'd given up everything that was really *her*.

Iris stepped forward but Alf said, "No." She looked at the other woman. "Just...let me talk to them, please?"

Iris's blue-gray eyes were gentle and understanding. "Of course." She turned and motioned for the maids to come with her to the far side of the room.

That left Alf and the boys a bit of privacy.

Alf bent—very carefully, because she was all dressed

now, ready for the ball tonight. Ready for the important job that Kyle wanted her to do.

"Peter," she said. "What's the matter, love?"

"You're all wrong," the little boy sobbed. "Your face is funny and you're a *lady*. Alf isn't a lady."

"I can be," she said. "It's just a dress and rice powder. Underneath I'm still Alf."

"But you *look* different," Kit said. He was still frowning—hard like his father.

She glanced at him and smiled. "Isn't that a good thing? Don't you like my ball gown?"

"I liked you as you were." Kit thought about this, his small brows drawn together. "It's a pretty gown," he added grudgingly.

Peter wiped his eyes, snuffling loudly. "Why're you in a big dress *now*?"

"I'm going to a ball," she said. "With Lady Jordan and your papa."

"A *ball*?" The younger boy scrunched up his face in apparent disgust. "But me and Kit were coming to tell you that we thought of a name for her."

Alf immediately knew who *her* was. She glanced at the little terrier. It had sat down, back legs splayed to the side, and was looking at her with sad eyes. That was what had made her pay a shilling for the puppy in the first place: its funny sad eyes.

"What is it?" she asked, smiling.

He leaned close and whispered as if it was a secret, "Pudding." He straightened. "I thought of it all by myself."

Behind him Kit snorted. "*Pudding*'s a lot better than what your other ideas were." He rolled his eyes in elder-brother exasperation. "*And* you cried until I said it was acceptable."

Fortunately, Peter didn't take offense at Kit's statement.

"I think it's a lovely name," Alf said, stroking the puppy with a forefinger.

Behind them Iris cleared her throat.

Alf swallowed. It must be nearly time to go. Time to face Kyle. Time to see if she could fool a room full of London aristocracy into believing she was a lady.

"I have to leave now," she told the boys. "But I'll come see you and Pudding tomorrow."

"Very well," Kit said, sounding like a small gentleman, which she supposed he was. "Good night, Alf."

He took his brother's hand and led him from the room, the puppy following.

"Are you ready?" Iris asked her.

Alf glanced at her. "Almost."

She walked to a table by the door where three of her daggers lay. She might be dressed like a lady, but she was still on a mission tonight—and that meant going in armed. She shoved a very thin, sheathed dagger down between her breasts, under her corset. The next she placed in her right garter against her outer thigh. And the third, the smallest, she carefully shoved up her left sleeve.

She made sure her skirt was straight and that the knife up her sleeve wouldn't fall out by accident, and then she nodded at Iris, who was watching her, wide eyed.

"Ready as I'll ever be."

Chapter Thirteen

*That night the Black Warlock returned home. He
summoned his son to him and said, "I have destroyed
the White Sorceress and her family. All that she had
is now mine. It is time, therefore, that you begin your
training as my heir to the Black Kingdom."
The Black Prince calmly inclined his head and said,
"Yes, Father."...*

—From *The Black Prince and the Golden Falcon*

Hugh stood waiting in the entry hall to Kyle House. Iris
and Alf should have been down by now—the carriage was
already outside.

He had an uncharacteristic urge to pace.

Was Iris unable to dress Alf? Perhaps the woman had had
a last-minute attack of nerves. That didn't seem like the Alf
he knew, though. Once committed to a course, she was brave
to the point of mulishness. In fact he'd hardly seen her in the
last day or so. She'd spent almost all her time in the company
of Iris, learning how to pass herself off as a lady.

On his orders.

Hugh cursed under his breath, making his butler glance at him. It had been the right decision—the *only* decision. Why, then, did he feel so restless now?

He needed her as a lady—as a *woman*—to infiltrate Dowling's study. He needed her as a woman to do the job. He needed her as a woman to...

Blast.

Perhaps he simply needed her as a woman period. As a man needs a woman. And if so, this was a fine time to come to that realization, just before an important and possibly dangerous mission.

And if he'd pushed her too far too soon?

He halted and bowed his head. Then he'd just have to comfort his little imp until she was strong enough to make the attempt again.

He drew a breath and straightened. Damn it, where the hell were they?

A step on the stairs drew his gaze upward. Iris was gliding down sedately.

Hugh strode to the bottom of the grand staircase.

"Where is she?" he asked softly as she made the bottom step. "Is everything all right?"

Iris lifted her eyebrows in what looked like amusement—which didn't make his mood any better. "Of course. Alf is right behind me."

She turned and looked up.

He followed her gaze.

Alf was there on the landing, standing in a purple dress that made her skin look like white rose petals, gleaming and soft. Her dark hair had been pulled away from her face into a knot at the crown of her head, revealing her delicate bone structure, her long, slim swan's neck, and her huge brown eyes. Her lips were erotically wide in that elfin face, lush and red and sensual, and he wanted to bite them. To take her into another room and smear the pristine powder and rouge.

He made his gaze sweep down, though it did little to calm his pounding heart. The dress was a ball gown and had a deep, square, and nearly indecent décolletage. Her small breasts were pushed into sweet mounds that made him wonder just how close her nipples were to the edge of the bodice.

Jesus.

He felt as if he'd been knifed in the gut.

Her eyes were on his as she descended the stairs slowly, her gaze wild and shy and so very brave. He held out his hand as her slippered foot touched the marble of the hallway.

She placed her hand in his.

"Well?" Iris whispered next to him. "Will she do? Is she adequate to your needs, my dear Hugh?"

He kept his gaze on Alf's as he raised her hand to his lips. He saw her eyes widen as he murmured, "She's perfect."

Beside him Iris chuckled. "Yes, she most certainly is."

Hugh cleared his throat and finally glanced at Iris—his friend Iris. "Thank you."

"I didn't necessarily do it for you, darling." She raised her eyebrows and gave him a slightly mocking look. "We'd best be away, hadn't we?"

"Indeed." He held out an elbow to each lady and led them out the door. "You have your masks?"

"Yes, Your Grace." Alf's upper-class accent was nearly perfect now. She shot a small smile at him as he helped her into the carriage. "Iris has them in her bag."

He glanced over and saw that Iris did indeed have a small silk drawstring bag on her wrist. He handed Iris into the carriage and then entered himself. He was wearing a black domino, but the ladies would wear only masks for the masquerade.

He knocked on the roof to let the driver know they were ready before sitting opposite Alf and Iris.

The carriage had been hired for the evening so that no markings could give his identity away.

Hugh stared at the women, Alf in her new incarnation, oddly self-possessed, Iris beginning to fidget nervously.

"It's a ball like any other," he told them, though it was Iris he was mainly speaking to. "We'll be masked. No one will be paying particular heed to us."

That was a bit of a lie. Dowling, if he was indeed part of the Lords of Chaos's inner circle, must at the very least be on the watch for him after the debacle over Crewe. Then, too, the man might be wary for other reasons with both Crewe and Chase recently dead under suspicious circumstances.

Alf looked serious. "Have you heard anything else from your men since Lord Chase's death?"

Hugh shook his head. "They've been quiet in the last week. Both Exley and Dowling have hardly left their houses. Of course they're the only named Lords that we know about. There are others who may be moving, may be warring with each other, and we simply don't have knowledge of them." He looked at Alf. "That is why tonight is so important. If we can find that list of members, we'll be able to open up and clean out the whole nest of them."

"I know, guv. You can count on me."

She lifted her chin as she met his gaze. The rouge on her lips drew a man's eye, making her even more alluring. Knowing what she was—what she *could do*—and seeing how she presented herself at the moment, he caught his breath at the possibilities. If he'd had a female operative when they'd been in Vienna a year ago, the things they could've accomplished. She thought like him, but she was his opposite: female to his male.

Dangerous, yet soft.

Intelligent and erotic at the same time.

His match, this urchin from St Giles.

The carriage jerked to a stop.

Hugh nudged aside the window curtain. "We're here." He glanced at the women. "Don your masks before we go in."

Iris tied a black silk half mask to Alf's face—making her more mysterious with only her red lips revealed. Iris took a painted oval mask of a woman's face on a stick out of the bag for herself.

The carriage swayed as the footmen got down. A minute later the door was opened and Talbot, wearing livery, held out his hand. "M'lady?"

They descended, and Hugh looked up at Dowling's house. It was a grand residence, only a few years old, with a row of Grecian columns across the front, staid and patrician. A lot of money had gone into building this residence. Dowling was a very rich man—odd, since, although he was an aristocrat, he'd neither inherited wealth nor married into it.

"Come," Hugh murmured, and ushered both women up the steps, already crowded with masked guests.

Inside the entryway was a press of bodies, moving slowly to proceed up a wide staircase. Some of the ladies were in costumes with elaborate headdresses. Others merely held oval masks on sticks like Iris. Most of the gentlemen wore dominos, though a few had gone to the trouble of a costume. He jostled against a devil, tail, horns, and all.

They made their way slowly to the first-floor ballroom, a large room that took up nearly the entire back of the house. Tall windows, some of them French doors, marched across one wall, though of course all of them were closed since it was winter. Hugh could already feel sweat sliding down his spine. The heat was overwhelming, and the stench of perfume, candle wax, and body odor oppressive.

Beside him Alf caught her breath. "It's so pretty."

Pretty? He glanced at her. She was gazing, rapt, at the chandeliers high above, the dozens of flat faceted pieces of blue cut glass sparkling as they reflected the candles.

He looked at her again. "Yes, I suppose it is pretty."

"We're lucky our host and hostess aren't greeting their guests," Iris murmured as she opened her fan.

"Mm," Hugh replied. "Do you see Viscount Dowling?"

"By the windows." Iris tilted her chin.

"Where?" Alf asked.

"The man in the mustard-colored suit. He's dressed as the sun, I believe," Iris said softly. "Do you see? He's wearing a mask, but Lord Dowling's red hair is quite remarkable, even in costume. He's standing next to another gentleman in scarlet."

Alf's eyes widened as she glanced at the group. "That's—"

"Exley," Hugh finished for her. Exley hadn't even bothered with a domino. Christ. What was the earl doing here tonight?

Dowling and the Earl of Exley stood together and appeared to be quite good friends. Although they were both on the list Montgomery had given him, in all the time watching both men's houses he'd never had word of them together, never known them to socialize.

Hugh drew a breath and tried to make note of the other men in the grouping—almost impossible since all except Exley wore masks—and wondered how many might be in the Lords of Chaos.

"We should stroll," Iris said nervously. "We risk attracting attention if we stand in one place too long."

"A good suggestion." Hugh offered his arms and they began perambulating the room.

"Are you calling it off?" Iris hissed.

"No," Alf said from his other side before he could reply. "There's no need just because Exley's here."

"She's right," Hugh said, his voice low. "We'll continue as planned."

Iris frowned. "But Exley *knows* you. He's seen Alf—she was there when you both discovered Crewe's body."

"I was dressed as a boy," Alf reminded her.

"What if there are more Lords of Chaos at this ball than expected?" Iris murmured. Her knuckles were white against her mask's stick. "For all we know the guest list is full of Lords."

"We already knew that Dowling was a Lord," Alf whispered, her voice calm and even. "Nothing's changed in that."

"It's dangerous."

"It was always dangerous." Alf's painted lips curved in an almost feral smile. There was his huntress, lurking under the lady's rouge and paint. He admired her even as he feared for her.

But she was right. He knew Alf was right, and he *needed* that list of names—or at least some sort of new information in this investigation.

And yet unease crawled up his back.

"Be quick," Hugh said to her, making his decision. "Find the damned room and take no more than two or three minutes. Leave if you hear anything, do you understand?"

She rolled her eyes at him. "I know my job, guv."

Their slow walk around the room had taken them to the far side and by a door that led to an inner hallway.

Alf winked.

And then she was gone.

ALF SMILED AND nodded to a lady as she walked down the hallway. The lady's necessity was down this way—that was a swell cove's name for a bog, Iris had told her. There'd be an outer room as well where ladies could repair their face paint, hair, and dresses if need be. Alf walked neither fast nor slow. She moved sedately, her skirts swishing down the corridor. She neared the door and stepped aside as two girls came out, tittering together. The girls turned and went down the hall, back toward the ballroom.

Alf glanced over her shoulder. The way was clear. Quickly she lifted her skirts and darted past the door, walking fast. Her panniers swung from side to side, silly things. She had to be careful that they didn't brush against anything in the hallway—a table or statue or other ornament—and knock something down. It wouldn't be good to bring the footmen and guests to her.

There. A staircase to her left. Just where her informant had said it would be.

She ran up it on tiptoe.

The floor above was the family's private apartments. Alf found herself in another hallway, this one much dimmer. She started creeping to the right, toward where Dowling's private study should be, and then realized she could hear footsteps approaching her rapidly.

Hastily she tried the nearest door, found it unlocked—thank God!—and ducked inside. She pulled the door to, but left a crack, peeking out.

She watched a maid hurry by.

She counted to twenty.

Then opened the door again and peered out.

The hall was empty.

Quickly she slipped down to the study, snatching a lit candle from one of the wall sconces as she scurried by.

She closed the study door, wincing as it squeaked, and held the candle high. The room was above the ballroom and about half as large. A huge desk sat by a fireplace, flanked by two chairs. Over the fireplace two crossed rapiers were displayed. Alf lifted her brows. Fine steel, possibly Toledo, judging by the lovely birdcage finger guard. A bookshelf and four cabinets were against the inside walls.

She snorted softly. Two or three minutes to search. Kyle was barmy if he thought she could do anything in that amount of time.

Alf set the candle on a candlestick on the desk.

A row of windows looked out over the back of the house, and she could hear the music drifting up from the ball below as she tested a drawer in the desk. Her informant had said that the desk was the most likely place. No point in even trying elsewhere, then. Not in the little time she had.

She sat at the desk. There were two drawers at the top, both locked. On both sides of the desk legs were more drawers—unlocked—and she quickly rifled these, finding nothing of interest.

She frowned and returned to the two locked drawers. At least that narrowed down her search. Alf took the dagger from her stays and wedged the point in the crack between the top of the right-hand drawer and the bottom of the desktop, above the lock. She searched the surface of the desk and found a marble bust.

She picked up the bust and bashed it into the hilt of the dagger. Once. Twice.

The lock broke.

Grinning to herself, she pulled open the drawer.

Inside was a stack of pound notes, weighed down by a small purse of golden guineas. She left those alone. Beside them were several letters. Those she stuffed between her stomacher and her corset—no time to look at them now. Nothing else of importance lay in the drawer.

She opened the left-hand drawer the same way.

Inside was a stack of papers.

She flipped through them, looking for names, places. They looked like contracts. Legal papers in any case. Were they important? She didn't know, and the papers were too many and too large to hide inside her dress. She placed them on the desk while she looked back inside the drawer to see if it hid anything else.

It didn't, but...

She opened the right drawer again, shoving everything out of it. Pound notes fluttered to the floor.

She examined both drawers.

The right-hand drawer was shorter than the left.

Alf yanked hard on the right drawer, pulling it all the way out of the desk. She bent and peered into the hole left behind, but of course there wasn't light enough to see anything. She angled herself and stuck her arm into the hole, wriggling until her fingers struck the back.

Outside the study door someone said, "Not here."

Alf froze, hardly breathing. Slowly she turned her head to look at the door.

"Damn it, Dowling," a different voice said. "When, then?"

Retreating footsteps.

She slid her fingers over the back of the hole. She could feel a crack. There was a door of some kind there.

She withdrew her hand and went back in with her dagger, wedging the blade in the crack and wriggling it.

The wood gave with a loud snap.

"...killing him only drew attention to us." They were returning.

There was a piece of paper wedged in the back of the drawer. Alf snatched it and the dagger and thrust both back inside her corset.

She whirled to the door.

"What would you have had us do?"

The door squealed as it began to open.

TEN MINUTES.

Iris glanced at Hugh out of the corner of her eye, keeping a small, politely bored smile affixed to her face. It had been ten minutes at the very least since Alf had left them. She and Hugh had continued their slow glide around the ballroom. He'd fetched her a small glass of punch.

And they'd somehow lost sight of both Lord Dowling and the Earl of Exley.

Alf had not returned.

She could feel the tension in Hugh's arm under her fingertips.

"It's taking too long," he growled under his breath.

Iris took a sip of the punch, her mask dangling from her wrist by a silk cord. "What shall we do?"

He shook his head, a muscle in his jaw flexing.

She swallowed and nodded to Lady Young, who was wearing an unfortunate shade of lavender. The ballroom was hideously hot. Lady Dowling ought to've ordered the windows opened, despite the January cold. It was only a matter of time before someone fainted.

"Damn, it's hot," Hugh muttered under his breath, using a handkerchief to blot his upper lip. "Promise me that after we marry you'll not have balls as crowded as this one."

Her head snapped around to him. "*What?*"

Beneath the mask of his domino she could see his brows knit. "I said—"

"Surely you don't still think we will marry?" she hissed under her breath.

"Iris, if I have offended you in any way, I do apologize." He'd stiffened in male pride.

"Are you an idiot?" She shook her head before he could answer and held up her hand. "No. Let me ask a different question. Do you imagine that *I* am an idiot? I have seen how you look at Alf. I have seen how she looks at you. And even if there were no affection or ardor between you and a woman whom I have come to regard as a dear friend, I do not wish to have another passionless and unhappy marriage. I'm tired of only being the hostess and mistress of a man's house. I had enough of that with James."

He blinked. "I... see."

She patted his hand. "I assure you, though, that I shall remain your good friend, dearest Hugh."

Someone exclaimed nearby and the crowd started murmuring, heads turning toward the door.

Iris glanced toward the entrance to the ballroom to see what the commotion was about, and saw Hades walk in the door. He was tall and lean and dressed all in black—as befitted the god of the dead. His dark hair was unpowdered and left loose about his shoulders as if he simply couldn't care less about what others might feel was proper. And his face...

His face was half fallen angel and half devil.

And he wasn't wearing a mask. He wasn't in costume at all.

"Why have you stopped?" Hugh muttered beside her.

"Who is that?" Iris asked, staring. It was as if she couldn't look away from that terrible face. He'd been scarred *horribly*. A single great gouge from his forehead, down through his eyebrow, somehow missing the eye itself, but digging a furrow into his cheek, twisting one corner of his mouth, and carving a divot out of the edge of his jaw.

"Dyemore," Hugh said.

The room had gone silent and his single word sounded overloud.

Hades turned his spoiled visage toward them as if he'd heard his name on Hugh's lips.

Iris felt the impact of that gaze across the room.

She inhaled, hastily looking away.

"Dyemore?" She licked her lips, turning aside. She had the oddest feeling that he could read her lips even across the room. "Who is he?"

"Raphael de Chartres, the Duke of Dyemore," Hugh murmured in her ear. "His father was the former leader of the Lords of Chaos, the Dionysus. The old duke died last fall. Dyemore turned up in London just weeks ago to claim the dukedom."

Iris frowned. "He was out of the country before that?"

"No one seems to know where he was. The father was estranged from the son." His voice sounded tight.

"What..." She inhaled. "What in God's name happened to his face?"

"All we know is rumors," he replied. "Some say it was a duel—a father angry over a daughter's corruption and subsequent suicide. Others that his own father did it to him when he was very young. And some, of course, say he was born thusly. A curse on the family."

She glared at him. "Well, the last is obviously nonsense."

He nodded. "Yes, but even the wildest rumors and gossip are interesting in their own way."

"Humph." She chanced another glance at the demonic figure by the door. "You think it significant that he's here tonight."

"Let's walk," Hugh replied. They began moving around the ballroom again, nearing the hall that led to the ladies' retiring room. "Dyemore hasn't been seen in society since his return. He's only ventured out to his banker and his lawyer and once to a coffeehouse."

Iris inhaled. "He didn't bother with any sort of costume tonight."

"Perhaps he wanted to be recognized," Hugh said. "The position of Dionysus—there are rumors that it's hereditary."

She felt a chill of horror even in the humid room. "Then he might be here to claim leadership of the Lords."

Hugh looked at her. "Yes."

They'd made the side of the room near the door to the hall.

"I don't like that Alf hasn't returned. She's now well past ten minutes late." Hugh leaned close to her. "Wait fifteen minutes. If I'm not back by that time, make your way to the carriage in the mews."

Iris turned her head in alarm. "But—"

He was already ducking out the door.

She turned immediately back to the ballroom. Best not to stare at the door. Best not to draw attention, either to herself or to him.

She inhaled slowly. This was a ball. She'd attended innumerable hot, boring balls since she'd come out more than a decade ago. This was simply one more.

"My lady," a voice like black smoke rasped behind her, "might I have the honor of this dance?"

She knew even before she turned and saw the pale-gray eyes, the left staring out of ravaged crimson scar tissue:

Hades had found her.

Chapter Fourteen

*Thenceforth the Black Warlock taught his son all that
was most evil of wizardry. Spells that maimed and
drove others insane. The mysteries of mesmerizing and
commanding armies. Every night the Black Prince
would return to his rooms weary and sore and with his
heart aching. The Golden Falcon would fly to his arm
then and butt her head against his cheek until he stroked
her feathers with his fingers.
But even she could no longer make him smile....*
—From *The Black Prince and the Golden Falcon*

Hugh took the stairs two at a time, and as he did so he had to keep reminding himself that she knew what she was doing. That she'd lived by herself in bloody St Giles for years. That she was smart and swift and brave.

And oh God, he'd sent her in alone, and if anything had happened to her he'd never forgive himself.

The upper floor was dimly lit, but even so he could see an open door farther down the corridor. It had to be the study.

As he neared, a footman burst from the room, shouting, "Thieves! Robbers! Help!"

Hugh punched the footman in the jaw, shutting him up, and threw himself into the study.

And heard Alf *laughing*.

She was by the fireplace to his left, a rapier in one hand, a sheaf of papers in the other, and she was fighting off Exley, Dowling, and three footmen.

Jesus *Christ*.

Both Exley and Dowling had swords. Hugh grabbed the closest of the three footmen and shoved him headfirst into the wall. The man crumpled. Hugh sensed movement behind him, though, and glanced around in time to see three more menservants rush in the room.

Bloody hell. They couldn't escape by way of the door, then.

That left the windows.

Instead of engaging the men by the door, Hugh charged the original two footmen and Exley and Dowling. The first of the footmen was a bruiser and tried to throw a balled fist at his head.

Hugh caught it on his left forearm and gave the footman one in return in the jaw. The footman fell back.

Dowling slashed at him with his sword, but Alf parried the blow as Hugh slid by. Which left her side open to Exley.

The earl stabbed at her.

For a moment Hugh thought it was all over, and his heart stopped.

But she swayed, lithe as a willow, and the point of Exley's sword swept into the empty air beside her.

Hugh drew his sword.

"Glad you could join me," she said, her voice high and light, and not even out of breath.

He shot her an incredulous glance. "You were *late*." He brought up his sword in time to keep Dowling from carving out his liver. "Window."

She laughed again and he thought, *I want her. Now. Tomorrow. Forever.*

But that was insane, so he thrust his rapier at Dowling, aiming at the bastard's gut, and backing toward the blasted window.

Four more menservants came in the room. It was a bloody army advancing on them. He wasn't even sure what was outside the windows. If it was a sheer drop he'd have to surrender. Or perhaps Alf at least could climb it. If she wriggled out of her damned dress.

He never should have made her do this.

But she was fighting as bravely as she ever had as the Ghost. Bravely and beautifully, a smile tilting up her painted lips under her half mask as she deftly parried Exley's thrusts.

He felt behind him. Found the latch of the window and opened it. He took a quick look over his shoulder. *Thank God.* There was a balcony running all along the back of the house.

He flung open the window just as Dowling lunged at him, shouting, "No! Don't let them get out onto the balcony!"

Hugh felt a slash across his thigh. The footmen rushed them, despite their swords.

Alf was beside him, still fending off Exley, who hadn't said a word.

"Go!" Hugh ordered.

She hiked up her dress and clambered over the windowsill almost before the word was out of his mouth. Hugh thrust savagely at Exley's belly, making him jerk back. Hugh leaped out the window onto the stone balcony, turning just in time to prevent Dowling from severing his ear. Exley and Dowling were right on their heels, forcing them back down the balcony. Dowling swore under his breath, his face red and shining with sweat as he swung his sword wildly. Exley was controlled and precise in his movements, and by far the more deadly of the two.

Hugh grunted and parried blow after blow as he and Alf defended themselves down the length of the balcony. The music drifted up from the ballroom, sedate and serene. The clash of blades striking was in odd disharmony. In front of Hugh, his breath was a white fog in the night air, his lip curled in a sneer of exertion and anger.

His hips hit the balcony edge.

They were at the end. He glanced behind him and didn't see Alf.

He looked back in time to find the point of Exley's blade at his throat. "Your slut has deserted you, Kyle."

ALF STOOD ON the terrace that ran across the back of the town house and peered up at the balcony she'd just jumped from. Where was Kyle? What was taking him so long?

Suddenly there was a shout, and a sword sailed over the balcony, clattering to the pavement at her feet. Kyle followed, vaulting over the stone railing. He caught himself only just in time, swinging for a second by his fingertips, even as both Exley and Dowling bent over the railing reaching for him.

Kyle let go and dropped to the terrace, landing neatly as a cat. "Move!"

He picked up his sword as she turned and raced to the wide steps leading down into the back garden.

There was a boom from behind them and the top of a stone vase exploded several feet away.

One of the footmen must've brought a pistol.

Alf flinched but kept running. Skirts were a bloody bother to run in. The panniers were an odd jostling counterweight, all the fabric heavy and dragging, and she wasn't at all used to walking, let alone running, in the pretty little heeled slippers.

They made the gravel path and she nearly turned her ankle as her foot twisted.

Kyle swore. "Don't you dare fall!"

"Not planning on it, guv," she shot back as she righted herself and kept running.

Shouts came from behind them.

A crack, and a lovely little tree shattered halfway up the trunk, making the top fall over.

"They're wrecking this here garden," Alf said with deep disapproval.

Kyle gave her a disbelieving glance as he opened the gate onto the mews.

They raced out and Kyle turned to the right—toward where the carriage would be waiting.

"No!" She grabbed his arm.

"What?" But he stopped and looked at her, though his face was dark with impatience.

"Do you *want* them to catch us at the carriage?" she demanded. "Better we go the other way." She tilted her head to the left.

He turned that way with her. "They'll catch up with us."

"Oh, aye, that they will," she said. "Here. Hold this."

She thrust the bundle of papers she still held into his hands. He shoved them into his waistcoat. Then she tore the layers of beautiful, beautiful lace from her sleeves. Lace like this, why, it probably came from somewhere lovely over the seas. Took months to make. Cost more than most people saw in a year.

And she threw it into the mud and stamped on it so it couldn't be seen by any passing light.

She hauled up her skirts and untied her panniers. Those she threw over a wall.

By now Kyle had figured out her plan. He pulled his domino over his head and tossed it aside and took her half mask from her. He didn't even blink when she wriggled her hand under her stays and pulled up her small breasts just enough so that her nipples showed above the neckline.

His eyes glittered.

They'd made the end of the mews now. The street beyond flickered with one or two bonfires, and it was crowded with carriages and waiting coachmen.

They could hear the pounding footsteps of their pursuers already. She didn't have time for nerves or second thoughts.

Make a plan, stick with it. Ned had always said that.

Alf snatched his sword and hers. She sank down with her back against a stone wall, the swords hidden under her pooled skirts, and knelt on the cold ground.

She looked up and saw the glint of his black eyes widening as he muttered, "Bloody hell."

His face taut, his beautiful lips parted in shock or desire or both.

Then he leaned over her, one hand on the wall, the long sides of his coat swinging forward and hiding her face and shoulders.

She worked at his falls with shaking fingers as the footsteps neared. He was *hard*, and she couldn't stop her lips from curving in anticipation.

Despite the danger.

Maybe *because* of the danger.

He and she were more alike than she ever would've guessed, that first time she'd seen him.

She got his smalls open as light flashed through the shroud of his coat, and she felt strong, stretched flesh. So close.

So hot.

She didn't think.

She put him in her mouth and breathed in his musk.

"What are you doing here?" A stranger's voice. One of the footmen?

"What does it *look* like?" he growled back.

She smirked at that, even with her mouth full of his hard cock. It tasted odd, it did, but not half as bad as she'd thought it would. Mostly it simply tasted of *him*. Of skin and man and salt.

"Have you seen a gentleman and lady run past?"

She sucked and moved her head up and down because that was what she'd seen the molls in St Giles do. Of course she'd seen this done. Many times. You didn't grow up in St Giles without seeing such. But she'd never done it herself and she'd never known...

Oh.

Never known that an act like this could give pleasure to the one doing the sucking and licking. And wasn't that an odd thing to discover here on the frozen ground, surrounded by their enemies?

Surrounded by danger.

Above her he groaned and she felt it between her lips. "God's blood, man, the King himself could run past and I wouldn't give a damn." His hand was suddenly in her hair. "Yes, luv, like that. Use your tongue."

She obeyed, licking around his stretched foreskin, tasting bitter fluid, and he responded by thrusting his hips, the broad head of his cock plowing against her tongue.

One of the men around them muttered something, someone laughed, and they moved off.

She could hear his rough breathing in the night air.

With her hand she squeezed the part of his cock that didn't fit in her mouth and then began stroking up and down.

"They're gone," he muttered, his breath hitching, his hips rolling in little pushes he couldn't seem to stop.

Oh, he wanted her. He wanted *her*.

She looked up at him and sucked harder.

It was dark, but she could just make out the glitter of his eyes. He was watching her. Down on her knees, with his cock in her mouth, sucking him.

His nostrils flared and that beautiful upper lip curled.

She rubbed the tip of her tongue underneath the head of his penis and he gasped. Slid his hand down her face in a caress.

Touched the corner of her wet, stretched lips with his thumb.

And came, flooding her mouth with his bitter seed.

She closed her eyes, feeling the pulses, listening to his grunts, trying not to taste what was on her tongue, wishing she could touch herself.

"Alf," he whispered.

His cock slipped from her lips and come and spit dribbled down her chin.

She felt him press a handkerchief to her mouth.

She spit into it and wiped her mouth, watching as he fastened his falls. His fingers were shaking as if he had the ague.

She smiled and stood, the swords in her hand.

He put his hands on either side of her face and kissed her hard and fast. "What in hell am I going to do with you?"

He took one of the swords and pulled her back down the alley, retracing their steps. When they passed Viscount Dowling's house again, she was surprised to see that the garden was dark.

They hurried past and were soon at the other end of the mews. Another turn, and there was the carriage.

As they neared, Talbot called softly, "Where's Lady Jordan?"

Kyle stared at him up in the driver's seat next to Jenkins. "She's not here yet?"

Both men shook their heads.

"Christ," Kyle whispered. "Iris is still inside."

THE THING WAS, she really oughtn't to be talking to, let alone *dancing with*, a gentleman she hadn't been introduced to, Iris thought a little desperately. She *had* declined his invitation to dance, she was quite certain.

And yet here she was, decorously moving through the steps of a dance with His Grace the Duke of Dyemore, who, despite a dukedom, was obviously no gentleman.

"Where is your minder?" he demanded of her in *that voice*, so dark it reminded her rather of brimstone, when the progression of the dance brought them together again.

"I beg your pardon, Your Grace?"

He sighed as if he were talking to a ninny. "The gentleman whose arm you were adorning when I entered the room." He glanced at her as he took her hand and they paraded down the center of the ballroom. She had to repress a shudder at the cold darkness in those gray eyes. "A lover, perhaps?"

She stared at him. "You are *very* mistaken."

"Am I?" He shrugged carelessly as if he hadn't just maligned her virtue. "You must admit it was a possibility."

"No, I don't think I need make that admission at all," she replied calmly.

"Ah." His lips curved, which was a rather disconcerting sight considering the scar deforming the right side of his mouth. "You're just a poor innocent, then."

She was still contemplating why his words should sound so terribly insulting when the movement of the dance separated them.

Iris spent the next several whirls trying to think of a cutting reply, which was why it was so demoralizing when they came together again and all she could say was, "What do you mean by that?"

"You're an innocent," the duke said, his eyes holding all the humanity of a lump of crystal, "because you don't appear to understand where you are."

Iris arched her brows. "And where do you think I am?"

"Hell."

She should laugh at him—his words were entirely too dramatic. They were in a *ballroom*, an overheated, crowded, slightly stale-smelling ballroom.

But the thing was, he was perfectly serious. And she knew that at least two members of the Lords of Chaos were here in this house.

Three, if the duke himself was a member as well.

Iris was fairly sure she kept her face expressionless—though her heart was beating extremely fast—as she simply looked at him.

His eyes narrowed when she did not reply. "What I'm wondering is why your companion left you here all alone like a pretty little ewe in a den of wolves. It must have been very important, whatever it was that called him away."

The horrific red scar seemed to make his lips sneer as his wintry eyes bored into hers.

She felt a thrill of pure fear as they circled one another, their palms held aloft, together, but not quite meeting. She very carefully did not look at the door leading out of the ballroom.

Iris inhaled. "Did you just call me a sheep?"

His eyebrow—the one not destroyed by the scar—lifted. If he draped the right side of his face, he might be the most comely man she'd ever met.

"Perhaps I ought to inquire why *you* are here tonight, Your Grace." She made herself keep her voice even. Almost bored. "Do you have special business with Lord Dowling? Something that can't be done by the light of day?"

The music ended and she sank into a curtsy.

He caught her hand as she rose and pulled her close.

Too close.

His breath, smelling of brandy, washed over her face as he growled at her, "Your companion is a fool to've brought you here, and a rank *idiot* to've left you alone. Run, little lamb. Run for your life."

He stepped back and bowed. Then pivoted and strolled away.

Well.

Iris swallowed and opened her fan.

Well.

She rather wanted to take the Duke of Dyemore's advice, but instead she calmly—at least outwardly—walked toward the entrance of the ballroom. She smiled and inclined her head. Even stopped and made small talk with a trio of ladies she knew vaguely.

And the entire time her hands wouldn't stop shaking.

She came to the door and spoke to a footman. Mentioned her wrap and that she had a headache. That her escort had already gone ahead to find the carriage.

A dreadful feeling that she might be followed out made her turn and glance back into the ballroom then.

No one was looking at her.

No one save the Duke of Dyemore, across the room, standing alone. He nodded to her and turned away.

She hurried down the stairs.

A footman waited by the front door with her wrap. She took it and thanked him and then was out the doors.

The carriage wasn't there.

She inhaled. This was to be expected and nothing to be worried about. She mustn't panic. Not now. The agreed-upon meeting place was around the corner. She picked up her skirts and began walking. There were carriages sitting idle in the street, waiting for the guests of the ball. The coachmen and footmen were gathered around bonfires to keep warm while their masters and mistresses danced inside.

Some cast glances at her as she passed.

She walked faster.

Where were Hugh and Alf? Were they still inside? Had they been caught? If so, she needed to find the carriage as soon as possible and send Hugh's men back. Well. If three men were enough to rescue them.

She bit her lip and realized that footsteps were echoing her own behind her.

Iris turned the corner into the lane where the carriage should be, trotting now, her skirts held up. It was darker here, away from the lights of the main road, and the cobblestones were icy. A carriage was lumbering toward her, moving slowly. Perhaps she should cross the street or—

She glanced up in time to see a big shape just beside her. "M'lady."

She gasped, flinging her arm up instinctively. "Talbot. Oh, dear Lord, you gave me such a fright."

"I'm sorry, my lady." He took her arm, an extraordinary breach of etiquette, but then it was a rather extraordinary night. "Come, the carriage is just ahead."

She nodded, but couldn't help a glance behind her.

No one was there.

They were at the carriage now and Talbot helped her inside before shutting the door.

Only Alf was inside, looking like she'd been dragged backward through a hedge, though she seemed well enough. "Where's Hugh?"

"He went back to look for you," the other woman said, even as the carriage rolled forward. "When we found you weren't already here, he was worried."

"Oh God." Iris laid her hand over her mouth. "Should we send Talbot back in for him?"

"No." Alf shook her head, though she didn't look happy. "He gave orders to go back to Kyle House if we were to find you."

"But—"

Her protest was interrupted by the door opening and Hugh swinging inside the moving carriage.

He flung himself on the seat beside Alf. "Thank God you made it."

Iris felt foolish tears start in her eyes. Her hands were *still* shaking. "I could say the same to you both. I never, *ever* want to do that again."

"What happened?" Alf asked.

"The Duke of Dyemore happened," Iris said. She looked at Hugh. "The minute you left the ballroom, he asked me to dance."

Hugh's mouth flattened. "Did he harm you?"

She shook her head. "He couldn't very well in the middle of a ballroom, could he? He merely called me a sheep and warned me to leave."

"A sheep?" Alf looked perplexed.

"Never mind that." Iris waved away Hades. "Did you find anything? Was all this worth it?"

"Oh, yes." Alf's satisfied tone made Iris look up. Even by the dim light of the carriage she could see the other woman was grinning. "I found Dowling's hiding place." She took a crumpled piece of paper out of her bodice. "And what was in it."

Chapter Fifteen

*The years passed and the Black Prince grew. In time
he became almost as powerful as his father. The sight
of the stern prince riding through the Black Kingdom,
clad all in black robes and with the Golden Falcon on
his arm, was a common one and nearly always caused
those who saw him to shudder and bow low in fear....*
—From *The Black Prince and the Golden Falcon*

She still had the taste of him in her mouth.

Alf watched as Kyle leaned over the dining room table in
Kyle House and spread out the letters, the stack of rumpled
contracts, and the single piece of paper she'd found in the
secret compartment in Dowling's desk.

He was staring down at the papers, arranging them with
his fingertips, a line between his brows. Jenkins had efficiently bandaged the wound on his thigh, despite his protests
that it was nothing.

He was tall and broad and he was hers.

It made no sense, not in any social or legal way, but she
knew it deep inside herself. This man was hers. She'd held
him in her hands and in her mouth. Tasted his seed. Run
with him. Faced her deepest fears for him.

Become a woman for him.

Even if she turned and walked out his front door right now and never saw him again, she knew that they would always be connected.

Forever in her heart.

She'd never thought she'd have this connection with anyone—any *man*—and she was a little awed by it. Awed and excited and maybe even afraid.

But not so afraid that she wouldn't enjoy it, this wonder that had been given to her, just plain Alf of St Giles in London.

Only a fool wouldn't seize with both hands when offered a drink after thirsting so long.

"This is everything Alf found," Kyle said, bringing her back to the present.

Iris leaned forward from her seat next to Alf. Across from them were Kyle's men.

Riley pulled the contracts to himself and started scanning the documents with Talbot.

Jenkins opened a letter and read. Next to him Bell peered over his shoulder and moved his lips, frowning in concentration as he scanned the letter as well.

"What is this?" Iris was looking weary, her face pale, her voice husky. She frowned as she picked up the folded piece of paper Alf had discovered in the secret compartment.

"I don't know, but Dowling made sure it was hidden well." Alf nodded at it, aware that Kyle was staring at her. Was he thinking of what they'd done in the mews less than an hour before? Was he thinking of what they might do later? She hoped so. "It was in a hidden compartment at the back of a locked drawer in the viscount's desk."

"And the other papers?" Kyle asked, waving his hand at them.

"The rest were all in the two locked drawers of the desk. That"—she jerked her chin at the paper Iris held—"was the only thing in the hidden cubbyhole."

"Then it's probably the most important," Kyle said.

"If it is, I can't understand it," Iris said slowly. She laid the paper flat on the table and they all leaned over it to look:

618165036183646592	81848372816504
726584927265	62619283659494
928462659294	638463756592
02748181746182	73848194
85737481817485	026181946592
02748181746182	029274727394
726584927265	637395926373
836194736183	9381846384826265
8374637384816193	94736163756592
947384826193	82610493

848164   9361748394   8261920493   8384929473   8471
02618585748372   848164   9394619293

"A ledger?" Riley asked.

"Not one that I'm familiar with," Jenkins said softly. "These numbers don't add up."

"And look at these numbers at the bottom." Iris tapped the series of numbers in a line at the bottom. She cocked her head, looking more awake. "If they weren't numerals, I'd say they resembled words."

Jenkins glanced at her and then at Kyle. "A cypher?"

"That makes sense." Kyle straightened. "Copy the numbers exactly as they're written. I want both you and Riley working on this as soon as possible. Don't forget the letters and other papers, though. We'll need to go through everything Alf found."

He gestured at her as he said her name, but didn't look at her. Almost as if he didn't dare meet her eyes. Was it from fear of what he might show if he looked at her in front of the others?

Or was he regretting what they'd done earlier?

She didn't know, and the *not knowing* was near killing her. She didn't want this to end so soon. *Not yet. Not yet*, a part of her cried.

But then she thought of how he'd looked when he'd gazed down at her in the mews. The glint in his black, black eyes. The curl of his upper lip.

And she thought—she *hoped*—he wasn't quite done with her yet.

Iris cleared her throat. "Would you mind making a copy of the cypher for me as well?"

The men all turned to her.

Her cheeks pinkened, but she held Kyle's gaze. "It's just...I've always liked puzzles."

Jenkins cleared his throat. "Won't take me but a moment to make you a copy, my lady."

Iris turned and smiled at the gray-haired man as he got a fresh sheet of paper and began transcribing. "Thank you."

Kyle nodded and glanced at the grenadier. "Talbot, I'll

have you ride in the carriage with Lady Jordan to see that she returns home safely." He glanced at Iris, his expression strangely formal. "That is, if that meets with your approval, my lady?"

"Of course it does, Hugh," Iris said briskly.

Alf frowned, watching them both. There seemed to be some sort of tension between them that hadn't been there before the ball.

Talbot rose to his feet. "Yes, sir. I'll just check that the carriage is ready."

The big man left the dining room.

"No doubt you're tired, Alf," Kyle said to her, still without looking her in the eye. "There's no need for you to stay up while we work."

She knew a dismissal when she heard it. "Good night, then, guv. Jenkins. Riley. Bell." She smiled at the other woman. "Iris."

The other woman nodded wearily. "Good night, Alf."

The men's good nights rumbled behind her as she left the room. Their heads were already bent over the papers when she closed the door.

She took a candlestick standing on the table outside the dining room and picked up her poor bedraggled skirts. A bit like Cinderella, wasn't she? Cinderella well past midnight.

Except Cinderella had never sucked her prince's prick, had she?

She mounted the grand staircase, dragging her muddy skirts over the marble steps. Some poor maid would have to get up before dawn to scrub the mess she was leaving. If she were a lady, she'd never think of that maid.

But she wasn't a lady. She was an urchin from St Giles who'd had to steal, scavenge, beg, and work *hard* for everything good she'd ever found in life.

It simply wasn't in her nature to sit back and *wait* for what she wanted.

What she *needed*.

She came to the second-floor landing and didn't even hesitate. She walked down the hallway, took the first turn, and tried the door there.

It was unlocked.

She smiled and let herself into Kyle's bedroom.

She shut the door behind her and set the candle on a table.

It was a grand, lovely room, made for a duke. Alf strolled around his bedroom as she unpinned her outer robes. The fire had been lit in here to keep the bedroom warm for his return. The bed was a big thing, draped with blue and gold cloth. She smiled as she let her dress fall to the floor. There were paintings on the walls, of green woodlands—massive trees and huge blue skies, with not a building in sight. Had he seen places like that?

She never had.

She shrugged her stays off and carefully draped them over a chair. She slipped off her poor heeled shoes and tutted over them. They were destroyed, the fragile embroidered fabric torn and caked with mud. Such a shame. The silk stockings were mud splashed as well, but she was fairly sure they could be salvaged if washed carefully. And her chemise as well. She might get a nice price for the both of them—secondhand clothing sold well in London. She pulled the chemise off over her head.

Naked, she walked to a chest of drawers where a pitcher of fresh water waited. Did Kyle ever think of all those silent people who moved in and out of his rooms serving him? Did he ever wonder where they came from, what their hopes and dreams were, and if they had any family?

Most masters didn't, but Kyle...Kyle might. He'd taken in Bell, given money to his mother's brother and his sons, seemed in fact to care for and to take care of many around him.

Including her.

She poured half the pitcher in the washbowl and took one of his cloths and washed her body and her face. She pulled the pins from her hair and combed out the locks.

Then she walked to his bed and climbed in, stretching in the fine sheets. He'd said he wanted her to be a woman for him. And she'd gathered her courage, her wits, her cunning, and her tenacity, and by *God*, she'd done it.

Now, *now* she wanted all the rewards of being a woman.

HUGH OPENED THE door to his rooms wearily. It was nearly dawn, and they hadn't found anything more about the papers save that the letters indicated a love affair between Dowling and a married lady and that the cypher wasn't a simple number-to-letter replacement.

He sighed and pulled off his coat. He'd turned to toss it on a chair by the fireplace when he noticed that the chair was already occupied by a pair of stays.

For a moment he simply stared, he was so tired.

Then he noticed the dress, the chemise, the muddy shoes, and Alf, asleep in his bed, her dark hair spread on his pillow, her breasts nude and beautiful, high above the crumpled sheets.

God.

Were he a better man he'd wake her and make her leave. Or leave himself.

Instead he finished undressing. Washed in what clean water she'd left him, and climbed into the bed.

"Guv," she murmured as he pulled her close.

"Go to sleep," he muttered into the soft skin of her shoulder.

"*Hmph*." She wriggled into him, her sweet arse against his cock, her back cradled by his chest. Then she went limp.

He slipped his arm around her waist and cupped one breast in his hand.

And fell into sleep, blessedly headache free.

"ALF." KYLE'S DEEP voice brought her swimming up out of her dreams.

She opened her eyes and saw him bending over her in the early-morning light of his bedroom. Joy, pure and wonderful, blossomed in her chest. She looped her arms about his neck and pulled him down to kiss him, opening her mouth beneath his.

He lifted his head enough that she could see the lines around his black eyes. "You should leave."

She chuckled. "Why would I be wanting to do that, guv?"

He frowned sternly. The stubble of his beard was black around his jaw, making him look like a pirate.

An irritable pirate. "I don't want to take advantage of you."

"Taking advantage." She lifted her eyebrows. "That's something rich coves do to fine-bred ladies, isn't it?"

He scowled.

She pressed her thumb between his brows where the lines were deep. "Now, what makes you think I'm anything like a fine-bred lady? What makes you think I'm someone to be worried over or protected, eh, guv?" She didn't wait for his answer, but kept talking because she knew this wasn't forever between the two of them. Wasn't something she'd hold for more than a day or so—a week if she was lucky. And she'd be *damned* if she'd lose it to his highborn morality. She'd never had much in her life, and certainly she'd never had a man. For once she wanted something—*someone*—like other women had. Wanted joy and tenderness and to feel beloved.

So she looked him in the eye and said, "I'm not some

delicate miss. Not some lady who can't take care of herself. Didn't I break into Lord Dowling's study last night?"

"Yes."

"Can't I fight any man with a sword—and make him sorry he'd ever took me on?"

The corner of his mouth curled at that. "Yes."

"And didn't I get us away from Dowling's men last night—and made you right happy while I was at it?"

He winced. "Yes."

She stared into his black eyes. "In this bed I'm your equal, guv. There ain't no advantage being taken."

"Have you ever done this before?"

"No. And that's why I want to do it." She stroked her finger over his bottom lip and looked into his eyes, black and surrounded by thick, curling lashes. "With you."

He closed his eyes. "*God.*"

She could feel his prick, hard and throbbing against her thigh. She wanted that. Wanted *him*.

"Please?" she whispered, heart in her mouth, running the palms of her hands over his cropped hair. "Please?"

He groaned then, as if he'd been holding himself back against a great tide and was suddenly overwhelmed by the waves. His mouth was on hers, gentle and sweet, parting her lips, his tongue nudging inside to lick and slide. He lowered himself onto her, his body big and hot, and she curled her legs over his hairy thighs. She was spread wide open, wet and wanting, and his prick was a hot pressure on the crease of her thigh.

She made a high sound in the back of her throat and wriggled under him, feeling his skin on hers. All that warm skin. His chest hair scraped and teased her nipples, and she arched her back to feel it again.

But he was sliding down now, his lips leaving hers, and

for a horrible, horrible second she thought he was going to get up and abandon her. Except then his mouth was on the underside of her jaw and she'd never known how sensitive she was there. Why should she? No one touched her neck save her. He kissed her, sweeping his lips down her throat, making her swallow, making her tremble helplessly. She didn't know what she was supposed to do, for this wasn't something she'd seen done in back alleys in St Giles.

This was saved for lovers and sweethearts. Husbands and wives. People who knew and cared for each other.

His tongue traced the hollow at the base of her throat and she whimpered, feeling so strange. He touched her as if she were something—someone—precious.

Someone beautiful.

His lips skimmed her skin until he found her nipple, and he licked around and around it until she was arching up, offering herself, moaning in want.

He took her into his mouth and suckled, but only for a second before moving to her other breast.

She cried out at the injustice and thought she heard him chuckle under his breath, flicking that wet nipple as he began to lick the other.

She was panting by the time he moved down to her belly, his big hands framing her hips, his tongue dipping into her navel. She tried to close her legs as he neared her quim, but he matter-of-factly took hold of her thighs and braced them apart. He glanced up once, lying there between her spread legs, his face so close to what made her a woman, and said, "Hold still."

And then he lowered his face and opened his mouth right over her.

She stiffened, completely shocked. He was licking her, *kissing* her right…right…

She made a strange keening sound because she'd never felt anything so wonderful in her life. His tongue was wet and strong, moving in slow lapping circles against her, and she might be going insane. Twinges of pleasure were sparking down her legs, across her belly, up her spine, all of it centered down there. Down at that place between her legs where he was kissing and tonguing her so crudely.

Without thought she brushed her hand across her stomach, feeling the prickling heat. The wonderful sensation. She couldn't breathe. She couldn't see. She was growing hotter and hotter and she wanted to scream.

Instead, when the pleasure hit her, she arched abruptly. He held her down, his palms firm on her hips as his tongue gave her such painfully sweet agony.

When she was limp and panting, her eyes half-closed, he slowly rose and crawled up her conquered body.

"Did you like that, imp?" he whispered against her lips.

He sounded so self-satisfied.

"You know I did." She licked his mouth, wanting to taste herself to make sure it'd been real.

She wound her arms about his neck and opened her mouth for his tongue as she felt him reach between their bodies.

Then she felt the heat of his prick between her wet folds. He slid up, until the head of his cock rubbed against her sensitive bud.

Once. Twice.

She'd just come. It was almost too much.

She whimpered.

"Like that?" he whispered against her jaw, and she couldn't quite draw breath to answer.

But he must've known her answer for he ground his hips down on her, making her squirm.

Making her want to move with him.

But he held her there. Held her still as he slid against her a third time, kissing her so sweetly all the while.

The air was thick with salt and sex and she was hot and wet.

"Put it in me," she said. "Please."

She opened her eyes and watched his face as he moved back and his prick slipped a little lower, notching into her entrance.

He pressed into her, wide and thick. Hot, so hot.

There was a pinch.

But she kept her eyes on him, staring. His lush mouth was almost grim, and his forehead shone with sweat. He'd propped himself up on his elbows above her.

He thrust again, more of him entering her—stretching her—and she saw him clench his teeth.

She wrapped her legs around his hips and stroked the back of his leg with one foot.

He jerked and his hips met hers, his entire length buried inside her. She was stuffed full of him.

He inhaled through his nose and his nostrils flared.

She raised her head and whispered in his ear, "Are you going to fuck me now, guv?"

"Little devil," he breathed.

She'd braced herself, thinking he might lose control, but he withdrew slowly.

Gently.

And pushed back in just as slowly.

Almost sensually.

This wasn't fucking—not as she knew the word, anyway.

This was making love.

She felt tears sting her eyes as he moved on her so carefully. So tenderly. As if she were a precious thing. As if he couldn't bear to hurt her.

And it felt so sweet, so real, that she felt herself open and fall in a way she hadn't when she'd seen stars earlier. This, this *care*, was far more dangerous than any orgasm.

This might break her.

Because she *couldn't* believe it was real for him or that it would last between them. Not and survive.

So she was grateful when he threw back his head and abruptly lifted up off her and withdrew his penis. He groaned deep in his chest, his hand on his cock as he fisted himself. When he closed those black, black eyes and a sort of anguish took hold of his face as his seed splashed across her belly.

Because then the most wonderful thing to ever happen to her was over.

Chapter Sixteen

*On the day of the Black Prince's twenty-first birthday
his father summoned him.
"You are almost ready, my son," said the Black
Warlock. "But in order to attain all of your powers you
must make a last sacrifice. Bring me the heart of your
Golden Falcon."
The Black Prince's expression never changed. He
bowed and said, "Yes, Father."...*
—From *The Black Prince and the Golden Falcon*

The scream woke Hugh.

He started up, his heart feeling as if it were beating right out of his chest. Beside him Alf swore.

The door to his bedroom burst open.

Talbot came in, dragging Milly, the new nursemaid. The woman was sobbing loudly. Behind them was Jenkins. The gray-haired man took one look at the bed and strode over to pick up Alf's chemise and give it to her.

"Tell him." The grenadier shook the nursemaid. "Stop your wailing and tell him now."

"I'm that sorry, Your Grace!" the woman wailed, sinking to her knees. "Please!"

Hugh looked from her tear-streaked face to Talbot's grim expression and felt his belly turn to ice. "What has happened?"

Alf wrapped her arms around his bare shoulders, and even in the midst of what might be tragedy, it gave him comfort.

"I…I…" The nursemaid broke into incoherent sobs again.

"Sir." Jenkins was handing him his breeches.

Hugh took them and stood, uncaring of his nudity as he pulled them on. "Someone tell me!"

"They took Peter." Kit stood in the doorway.

Everything stopped as Hugh stared at his eldest son.

Kit's face was white, a long scratch along one cheek, his hair a mess. He looked…lost.

His black eyes met Hugh's. "Father, they took Peter."

Hugh inhaled and opened his arms. "Come here."

The boy ran to him and into his embrace. Hugh sat back down on the bed, gulping air, trying to think, holding Kit tight.

"Tell me what happened," he said as he stroked a trembling hand through his son's curling hair.

"Milly took us on our morning walk," Kit said. "Me and Peter and Pudding."

"Nine of the clock every morning for their health," the nursemaid said, sounding desperate. "I took a footman like I always do. Please, Your Grace—"

Hugh glared at the woman, and she abruptly snapped her mouth shut.

Kit's lips crimped for a moment, but he took a shuddering breath and continued. "We were almost home again but Pudding saw a cat and she chased it. Peter went running after her. He went around a corner. But when the footman and I came after him, he wasn't there anymore. Only Pudding was there, trying to chase after a carriage. The carriage was already going away, but I saw Petey inside, looking out the window." He lifted tear-filled eyes to Hugh. "I wanted to run to the carriage, but the footman wouldn't let me, Father. He wouldn't let me help Petey."

Hugh hugged Kit close, glad that the footman had had the intelligence to hang on to the boy.

"What did the carriage look like?" Alf asked beside him.

"It was black," Kit said to her.

He didn't seem to find it odd that she was in his father's bed, but then he must be in shock.

She turned to Talbot. "Did the footman say anything else?"

The grenadier shook his head. "No, miss."

Hugh closed his eyes. It had to be the Lords of Chaos. This early in the morning after last night's raid on Dowling's house, it couldn't be a coincidence. He'd been masked, but Exley had called him by name last night. The earl must've recognized Hugh's voice. Christ, if his investigation had led to Peter's kidnapping, led to his...

He shook his head hard, cutting off the dreadful thought. He couldn't think of that. He'd be driven mad if he did.

Riley slipped into the room, walking softly. He held a letter in his hand. "This just came for you, sir. The boy who delivered it is downstairs, but he doesn't seem to know anything."

Hugh took the letter, ripped it open, and read:

Bring everything you stole last night to Crewe's house at noon. Do not try to attack the house. The boy is not there. Once we have the items in our possession, we

*will transport you to where he is hidden and we will
let you both go. Refuse our generous offer and you
will never see him again.*

The letter was signed with a crude drawing of a dolphin.

Hugh passed the letter to Alf. She made one sharp exclamation as she read it and then was silent again.

He had no doubts that the promise to let him and Peter go was a lie. Once he was in the Lords' hands they would kill him. He knew too much at this point. Had come too close to their affairs.

He breathed in and then out, trying to think. "Kit, was there anything else you saw on the walk? Anything else different or unusual?"

The boy knit his brows. "No, but you could ask Uncle David."

Hugh stilled. "Uncle David?"

Kit nodded. "We saw him on the walk. He waved to me and Peter. He asked if we wanted to come with him for some tea and cake, but Milly said we needed to be back for our lessons."

Hugh felt molten rage flood his veins. He looked at his men. "Bring my brother-in-law here. Now."

FORTY-FIVE MINUTES LATER Alf was dressed in her boys' clothes and sitting in the library with Kyle as David was brought in by Talbot and Riley. The man was bright red with either anger or embarrassment or both, and she watched as he tried to regain his self-possession before Kyle.

He did it by blustering, which she could've told him was a very bad idea.

"What do you mean, sending your lackeys to drag me in here like a debtor?" he demanded.

Kyle stood by the fireplace not moving. It was eerie the way he'd become so still and calm since he'd read that awful letter. All emotion was gone from his black eyes. Any anger or grief torn from his face.

She wanted to go to him. To put her arms around him and bury her face in his big chest and weep the tears he wasn't letting himself shed. She wanted to tell him that they'd find funny, sweet little Peter. That he'd be back soon, playing with Pudding and arguing with Kit and complaining about having to do schoolwork and dine on whatever it was they made little lords eat for luncheon.

Except she knew better.

The men they were dealing with were bad. Bad like the monsters who walked in the dark woods of St Giles. These Lords of Chaos might've already killed little Lord Peter. She pressed her fingers to her lips at the terrible thought. Kyle was the sort of man who knew a bit of the world—who knew that there were those in it who had no souls.

He knew that his son might not be alive.

And he was still upright.

She closed her eyes and looked away, her heart aching for the little boy, aching for his brother, aching for the man who would survive this, but might lose his soul in the process.

The thought made her heart shrivel. Made her want to run and run until she never had to think of blond little boys being hurt again.

Oh, it was *painful* to love.

"What do you want?" David shouted, making her jump and open her eyes.

Apparently he'd been unnerved by Kyle's silence.

"Why won't you speak?" the man cried. "You drag me here but won't answer me? What can possibly be the point? What do you want?"

"I want," Kyle said very quietly, "my son."

"I don't—"

Kyle moved at last, fast and decisively. He took three steps and grasped the smaller man's neckcloth, then twisted it in his fist until he lifted David up onto his toes.

Until David choked, his fingers clawing at Kyle's fist.

Alf swallowed, wondering if Kyle would strangle his brother-in-law. Wondering if anyone in the room would stop him.

Kyle relaxed his grasp, but still kept hold of the neckcloth. He leaned close to the other man's face and rasped, "I want. My. Son."

"They'll kill me," David said.

"And you think I *won't*?" Kyle's lips lifted in a snarl as he twisted the neckcloth again.

"No—!" David coughed, gasping as Kyle let him breathe. "The Lords of Chaos have him."

"Where?"

"I...I don't know. They didn't tell me. That's the truth!"

"Who in the Lords? Who is behind the kidnapping?"

"I...I...no!" David closed his eyes. "The Earl of Exley. Dowling. Probably others. That's all I know, truly! The Lords don't reveal themselves in numbers. That's how they keep their secrets."

Kyle narrowed his eyes. "And you keep their secrets as well?"

"I...yes." David swallowed. "Yes, I'm a member."

"Loyal enough to betray your own blood." Kyle shoved him away as if touching David dirtied his hands. "Christ, have you no honor, man?"

"Honor?" the other man spit, his hands at his throat. "*Honor?* If you hadn't cut me off I'd never have helped lure the boy. Christ, he wasn't even the one we wanted. We were supposed to kidnap Christopher, not Peter. Why would you even care about Peter?"

Alf's eyebrows drew together. Was David insane?

Kyle was staring at him. "Peter is my *son*."

David threw back his head and laughed. "No, he's not. He *can't* be. Katherine told me."

"I don't give a damn what Katherine cared to tell you," Kyle said, his voice precise and controlled. "Do you take me for as much of a fool as you are? I've known that Peter wasn't from my blood since before he was born. I had the choice of ignoring that innocent babe—the brother to my own flesh and blood—or bringing him up as my own. I chose the latter. Wholeheartedly. Without reservations. Peter is and always will be my son. Whom Katherine slept with to make him doesn't matter to me. He is my son."

Alf blinked back tears, amazed by Kyle's love for Peter.

"Of course it *matters*." David's mouth twisted, disgust and confusion crossing his patrician face as he stared at Kyle. "He's not yours despite your justifications. Why you would even make this much fuss over the little cuckoo—"

Kyle struck him hard in the jaw, laying David out flat on the floor.

Jenkins raised his eyebrows and bent over the man. "Out cold."

"Take him and lock him up—somewhere he can't escape, mind." Kyle shook his hand. "Get the papers ready. I've an appointment to make at Crewe's house."

Talbot threw David over his shoulder and Jenkins and Riley followed him out of the room.

"They're going to kill you," Alf said.

"They're going to try." Kyle was examining his knuckles. They looked as if they were bleeding. "Doesn't mean they'll succeed. He's my son."

"I know," she said softly. "Give me your handkerchief."

She got up and found the decanter of brandy in the corner. She wet the handkerchief with the liquor and came back with the cloth.

He watched as she dabbed at the broken skin on his knuckles. "He's so small. I can't stand to think of him alone and afraid." He swallowed. "Maybe hurt."

She looked up at him and placed her palm on his cheek. She couldn't fathom the wonder of him. Men—especially aristocratic men—put everything into their lineage. Into their bloodlines. Into whether or not their children were their own. Even in St Giles the very worst thing you could call a man was a cuckold.

Yet Kyle had knowingly brought up his wife's bastard as his own son. More, he'd not shown any bias in his dealings with either son. If David hadn't blurted out the truth, she would have never guessed that Peter was any different from Kit.

He sighed and leaned his forehead against hers. "I'll need to have my men follow me to wherever they take me. I don't want to put you in danger, my darling imp, but you're the only one who can climb those rooftops. It may be the sole way to keep up with them unseen. Will you do this for me?"

She kissed him gently, her lips closed. "Of course I will."

"Thank you."

She looked at him, his determined black eyes, his black bristly pirate's face, his sinfully full lips, this man who was going to almost certain death for a son not of his blood.

She loved him.

She loved him and she was going to let him go.

HUGH PAUSED OUTSIDE the boys' room and took a breath before entering.

Kit was on the bed, the puppy curled asleep beside him.

He glanced at the dog. Doubtless it shouldn't be on the furniture, but he would not be the one to scold his son today.

Not if it might be the last memory the boy would have of him.

"Father?" Kit had looked up at his entrance.

Hugh tried to smile, but it seemed an impossible task just now. He sat by the boy instead.

"Are you going to bring Peter home?" Kit asked.

"Yes," Hugh said. "I want you to know..." He cleared his throat as he reached out and stroked back the boy's dark curls. His hair still hadn't been properly brushed this morning. "I want you to know that I love you and I love Peter."

Kit frowned. "Then why did you leave us?"

Hugh blinked, something inside him squeezing. He hadn't... well, he supposed he deserved that question, but now? Now he needed to get to Peter.

And...oh hell. He might never have another chance to answer the question.

Impossible as it was to answer properly for a little boy. "Your mother and I argued. We didn't get on and we couldn't live together. But I've always loved you both."

Kit was still frowning, but he nodded. He peeked up through his tangled hair. "You shouldn't leave again."

He had to clear his throat to answer, and even then his voice was husky. "No, I won't."

He hoped that Kit would forgive him if it turned out he was lying. If he didn't return tonight with Peter. But he was going to do everything in his power to fulfill this promise to the boy.

To come back and become the father he should have been all along.

Hugh squeezed his eyes shut, praying to a god he wasn't even sure he believed in anymore. Then he kissed his son's forehead and got up.

Kit was crying, trying to hide it bravely, his little lips pressed together, but the sobs shook him.

Hugh placed a hand on his head for a second, his fingers trembling, and then turned and strode to the door.

He had to stop for a second with his hand on the knob and draw breath. Dear God, let him come back alive. A boy shouldn't grow up without a father. He knew that firsthand.

He shoved the thought aside. Shoved it deep within a corner of his mind, because he had to make sure he came out of this alive and with his younger son in his arms.

Outside Kit's room he found Bell and Riley.

He looked at the boy first. "Will you stay with my son for me, Bell?"

"Yes, Your Grace." Bell's eyes were red-rimmed, but he stood straight and tall.

"Good lad." Hugh opened the door for him.

Then he met Riley's eyes. "Guard him well for me."

The former soldier wore a brace of pistols and had a sword on his hip. "Aye, sir, I'll guard him with my life."

Hugh nodded and then turned and ran down the stairs and to the front entry hall, where Talbot, Jenkins, and Alf were waiting for him.

He looked at them each in turn, lingering on Alf's lovely face because he couldn't help himself even now. "Remember: no matter what, don't reveal yourselves until you see Peter."

All three nodded. Hugh waved the men to the back of the house. They would be following his carriage, each in his own way.

He turned to Alf. "Do I have your word?"

She tilted her head. "Of course."

He took her shoulders and couldn't refrain from a little shake. She was such a passionate thing, and he knew she had some affection for him. "They may beat me or even try and kill me. You *must* not intervene. This mission has only one goal: to rescue Peter. If you show yourself before they take me to him, all this will be in vain. We will have lost him."

She set her jaw, her big brown eyes serious, and for the first time he saw in her gaze all the years that she'd lived on this earth.

"I know," she said as she cradled his face in her palms. "We'll bring back your son, safe and sound. Together."

"Be careful," he said fiercely, and kissed her hard.

He turned and went out the front door.

The carriage ride to Crewe's house seemed to take an age. He watched from the windows, though he couldn't see either of his men or Alf.

That was a good thing, he reminded himself. If he couldn't see them, then any of the Lords watching wouldn't be able to see them, either.

When the carriage finally stopped, Hugh stepped out with the papers in a folder under his arm. He mounted the steps to Crewe's house and knocked.

The door was opened by Dowling, looking nervous. "You're by yourself?"

Hugh nodded. "Where's my son?"

Dowling ignored his question to peer at the street behind Hugh. "Come inside."

Hugh stepped into the house. Immediately two men came at him, one from either side, and took his arms. He didn't resist. Dowling snatched the file away as the men found and removed the dagger in Hugh's coat pocket.

Dowling nodded to the bully on Hugh's right.

They led him farther into the house, down a hall, and into a sitting room.

Exley was waiting there, drinking tea, and looking more like a cadaver than ever.

He glanced up on their entrance. "Did he have the papers?"

Dowling stepped forward, handing over the file.

"Where's my son?" Hugh demanded again.

Exley flicked a finger without looking up from the file.

One of the rogues holding Hugh punched him in the side of the head.

He fell to his knees, his ears ringing. Hugh planted one hand on the floor to brace himself and stood up, glaring at the earl.

"They seem to be all here," Exley drawled after another minute. He finally looked up at Hugh. "Your son is ... safe." He smiled. "For the moment, in any case. Make any attempt at escape or at harming any of us and he won't be, I can promise you that. Do you understand?"

"I've already brought you the papers," Hugh said calmly. "All I want is Peter back."

"Good." Exley nodded at the toughs.

Immediately a hood was thrown over Hugh's head. He fought not to struggle, not to resist in any way, but it was hard. Especially when their next step was to tie his hands together in front of him with cord.

They marched him through the house and out the back door—he could tell from the smell of the kitchens. Through the gardens and into the mews. He hoped his men and Alf could see him. A carriage was in the mews, and he was roughly bundled in.

The carriage rocked as they set off, but then jolted to a stop not five minutes later. Hugh tensed and felt himself being shoved out one carriage door and into another without even touching the ground. The carriages must have been side by side.

Immediately the second carriage pulled away.

Had his men noticed the switch?

He turned his head, inhaling, listening, trying to discover where they were in London.

Once again they stopped abruptly, and once again they changed carriages.

Now he could smell the rot of fishes. The river? Were they headed to the wharves?

The carriage stopped for a third time, and Hugh prepared to stand.

"Just a minute, Your Grace," Exley said, and a hand pressed the hood to Hugh's mouth and nose, while others held his arms and legs.

He bucked. Despite the warning to submit. It was an instinctive reaction to the lack of air.

He heard Exley's laughter as his body jerked and his lungs seized, and he knew: he'd failed.

He'd failed.

Then everything went black.

Chapter Seventeen

*The Black Prince rode far away from the castle and
cut the belled jesses from the Golden Falcon's legs. He
tossed her into the air and shouted, "Go!"
The bird wheeled and tried to return to his arm, but he
threw pebbles at her until she at last screamed her grief
and flew away.
He watched until he could see her no more. Then he
returned to his father and presented him with a still-
bleeding chicken heart.
The Black Wizard smiled. "Well done, my son."...*
—From *The Black Prince and the Golden Falcon*

She'd failed.

Alf slid down a balcony roof, jumped to a stack of crates,
and hopped down to the cobblestones, desperately scanning
the carriage she'd been following from the rooftops. It was
drawn by a pair of blacks, the one on the right missing half
an ear. The carriage was the second one they'd tossed Kyle
into. Now it was stopped, the horses standing with their
heads lowered, dozing, and the driver smoking a pipe. Her

worst fears were confirmed when she ran around the back and saw the interior was empty.

She'd lost Kyle.

"Bloody hell!"

Alf turned in a circle, searching the street, searching the crowd. He'd been hooded. Had they somehow left the carriage without her seeing? Bundled him into one of the buildings along the way? Should she retrace the carriage route?

But what if they'd pulled that trick again? What if they'd put him into yet *another* carriage? Or a wagon under a blanket? He could be halfway to Bath and she none the wiser.

"*Fucking* hell!"

She began jogging back the way she'd come. Maybe Talbot or Jenkins had been more observant.

But that hope was dashed when she turned a corner and saw Talbot peering under a tarp on a cart, ignoring the swearing driver.

Talbot turned and saw her and started in her direction. "Do you know where he is, miss?"

She shook her head bitterly. "I lost him in the second carriage they put him in."

"Better than Jenkins and me," Talbot said bitterly. "We followed the first until we saw it was empty."

Jenkins came jogging toward them, his brow damp with sweat and his face grim. "Nothing. I looked in all directions at the crossroads. There wasn't even a carriage in sight. We've lost him."

She closed her eyes, trying hard to *think*. "Where would they take him?"

"I don't know, miss," Talbot said.

"Well we can't just *stand* here," she growled, hands on hips. She made a decision. "Right. Back to Kyle House.

We'll consult with Riley. Maybe send out Bell and some footmen to St Giles. I have contacts I can direct them to. At least *try* and get some information."

"That's a good idea, miss." Jenkins began walking swiftly. Alf had to jog to keep up with the two men. "I'll work at the cypher. It seems strange that the earl reacted so violently to the theft of the papers. Other than the cypher, they all seemed innocent enough."

Alf nodded, feeling bad for taking out her worry for Kyle on the two men. "We ought to send word to Lady Jordan as well. The more minds the better."

But when they returned to Kyle House, they found Iris already waiting in the library.

She looked up as Alf and the two former soldiers entered. "Is it true what Mr. Riley tells me? That Peter..."

Alf nodded once. "Yes. Kyle brought the papers to Exley, and we followed them when they took him away, but..." She shook her head. "We lost them. We lost *him*."

"Oh." Iris sat suddenly in Kyle's chair, her face paper white. "*Oh*."

"We don't know where they may've taken him," Alf said, feeling restless and useless. "Where they might have Peter."

Iris suddenly looked up. "But I might help." She fumbled in her pocket.

"What do you mean, my lady?" Talbot asked.

"I solved the cypher," Iris said, drawing her copy out of her pocket. "It was quite a lovely little puzzle and it did take me a while, but around seven this morning I remembered Polybius and his checkerboard, and after that it was quite easy, really."

She pointed to a strange little diagram she'd drawn beside the two columns of numbers:

	1	2	3	4	5
6	A	B	C	D	E
7	F	G	H	I/J	K
8	L	M	N	O	P
9	Q	R	S	T	U
0	V	W	X	Y	Z

"You see? Each letter is composed of two numbers. So, for instance, *A* is 61 and *CAT* would be 636194. It's quite clever." Iris glanced up from her cypher and seemed to realize that none of them—with the possible exception of Jenkins—had any idea who Polybius was, let alone what she was talking about.

Iris cleared her throat. "The point is, it's a list of names. But at the bottom, you remember those longer numbers?"

"Aye," Alf said, looking over her shoulder.

Iris smiled. "That's a location."

"Oh," Alf breathed. Hope suddenly rushed into her breast. She looked up and caught Talbot's eye. "Have the carriage brought around."

"Yes, miss!" The big man was already rushing out the door.

She turned to Jenkins. "Find three footmen to guard Kit. We're going to need Riley. And we'll need to arm ourselves."

Jenkins raised his eyebrows. "*We*, miss?"

She nodded. "I'm going, too."

"I don't know that the duke would want you putting yourself in danger, miss," Jenkins said gravely.

"Well, he'll just have to tell me that himself after we rescue him, won't he?"

She was out the library door and rushing up the stairs while Iris was still protesting. She had her daggers hidden on her body, but her swords were still under the bed in the servants' room.

Five minutes later she was back down the stairs, buckling on her swords. Iris and Kyle's men were gathered in the hallway.

Riley looked intently at her. "You know how to use those, miss?"

Alf raised her chin. "Yes, I do."

The three men—all former soldiers and older than she—exchanged glances. Then Jenkins nodded. "Good enough."

Alf turned to Iris. "Please send word to Copernicus Shrugg, the King's secretary, about what has happened and where we think the Lords of Chaos have taken Kyle."

"I'll send a man on horseback at once," Iris said, and then blurted, "dear God, be careful."

She hugged Alf hard.

Alf squeezed the other woman back, inhaling her delicate rose scent. "Can you take care of Kit while we're gone?"

"Of course I can." Iris stepped back with tears rimming her eyes. "Now go."

They ran out the door and down the steps and into the carriage. Jenkins and Talbot sat on one bench, she and Riley together across from them.

The carriage rattled into motion.

Alf sat tensely, watching out the window as the carriage rumbled through the streets. The address Iris had deciphered was east, by the river, and she wondered now if they should've tried to take a wherry. Exley had a head start. They might not even arrive in time, before...

But it was too late to second-guess herself. Better to make a plan and stick to it.

She glanced at the others in the carriage. Riley was jiggling his leg up and down, but he shot her a quick grin when he caught her eye. Jenkins was stoic. Talbot had his head back against the seat, his eyes closed, and appeared to be whispering to himself.

"Likes to pray before we go in," Riley murmured, tilting his head at Talbot. "He's a religious sort."

"Ah." She nodded, fingering her long sword.

"You're the Ghost, aren't you, miss?"

She glanced at him out of the corner of her eye, her brows raised.

The Irishman grinned as he swayed with the carriage's movement. "He was taken with you, miss, right from the start."

Across from them Jenkins cleared his throat.

Riley flushed. "What? You know it's true."

Jenkins sighed. "Yes. It's most certainly true." He cleared his throat. "We were all quite pleased when we realized you were the Ghost, miss. Quite pleased indeed."

Alf bit her lip and looked down because she didn't want to cry in front of these seasoned soldiers—not after she'd assured them that she was capable of handling herself in battle. But she was unaccountably touched by their words. By their acceptance.

In that moment she realized that she might have a place, here among them. Here with Kyle and his sons. In his life. In his bed. Perhaps even in his heart.

If she could find the courage within herself to ignore Ned's long-ago advice and let herself become close to someone else. Let herself rely on someone else.

If they could get Kyle and Peter out alive.

She drew in a breath, straightening and bracing herself. There was no point in returning to Kyle House or even St Giles if they didn't rescue Kyle and Peter safe and sound. There wasn't anything left for her there.

So she'd just have to make sure they succeeded.

HUGH GAGGED AND desperately fought down the urge to vomit. He still wore the hood, and if he expelled the contents of his stomach he might choke to death. He could hear the sound of oars and feel the sway of the river.

And his arse and shoulders were wet.

He was definitely lying in the bottom of a boat.

The boat thudded against wood, and someone kicked him in the ribs. "Get up."

He clumsily rolled to his knees and then stood. Rough hands grasped his elbows and helped him out of the boat. At least they didn't want him at the bottom of the Thames.

Yet.

He wondered how long he'd been unconscious. How far they'd rowed down the river. He could feel stone under his feet as he stumbled up the river steps. He was led down a gravel path, up more steps, and into a building.

"Welcome, Hugh Fitzroy, Duke of Kyle." That was Exley's voice, echoing oddly. "You wanted to know about the Lords of Chaos. Our members. Our business. Our private, sacred ceremonies."

The hood was pulled from his head by one of his guards.

Hugh blinked. He stood in what had once been a church, by the look of the carved stone pillars marching in parallel rows. But there were great gaps in the ceiling and jagged, blackened beams outlined against the blue of the sky.

Exley stood in front of what looked like a crude stone

altar—certainly not the one original to the church. He was highlighted by a beam of sunlight, his arms raised in a parody of a blessing. Surrounding both him and Hugh was a circle of men in black robes, their faces entirely covered in animal masks, at least a dozen in all.

Exley grinned a ghoul's grimace. "Are you glad to have your wish fulfilled?"

Hugh tested the ties on his wrists. "Where is my son?"

The earl's grin dimmed a little. "You grow repetitious, and I assure you, you are not the important one here." Exley raised his arms again, his voice louder. "Lords of Chaos, welcome! We have had a winter of travails, a time of testing. Only the strongest, the most intelligent, and the most ruthless Lord is fit to lead our body."

The earl paused to gaze at his audience. His upper lip curled. "Sir Aaron Crewe thought himself capable of leading us. Yet he brought the prying eyes of Kyle down upon us by his folly in murdering the Duchess of Kyle."

The masked figures hissed their disapproval.

Exley raised his hand to quiet them. "Never fear, my Lords. I have dealt with Crewe as I have dealt with Chase, another who sought to contest my leadership, for I—*I* am your rightful leader, your Dionysus!"

Exley made a slight bow as the Lords cheered. "Today, my Lords, we celebrate. We celebrate a new Dionysus and we celebrate the destruction of our enemy. We are all-powerful, my Lords. Not even a duke—the son of a king!—may seek to bring us to our knees."

The man was mad.

Exley snapped his fingers, and a robed man wearing a mole mask led Peter into the ring of figures.

Thank God. He was alive. Hugh felt his throat close.

Peter had no such problems.

"*Papa!*" he shrieked. "Papa! Papa! Papa!"

The man in the mole mask must not have been expecting such a strong reaction from a little boy, for Peter wriggled from his grasp and ran to Hugh.

Hugh knelt and swung his bound hands over the boy's head, hugging him close. Peter was crying, his face a wet, hysterical mess.

The man in the mole mask clutched at the boy's shoulders, trying to tear him from Hugh's arms.

"Get your bloody hands off my son!" Hugh growled, backing away. He picked Peter up and clutched the boy to his chest.

Two other Lords started for him.

"Come now, Your Grace," Exley crooned. "Don't be foolish. Let my men take the sweet little boy. It will be far more pleasant in the long run, I think. For both of you."

Hugh looked at Exley. Looked at that damned mockery of an altar behind the earl.

He had Peter in his arms, and yet Alf and his men weren't making an appearance.

They had lost him.

There was no rescue.

And he knew what the Lords of Chaos did at their revels to sweet little boys.

He couldn't give Peter up, couldn't back down, couldn't escape.

He was going to have to do this alone.

Hugh bent his head to his son's wet face and whispered in his ear. "I love you, Peter."

Then he put his head down and charged the man in the mole mask.

Mole Mask hadn't been expecting his charge. Hugh hit the man in the belly with his shoulder and head and knocked them all to the ground. Peter was screaming, terrified. Hugh rolled, putting his son underneath him, and felt the blows as the other two Lords piled on top of him. He grunted, elbowing and kicking as best he could while still shielding Peter. Somehow he had to make it through the ring of robed men.

Someone kicked him in the head and then the side.

Hugh grunted. Got to one elbow and both knees and started crawling, awkwardly holding Peter in one arm.

Dragging three men on top of him.

And then all hell broke loose.

Two shots rang out in rapid succession.

Hugh jerked at the sound, nearly falling on his face. He glanced up in time to see Exley lurch, his eyes wide in astonishment, as he fell backward, scarlet spreading over his chest.

Bloody hell, maybe they were about to be rescued after all.

Then he caught sight of Riley, grinning as he holstered his pistols and drew his sword. The Lords were shouting, some fighting, though by no means all. Some seemed stunned by this turn of events.

Hugh grinned.

He bent to Peter and kissed his cheek. "Listen to me. Stay down, cover your head, and close your eyes. Do you understand?"

The boy immediately screwed his eyes shut. "Yes, Papa."

Hugh unlooped his arms from Peter's body, clasped his fists together, and slammed them into the side of Mole Mask's head. He shook off the man still on his back, elbowed him in the throat, making the man gag, and then brought both fists down on the back of the man's head.

Two down.

He turned to his third assailant, but Jenkins was already there, clubbing the man down. "Is the boy all right, sir?"

"Yes," Hugh replied. "He'll be fine as soon as we can get the hell out of here."

The gray-haired man nodded, unperturbed. "We're working on that, sir."

Hugh staggered upright, his feet braced over Peter's prone form to guard him, and saw Talbot, wading into the black-robed figures, his bloodstained sword swinging.

A man in a badger mask charged him. Hugh put his shoulder down and braced himself, catching most of the force of the attack. The man reeled, his mask falling off. Hugh caught the back of his head, looked him in the eye, and slammed his forehead into the other man's nose.

Badger crumpled to the floor.

Hugh glanced up again and finally saw Alf. She was whirling, graceful and free, both swords working at once, one blocking, one thrusting, laying her enemies out with ruthless, feminine precision.

"I think it's time to leave, sir," Jenkins said.

Hugh picked up Peter, holding him close. "Are your eyes still closed?"

"Yes, Papa."

Hugh put his head down and ran to Alf with Jenkins by his side.

"This way, guv," Alf said, pointing to a side door.

Talbot and Riley were covering their retreat.

They ran, Hugh clutching Peter, aware of his son's legs wrapped around his waist, of the boy's wet face pressed against his body, of how glad he was of the slight weight.

A carriage was outside the ruined church, but as they came abreast of it, another vehicle rumbled up, accompanied by the thunder of a dozen mounted soldiers.

"Kyle!" Shrugg was waving to him from the open carriage window, his gray wig slightly askew. "I say, Kyle! Are you and the boy well?"

"We are indeed," Hugh called back. "But if your men would care to do the honor, there are the remains of the Lords of Chaos to be cleaned up inside that ruined church."

Shrugg looked positively gleeful. "Consider it done!"

Hugh turned back to his own waiting carriage, where Talbot swiftly sawed through his bindings. His men scrambled to climb on the outside, and he and Alf ducked inside with Peter.

The carriage jolted off.

"Peter?" Hugh said, prying the boy's face away from his chest. "Are you all right?"

The boy inhaled noisily on a sob. "Uncle David said he'd buy me a bag of sweets but then he wouldn't take me home, and he went away and left me with those bad men. I don't like Uncle David anymore!"

"Neither do I." Hugh sighed and kissed the boy's sticky, sweaty face. "Did the bad men hurt you?"

Peter looked up, his big blue eyes betrayed, his lower lip trembling. "They hurt my arm when they made me go to that place."

Hugh closed his eyes, thankful that had been the only damage done to Peter.

Then he took his son's face in his hand. "No bad man will ever hurt you again."

Peter frowned as if he wasn't entirely certain. "Promise?"

Hugh nodded.

"Good." The little boy put his head back on Hugh's chest, then rolled his eyes to look at Alf. "Can you sing me the moon song, please?"

Alf blinked hard and smiled. "Of course."

Peter sighed and thrust his grimy thumb into his mouth as Alf began to sing huskily about a moon and seeing someone you loved. At any other time Hugh would've reprimanded him.

Not today.

Instead he wrapped one arm around his son and the other around Alf and tugged them both closer to his heart.

Chapter Eighteen

*After that the Black Prince rode by his father's side,
silent and grave and feared, and if he sometimes seemed
to search the sky for something, no one made note of it,
least of all the Black Warlock himself....*
—From *The Black Prince and the Golden Falcon*

Alf watched from the doorway as Kyle laid his hand lightly on first Kit's and then Peter's back.

The boys' bedroom was lit only by the banked fire, the embers glowing warm in the little fireplace. Despite their being tired from the drama of the day, it had taken a long while for the children to fall asleep. Kyle had read to them and Alf had told them heavily edited stories of growing up in St Giles.

Now the boys lay curled together in the same bed, Pudding the puppy a little furry lump against Peter's bottom. Alf smiled crookedly at the sight. Kyle hadn't said a word when Peter had lifted the puppy into the bed.

Her smile faded when she looked at him again. Kyle's men were still celebrating their victory downstairs with the help of a half-dozen bottles of wine, but he had grown quieter and quieter as the day had worn on. She didn't quite understand his mood, but it made her uneasy. Shouldn't he be happy—or at least relieved? Peter was safe. The Earl of Exley was dead. All the Lords of Chaos who had been at the ceremony at the ruined church were either dead or injured and captured by Shrugg and his soldiers.

Kyle had done his job, just as he'd vowed he would. He had brought down and destroyed the Lords of Chaos. He'd avenged not only his own near assassination but also the murder of his wife.

He should be glad.

But he was brooding instead.

She watched him, this aristocratic man, born to an actress and a king. This man who had joined his flesh with hers. This man who had fought alongside her, who had forced her to confront her deepest fears and overcome them.

This man she loved.

This man she'd almost lost.

This man she still didn't understand. Strange that you could love a man with every particle of your being and not know why the corners of his mouth turned down.

The thought made her sad. "Are you coming to bed?"

He glanced up at her.

"They're safe now," she said gently. "You can leave them here for the night. The nursemaids are next door, and two footmen are on watch."

A muscle bunched in his jaw, and he nodded tightly before straightening and walking to her. They went down the stairs and he was silent, but he didn't send her away, so she was content.

He opened the door to his room and stood aside as if she were a proper lady.

That amused her. She trailed a fingertip across his chest as she walked by him. "Thank you, guv."

She stopped short when she saw that Jenkins was in the room, holding a pile of cloths by a steaming copper tub of water.

She suddenly wondered if she'd taken too much for granted. She wanted to be here in his room with him, tonight and all the nights after, and she thought that was what he wanted, but he'd never said that aloud to her.

Perhaps she'd misread him.

"I think we'll have no more need of you tonight, Jenkins," Kyle said from behind her. "Go and have a drink with Riley and Talbot—and make sure that Bell doesn't have more than half a glass of wine."

"Sir." The former soldier bowed, casting a very small smile in her direction before setting the cloths on a chair and letting himself out.

Kyle cleared his throat, gesturing to the bath. "It's for you."

She looked from him to the tub, her heart shriveling small like a salted snail. "Do you . . . do you think I smell?"

"No!" He thrust his hand into his hair. "I thought . . . *goddamn it*, I merely thought you would like a bath after today. If you don't want it, I can . . ."

He cut himself off, maybe because she'd walked past him and was peering in the tub. It was lined with fine white cloths, the water clear and hot. She'd never had a bath before.

Alf took off her coat and tossed it over a chair.

"Ah," he said behind her, "do you want me to leave?"

She glanced at him. "Why?"

"So that you might have some privacy."

She shrugged off her waistcoat, biting back a smirk. "Why?"

He shook his head at her and sighed. "I've no idea."

After that he simply watched as she swiftly shed the rest of her clothes. Maybe she should've tried to do it seductively, but she wasn't some fine lady or courtesan. She was just Alf. And she wanted that bath.

She shivered in anticipation as she crept up to it naked and set her hands on the warm sides. Maybe there was a graceful way to get in, but she just shoved a leg over and climbed in.

And oh, but it was fine! Lovely hot water all around her, lapping at her shoulders and warming her bones. This was what queens must feel like in their palaces. The copper tub was probably only big enough for Kyle to sit in, but she could draw up her knees and dunk her entire head.

She pinched her nose and held her breath and did just that, and the warm water closed over her ears and mouth and eyes and it was as if she were in her own little cave. No sight, no sound. Just warmth.

But then she ran out of air and had to come bursting out of the water, sputtering and laughing.

Kyle was staring at her, his coat in his hand as if forgotten. His black eyes held an odd light. He threw the coat aside, not even seeming to care as it fell to the floor, and began working on the buttons of his waistcoat.

She eyed him for a moment and then shrugged and reached for the soap sitting on a small stool next to the tub. It was lovely soap, fine and white. She held it cupped in her hands and brought it to her nose. Oh, it smelled of flowers and rich things, and when she dipped it in the water it made a creamy lather. Not like the nasty brown lye-and-animal-fat soap she'd sometimes used. This soap was fit for a queen, and she sighed as she smoothed it over her face and arms.

Kyle was down to his breeches, his chest hair dark and curling against his skin.

She shivered.

"We used to dream of this, Ned and me," she said softly

as she cleaned between her toes. "Enough hot water to fill a tub full, and soap so fine it was white and pure."

"Did you?" he murmured as he poured water into a basin. He wet a cloth and washed himself with efficient briskness. "What else did you dream of?"

"Oh, all sort of things." She sucked in a breath as she passed the soapy cloth over a scrape on her knee. It stung. "Tables crowded with roasts, meat pies, gravy, and cakes. Shoes that fit and had no holes. Warm coats. A bed." She shook her head because her voice had cracked on that last one. She didn't want to think of sad things tonight. She cleared her throat. "Once when I was ten or so Ned and I saw a lady with such a beautiful muff. It was a deep red—so elegant! and embroidered all around the hand holes in gold thread. Oh, I dreamed on that muff for years afterwards. I wanted one made of cream silk with violets embroidered all over it. I used to lie awake and imagine my muff until I could picture it, so real in my mind I could almost touch it." She sighed, remembering, and then looked at him. "Did you dream of things when you were little?"

He raised his head, dripping, over the basin, and reached for a cloth. "No. I had everything I needed."

"But..." She wrinkled her nose in thought as she looked at him. He was an educated man, she knew that. An aristocrat who had been sent to the finest schools in the land. And yet, she thought, in this she might have the better learning. "But isn't dreaming about what you *hope* for, not what you need?"

He stared at her. "Why would I hope for more than I need?"

"I don't know," she said gently. "But it seems like something people do, dream. It's just the way we are. After all, I never *needed* a muff when I was but a little thing running the streets of St Giles—not like I needed food or shoes that didn't have holes in the soles or a proper bed. What would I have done with a fine embroidered muff except maybe sell it? But that isn't what mattered. I knew I wasn't ever going to have a pretty muff, but that didn't mean I couldn't *dream* about having one of my very own. It passed the time, didn't it, when nights were so cold and bleak? Thinking and hoping for something better than what I had." She looked at him, so strong, so implacable. Was he ever weak or worried or sad? "If you can't dream of something you don't *need* but *want* so much it makes your heart sing, well, you might as well just lay down right there and breathe your last, I reckon. Some things are worth more than bread or shoes or a warm bed."

He stared at her, looking puzzled, almost as if he didn't know what to make of her. "Maybe for you. As for me, longing for something more than I need, something that is unattainable..." He trailed away, looking down as he began unbuttoning his breeches. "That way leads to...dissatisfaction. Unhappiness."

She felt her pulse beating so very near the surface of her skin, like the fluttering of a bird, trapped there. "But if the thing you longed for *were* attainable, surely then—"

He glanced up, his brows drawn together quite fiercely. "You just said you could never have a muff."

She felt a sad little smile curve her lips. "I wasn't sure we were still talking about muffs, guv."

He didn't answer her.

Well, and that was answer enough, wasn't it? She let out a breath, her heart aching something fierce inside her breast.

He shed his breeches and smallclothes and turned to his dresser, naked.

She watched him as she lathered his fine white soap between her palms and washed her hair. He had a lovely back, had Kyle. Broad and muscled, narrowing to fine trim haunches. She'd never ogled a man's buttocks as much as she had since meeting him. He had a way, when he wasn't in a great hurry, of ambling. It was a very male walk. It caught a person's—a *woman's*—eye, especially from the back. Pity gentlemen wore such long coats, hiding all the best parts of themselves.

She leaned back in the bath and dipped her head below the water to rinse her hair, and when she straightened again he was beside her, holding out a drying cloth.

"Are you done yet?" he asked, his voice gruff.

His cock was half-hard, though, so he wasn't as uninterested as he pretended. And she hadn't forever with him in which to sulk.

So she smiled at him, just for having a cock that couldn't hide his fondness for her. "Yes."

She stood in the tub and he steadied her as she climbed out, but as he made to wrap the drying cloth around her, she simply twined her arms about his neck and kissed him.

"You'll get me wet," he said against her lips, but neither he nor his cock seemed to mind, and then he opened his mouth over hers.

He was slow as he explored her mouth, and for a long minute she forgot all about the drying cloth. About dripping on the floor. About tomorrow and the world outside.

About everything else except his tongue sliding against hers. His hands holding her face. His chest hair rasping against her wet nipples. His hot thigh nudging confidently between her legs, rubbing against her mound, making her gasp into his mouth. And still he kissed her slowly, his mouth open on hers, his tongue thrusting inside. It was luscious and sweet. Explicit and thorough.

"God, how I want you," he raised his face to whisper. "I can't seem to help myself, no matter how I try."

He nipped her bottom lip and plunged in again, angling his head over hers.

She felt surrounded. Protected.

Cherished.

He wrapped the cloth around her and bent suddenly. He picked her up, high in his arms, cradled like a child, and she gasped, startled.

He raised an eyebrow at her, his beautiful lips quirking just a bit, and she thought, oh, if only this could be forever. Hoping, because she was the one who still longed and hoped even if it was impossible.

He laid her on the bed as if she were something special to him, and she smiled up at him, holding out her arms.

"Your hair is wet," he said.

"I don't care," she replied, because she didn't.

"You'll catch a chill." He bent over her, an intent line between his brows, and blotted her hair with the cloth. "It'll tangle."

"Are you a lady's maid now, guv?"

He winced and stood, crossing to his dresser to bring back his comb. "Why do you never call me Hugh?"

He sat down on the bed beside her.

She blinked at him, sitting up so he could comb her hair. "Do you want me to?"

He drew the comb through her hair so gently it didn't even pull. "Here, in my bed, yes."

She inhaled and said carefully, "Well, then. Will you make love to me, Hugh?"

He tossed aside the comb. "God, yes."

He sprawled back against the big headboard and pulled her into his lap. She didn't know where to put her legs at first, but then he showed her, carefully drawing them over his thighs so she was almost astride him.

She looked down at him gravely and took his face in her palms. The scar from that first night in St Giles when she'd been the Ghost and he'd been fighting off a pack of footpads was nearly healed. It was a pink scrawl against the upper corner of his forehead. In another month or so it would be barely noticeable.

Would she be here to see it heal entirely?

She bent her head and kissed the scar, and then between his brows, on that line where he always frowned. His high cheekbone, bruised from the fight tonight. The corner of his wickedly pretty lips, where there was always a bit of a curl.

He turned his face a fraction, and then she was drawing from his mouth. Inhaling all his hurts, all his needs, all the hopes he could never dream.

This man. This man she couldn't have for her own.

She rose, balanced over his cock, heavy between her legs, trembling on her knees. She wanted to take him in and hold him forever. To never let this night go.

"Easy," he whispered, his voice rough.

He put a hand on her hip to steady her, his thumb brushing back and forth on her skin as they kissed.

She felt tears start in her eyes, and she closed them fiercely. She wouldn't let him see her cry. She was Alf of St Giles and she wasn't weak or scared or to be pitied.

She felt his palm on her breast and was grateful for the distraction. The stab of sweet pleasure as he pinched her nipple.

She gasped, breaking their kiss, and saw that he was watching her.

"Are you still sore?" he asked, and it was such an intimate question she nearly hid her face.

"No," she lied, for she was a little. Not much, though—certainly not enough to pass up a night with him. "I want you."

He closed his eyes as if he were in pain, and his prick jerked against her thigh. She looked down at it, such a splendid thing, all ruddy and alive. Thick and hard, the foreskin stretched back, the eye weeping a little.

"Come here," he said, interrupting her inspection.

He urged her up higher and took a nipple between his teeth.

She gasped, watching him through lidded eyes as he suckled her, those pretty lips ruby against her breast, making her feel such things. Making her feel wanton.

His black eyes flicked open and gleamed up at her, and she couldn't keep her hips from moving. Seeking something.

He lifted one knee, wedging it between her legs, firmly against her folds.

Oh. Oh, that felt good.

She closed her eyes and slid against him as he lifted his head and blew on her wet nipple.

She whimpered.

He moved to suck her other nipple while he thumbed the first, pulling pleasure from the two points, holding her captive. She'd never known her nipples could be so sensitive. That *she* could be so aware. She'd covered and hid and disguised herself for so many years, and now she was naked with him.

It was like being reborn. Her skin alive and new.

She ran her fingertips over her sides, feeling her skin prickle and spark. Feeling the sweet, wet ache between her legs. Feeling the tight pull of his lips.

Until she cried out loud, gasping, her head thrown back, her body bowed, her legs spread crudely over his knee. It was as if a great hand seized her, squeezing life into her. Hope and dreams and every sensation she'd denied herself living as a boy.

If his hands hadn't grabbed hold of her she might've collapsed to the bed.

But he held her, safe above him, and she opened her eyes and saw him. His eyes were black and fierce, his lips parted.

He wanted her.

"Ride me," he rasped.

She blinked, not fully comprehending, but he was spreading her legs farther apart, taking away his knee and lowering her to his cock.

Oh, if she'd thought it large before, that was nothing to how proud he was now. A dark, angry red, heavy and full, thickest at the middle, and the foreskin stretched taut about the ridge of the head. She wanted to stare. To look her fill and perhaps feel it with hands and tongue.

He had other ideas.

He took hold of himself as she watched and rubbed his prick against her wet quim. "Sit."

She could feel him at her entrance—*there*—big and waiting. She leaned a little forward, placing her hands on his shoulders and meeting his eyes.

Staring into his eyes as she tilted down and felt him breach her.

His nostrils were flared, his gaze implacable. "More."

She nodded, lowering herself, *pushing* down, forcing that big wedge of hot flesh past her fragile folds and into her. It felt...it felt as if he were taking her, even if she was the one doing all the moving.

She bit her lip at the realization, her gaze flicking up to meet his, even as she felt a pulse of desire at her center. She could *smell* how wet she was for him, which meant he could, too.

"Almost there," he whispered, and flicked a thumb over her nipple.

She jolted, the movement bringing her down another inch, and she thought she saw the shadow of a smile on his face.

So she lifted her chin and slammed herself all the way on him, taking his penis fully within her.

"Good girl." He took her mouth in a savage kiss, lunging up at her, his pelvis grinding into hers.

She moaned, for she was still oversensitive from her earlier orgasm. Every movement, every rough thrust of tongue and cock was a spark on her skin, so pleasurable it was nearly painful. She couldn't stop, couldn't hold back, could only cling to him as he bucked beneath her.

Driving himself into her again and again.

And then he put both his thumbs in her cunny, right where his cock stretched her flesh tight, and circled her wet, aching pearl until she shoved a fist in her mouth and screamed.

He growled and pulled her up and off his cock, and she felt his hot seed spurt against her stomach and thigh. For a moment she leaned against him, her head against his heaving chest, his face on her shoulder. Then he gently rolled her to the bed and got up.

Alf lay with her eyes closed, half-dreaming, before she felt a damp cloth cleaning her belly and thighs. She opened her eyes and looked at him, a duke, wiping his come from her body.

But perhaps here he was simply a man and she simply a woman.

He got in the bed and she settled against him, his big arms around her.

She could dream, at least.

Chapter Nineteen

*On the twelfth anniversary of the defeat of the White
Sorceress, the Black Warlock caused a great celebration
to be held at the ruins of Castle White. He stood with
his son in the exact spot where the sorceress had died
and spread wide his arms as he crowed in triumph to a
gathered crowd.
And as he did so a circle of magical fire sprang up
around him and the Black Prince. The White Sorceress's
dying curse was finally being fulfilled....*
—From *The Black Prince and the Golden Falcon*

Hugh woke to peace. To the sun at the window and a warm
breast against his arm, and truly his first emotion was joy.

Followed immediately by fear.

For it wasn't as if he'd never felt joy before in his life.
He'd thought himself blissfully in love with Katherine once.
That had led to screaming arguments, anger the like of
which he'd never known, and exile from his land, his home,
and his family.

He turned to look at Alf. She lay with dark lashes on
her delicate cheeks, her pink lips parted in sleep. Her hair

was tangled about her head, a lock almost across her closed eyelid.

He gently brushed it aside without waking her.

Alf was nothing like Katherine, in looks or temperament or station in life. Alf was lovely and quick and cocky, where Katherine had been an elegant dark beauty. Alf made him laugh with her teasing.

Katherine's teasing had led only to sex or bitter arguments.

And of course Katherine had been the better match. She had been an aristocrat, born and bred to be the wife, if not of a duke, then certainly of a titled gentleman. She'd been taught how to plan balls, how to talk to foreign princes, how to pour tea.

Alf knew none of that. She simply brought him joy.

That was what sent a thrill of unease down his spine. In this emotion he could not trust himself.

But he could not draw away, either. He'd tried to keep himself apart from Alf and failed.

He watched as she sighed and turned her head on the pillow, her palm curling against her cheek.

He *wanted* her. Not just her body. He wanted her laughter. He wanted the spark he saw in her eyes when she teased him. He wanted the way she ate too fast, the appetite and enthusiasm she had for jam. He wanted the way she held his sons and told them unsuitable stories. He wanted her worldly cynicism and her innocent wonder. He wanted her running beside him, in the night or in the day. Hell, he wanted to cross swords with her and then make love to her afterward, still panting with their exercise.

He wanted her beside him always.

And he couldn't trust his want.

He must've made a sound then, for she opened her eyes and looked up at him.

Her pink lips curled in welcome. "Hugh."

"Alf." He bent—he couldn't bloody stop himself—and brushed a kiss across her mouth. She was warm. Humid. Smelling of woman and him. He was hard against her—he'd woken hard—and his hips shifted, his cock sliding on her thigh.

He raised his head and her smile widened beautifully. The hand by her cheek disappeared underneath the coverlet and he knew where it was headed.

He caught her wrist.

That beautiful smile died. "Guv?"

He cleared his throat. "I need to speak to Shrugg."

"This early in the morning?" She glanced at the window and then back at him, her smile uncertain now. "I never knew swell coves were up and about before noon."

He hated that he'd made her doubt herself, but he needed to think.

And he couldn't think naked and in bed with her. "Some of us are." He let go of her and rolled to the edge of the bed. "I should have seen Shrugg yesterday to give him my report on the Lords of Chaos and to hand over both the list of names and the cypher that Iris decrypted, but I didn't want to leave Peter and Kit. I'm surprised he didn't send messengers to pound on my door at dawn's first light."

He stood and began dressing. "I'll make sure that Cook prepares some breakfast. You can have it either here or in the dining room, whichever you'd prefer."

God, he sounded like a bloody stiff ass. He knew it even as his mouth was forming the words, and yet he couldn't stop himself.

She sat up, wrapping her arms around her legs, but didn't reply.

He frowned, feeling ill at ease as he donned his waistcoat. Would she find herself bored in the house without him?

There were the boys and his men, but perhaps she didn't consider them adequate company. Of course she could go out.

The thought reminded him.

He crossed to a heavy chest of drawers and took a key out of his pocket to unlock the top drawer.

Inside he found a purse of coins, and he turned with it in his hands. "I owe you this, I think. You've more than done the job I originally hired you for, and I never gave you the second payment."

He handed her the purse, a slight smile quirking his lips. What would she spend the money on? Would she tell him when he returned? Or did she hoard her coins like a small fiery dragon?

"Thank you, guv," she said, her voice gruff. She'd bent her head over the purse, held in her lap, so that he couldn't see her face.

"You're welcome," he replied, turning to the door. "I have my son's life because of you. Don't think I'll ever forget that, Alf."

"I'm not likely to forget anything about you, guv," she called.

He turned.

She'd straightened in the bed and was staring at him, the covers pooled in her lap, her breasts proud and bare. She looked like an Amazon warrior.

He hesitated. This was all wrong and he knew it. He almost returned to her and that warm bed, but he was already dressed and he hadn't lied about Shrugg. The man had sent two urgent letters yesterday, demanding information.

He shook his head. When he got back maybe he'd have lifted himself from this awkward humor. "Good-bye, Alf."

"Good-bye, guv."

He left then without turning back, because if he did he

wasn't at all sure he'd be able to resist temptation a second time.

He walked to the palace and then spent nearly three long and tedious hours explaining and going over everything that had happened in the last three weeks with Shrugg.

At the end of that time the older man sat back and nodded with evident satisfaction. "I'll task my men with checking the names on the list you've given me against the gentlemen we arrested at the church, but I can tell you now that there are very few names on that list that I don't recognize and already know to be dead or in prison. I think the Lords of Chaos are done."

"Yes," Hugh replied. "They're finished. We don't have Dyemore, but what can he do without a society to lead? Everyone else is gone." He rose and smiled grimly. "Besides, I'll be watching him."

"Thank you, Your Grace." Shrugg stood as well. "His Majesty is most pleased with the result of your endeavors." He hesitated. "Are you still interested in traveling? I've word that a gentleman of your talents will soon be of use in Vienna. Especially when you marry Lady Jordan. An intelligent and sophisticated wife can be a very helpful tool for a diplomat."

Hugh's lips firmed. "I'm afraid Lady Jordan has informed me that we no longer suit."

"Indeed?" Shrugg's bushy eyebrows nearly reached his wig. "I'm sorry to hear that, Your Grace. But never fear, there are other ladies in society of equally old lineage. When you find your new duchess I'm sure she'll be the sort to be able to move in the courts of Europe."

Hugh opened his mouth…and then closed it. The fictional woman Shrugg described was exactly what he had wanted when he'd considered marrying Iris. A member of society. A lady from a good family. Someone who could manage his household. Someone who wouldn't disturb him. Someone who would never cause him pain or passion.

And he knew in his heart and in his soul and in his *gut* that he didn't want that anymore.

He wanted Alf.

No one else.

He took a breath and looked at Shrugg. "I won't be able to travel to the Continent. Not while my sons are so young. I'll be staying in England for the foreseeable future."

"A pity." Shrugg sighed heavily and then brightened. "But I'm sure we'll find something for you to do here as well."

"Hmm," Hugh replied noncommittally. The truth was, he might want to take some time to simply be with his sons.

And Alf.

He inhaled. He couldn't think of a future—a family— that didn't have her in it. Even if she never learned how to hold a ball or pour tea properly. Alf was part of the whole that was he, Peter, and Kit.

And really he'd rather be convincing her of that for the next several years than running all over London destroying secret societies.

He nodded to Shrugg, made his final farewells, and left.

Outside, the day had brightened, and he strode briskly toward his house, wanting to get home to Alf and the boys. If Alf was still at the house, perhaps they could liberate the boys from the nursery. Take them for a ride or simply sit in the library while they played with Pudding.

By the time he ran up his own front steps he was smiling.

The butler took his hat and cloak and Hugh asked, "Is Alf still in?"

"No, Your Grace," Cox replied. "Miss Alf left several hours ago."

He grimaced in disappointment. "Did she take the carriage?"

"She left on foot, I believe—"

Damn. He should've told her she was free to use the carriage.

But the butler was still speaking. "—carrying a bag."

For a moment Hugh stared at Cox. A bag? Why would she be carrying a bag?

He walked to the staircase, his muscles tensing for some reason, and then he was running. All the way to the top, to the servants' floor. He strode down the hall and flung open the door to the room that Alf had been using.

The bed was neatly made. The room was empty.

He checked the tiny chest of drawers to be sure, his breath coming faster for some reason, and then descended to his own room.

He startled Jenkins when he burst into his bedroom.

"Sir?"

Hugh ignored the former soldier, scanning the room. Nothing remained of Alf.

His chest was heaving now as he stared. She hadn't had much to begin with, he reminded himself. The clothes on her back. Her Ghost attire. The bag of money he'd given her this morning. Was there anything else?

He couldn't remember.

There was no point in panicking. She'd probably only left for the day. She was a woman used to going about by herself. If she returned...*when* she returned, he would talk to her very strongly about changing that. About at least telling someone where she was going and when she'd be back.

Until then he'd just have to wait.

Which he did.

All day and into the night.

But when the clock struck midnight Hugh had to finally believe it: Alf was gone.

SHE HAD NO true place in the world anymore.

Alf stood on a corner and wrapped her arms about herself. She wore her one dress—the blue dress that used to belong to Iris's maid. Why, she wasn't sure, because it wouldn't be wise to go into St Giles as a woman. But she'd not exactly been in a thoughtful frame of mind when she'd donned her clothing this morning.

All she could think about was that it was over. Kyle—*Hugh*—had paid her off. Let her know that he considered their liaison at an end. She'd just wanted to flee and lick her wounds a bit.

And she had. All day. Walking up and down London Town, her bag in her hand.

The problem was this: she'd had a life as a boy in St Giles. A place to stay. A means of making money. A way of *being*. It hadn't been exactly the best life in the world, but it had been hers and hers alone.

But Hugh had come along and picked her up, looked her in the eye, and shaken her. Told her she could be *more*. Turned her inside out and upside down and now, *now* she was a woman.

She didn't know how to make her way as a woman. Well, aside from on her back, and she'd rather not, thank you very much.

She started walking, her feet weary and sore. She was so tired, and it was cold and dark now. She just wanted a place to lay her head so she could *think*.

Because she wasn't sure she was the same person anymore. She'd spent the last weeks not only wearing a dress, but hoping and laughing and holding little boys who held her back. It was as if her heart had been a tiny seed, alone in a dark box, and Hugh and his boys had shone light on it. Her heart had grown right out of that box, thriving on all the love she'd felt, and now it was hard, so hard to try to shove her heart back into that too-small box. To try to forget what she'd felt. To forget the warmth and comfort of others.

To be alone again.

Strange, that once it had seemed easy to be alone. But perhaps she'd been deceiving herself before. Perhaps it had never been easy to make her way in the world, depending solely upon herself. But it wasn't until she'd had the comfort of a warm strong shoulder to lean on—had that shoulder and *lost* it—that she felt her terrible solitude.

She stumbled over a cobblestone and looked up.

She was at Saint House.

The windows of the house were dark, but two lanterns were lit at the door.

Alf swallowed. She hadn't been back since she'd spied upon St. John and his wife and babe in the nursery. Hadn't spoken to him since she'd run away after their sparring lesson weeks ago.

But he was a kind man. And she had nowhere else to go.

She went to the front door and knocked. Then stood, shivering in the wind, waiting to see if anyone would answer. It was past midnight. They might not.

But then a light shone at the cracks of the door, and an elderly and rather cranky-looking manservant in a nightcap and coat opened it. "Who might you be?"

"Is Mr. St. John in?" she asked, realizing what a stupid question it was.

"No, miss," the butler said, and her heart plummeted. "He's not returned from dinner yet."

"Who is it, Moulder?" came a woman's voice.

Alf was already backing away, but she wasn't quite fast enough.

"Stop!" It was Lady Margaret, St. John's wife, looking quite fierce for a heavily pregnant woman in a pink-and-peach wrapper. "Don't you run away, Alf."

Alf turned to stare at her. "Lady Margaret. How—?"

Lady Margaret stomped forward and grabbed her wrist. "You come inside," she said, pulling her into the house. "How do I know who you are? Don't be silly. Godric talks about you all the time. He's been worried sick over you. Not of course that he's actually *said* much of anything. Oh no, he's simply *brooded*. Where have you been? Oh, and do call me Megs, I feel we know each other already."

It might've been the big dim hall, it might've been all the scolding yet worried chatter, or it might've been that last. The offer of friendship.

Alf burst into tears.

Megs wrapped her arms around her. "Don't worry. You're here now."

THREE DAYS LATER Hugh sat in his dark library with his pounding head in his hands. He'd sent his men into St Giles. He'd spent hours scouring the streets, made inquiries of every informant he had, ducked into countless taverns and tiny shady gin shops and even checked at the Home for Unfortunate Infants and Foundling Children.

No one had seen Alf, and he was half out of his mind with worry for her. Had she gone back to St Giles and been taken by the Scarlet Throats? Was she even now some nameless corpse floating in the Thames? Or had she disappeared like so many others—like her childhood friend and protector, Ned? Had she gone out one day and simply vanished?

He might spend the rest of his life never knowing what had happened to her.

Then he truly would go insane.

Two things only were keeping him in his right mind. One, that she'd survived on the streets by herself so long—she was strong, canny, and tenacious, his Alf.

Two, that he was almost certain she was deliberately hiding from him, which was his own bloody fault. He'd gone over and over that last morning with her and damned himself for what he'd neglected to say to her.

What he should've told her immediately.

Stay.

Don't leave me.

We'll talk when I return.

I care for you.

I want you in my life.

He groaned into his hands. He'd let his cynicism and fear make his words too cold toward her on that morning, and he'd driven her away.

What a bloody damned idiot he was.

"Papa?"

The small voice was Peter's, and Hugh looked up, though his eyes were damp with pain.

His son stood in the doorway, Pudding in his arms. The puppy looked half-asleep even though Peter held her under her front legs, her back end drooping. The boy looked uncertain and lost.

"Peter." His voice was rough, and he cleared it. "Come here."

The boy stumbled over, the puppy swaying in his arms.

"You have to hold her bottom, too," Hugh said gently, showing the boy. Then he picked up both his son and the dog and settled them in his lap. "Where are your nursemaids?"

"Getting tea." Peter's lower lip was trembling.

"What is it?"

"Where's Alf?"

Hugh inhaled, closing his eyes for patience. He'd already had this conversation with both boys—many times over the last three days. Kit was barely speaking to him. Peter had had two magnificent tantrums—and both boys had spent all three nights sleeping with him. His bed now smelled vaguely of puppy and boys.

"I don't know," he said, "but I'm looking for her. I will bring her back."

"When?" Peter demanded, his lower lip beginning to tremble as he fingered one of the buttons on Hugh's waistcoat.

Hugh closed his eyes, knowing he was priming the cannon when he replied softly, "I don't know."

"I miss her."

He looked at his son. Instead of the boy falling down and screaming, Peter's blue eyes were welling with terrible, sad tears.

He met his father's eyes. "I want Alf."

"I do, too." He laid his cheek against the boy's soft head.

Not long ago he'd not even known Alf. He'd met her only once and believed her an urchin boy. Now her absence was like a ghost haunting his and his sons' lives. When he walked into a room, it seemed empty without her. When he heard a woman's laughter he turned and sought her smile. When he sat down to dinner, he looked across the table and remembered her smearing jam on her bread. And at night, lying in bed, when he listened to his children breathing in sleep, he ached to be able to reach over and touch her shoulder.

She'd left, leaving a hole in his very soul. He wasn't sure a man could stagger on thus injured.

"Your Grace."

He lifted his head and saw Jenkins.

The gray-haired former soldier approached, his grave face looking uncharacteristically excited. "Riley has discovered one of the former Ghosts of St Giles. The man is in London now."

Hugh's head was suddenly clear. He'd known all along that someone had taught Alf. Someone had shown her how to fight with swords and perhaps given her the Ghost costume.

And maybe that someone knew where she was now. "Who?"

"Godric St. John."

Chapter Twenty

*The Black Warlock screamed his rage and ran through
the fire. But it was just as magical as the one he had cast
twelve years before, and, like the White Sorceress, he
burned alive.*
*The Black Prince stood alone and knew that nothing his
father had taught him could quell these flames.*
Then from the sky the Golden Falcon swooped down.
"No, go back!" shouted the Black Prince.
*But the bird ignored him and landed within the
fiery circle. At once she transformed into a
golden-haired woman....*
—From *The Black Prince and the Golden Falcon*

Baby Sophie was simply adorable.

Alf watched as the toddler, clad in a white chemise with
a wide, sky-blue girdle, determinedly placed her fat little
hands on the settee and pulled herself upright. She grinned
at her accomplishment, revealing tiny perfect teeth in her
chubby little face.

"Well done, darling," Megs told her.

The three of them sat in Megs's newly refurbished sitting

room, taking tea. Well, she and Megs were drinking tea. Sophie had gummed a bit of hard biscuit—abandoned under the table now—and was making it her mission to explore as much of the room as possible.

The baby placed her hand next to Alf's skirt and carefully sidled toward her, keeping a grip on the settee the entire time. Her goal appeared to be the gold-edged plate on Alf's lap, which held a slice of lemon cake.

"You could become a governess of some sort," Megs mused, rubbing her belly absently.

Alf looked at her doubtfully. "All I know how to do is break into houses, gather information, and sword fight." She thought. "Oh, and climb buildings."

"Well, it would certainly make for an interesting curriculum." Megs took a sip of tea. "Really, you don't have to look for work at all. I quite like having you here, and with the new baby coming soon, I'll need the extra help."

Alf tried to smile at the generous offer, but it was hard. She was heartbroken, plain and simple. She'd told everything to Megs and then St. John after she'd arrived on their doorstep three nights ago. Even their kindness and the sweet adorableness of little Sophie couldn't replace what she'd lost.

She wanted Hugh. She wanted Hugh and his boys, and she wanted...

She caught her breath as Sophie reached her lap and laid a tiny hand on her knee, grinning up at her with infant charm.

She wanted a child of her own. A child with Hugh.

Alf bent her head and hid her face as tears welled in her eyes, blurring her vision. That wasn't going to happen. Ever.

She had to somehow make herself understand that, not only in her mind but in her heart as well.

She had to find a way to give up hope.

There was a crash and a terrific shout from downstairs.

Sophie startled, her hand hitting the plate on Alf's lap. The plate slid to the floor and smashed.

The baby opened her mouth and let out a loud wail.

Megs moved very fast for a woman with an enormous belly and snatched her child up. "What was that?"

Alf was already on her feet. She caught up her skirts and ran into the hall.

The sitting room was on the floor above the entrance hall, and the staircase was open, with a balcony rail running around the upper floor. She leaned over and looked straight down. St. John had his hands fisted and was facing Hugh, who was sprawled over one of the hall tables. Behind him a mirror on the wall had been smashed to pieces.

Alf felt her heart expand and suddenly start beating fast, as if it'd been frozen for days.

"Bother," Megs said from beside her. "I liked that mirror." She hoisted a sniffling Sophie on her hip. "I take it that's the Duke of Kyle?"

Alf nodded, unable to speak.

He'd turned his head at Megs's voice and was staring up at Alf now, his eyes black and intense. She could only stare back, her heart pounding in her ears so loudly she couldn't think. Why had he come?

"You may return, Your Grace, tomorrow at a more convenient hour," St. John said to Hugh, sounding cool and collected. Only those who knew him well could tell how furious he was. "I believe we are to sit down to dinner soon and I am not used to receiving guests without prior introduction or invitation."

Megs cleared her throat. "I don't think dinner is all *that* soon."

"I don't particularly care what you have to say to Alf," St. John continued.

"*I* do," Megs muttered.

"But you will keep in mind that she has many choices, and I am not entirely certain that you are the best of them."

There was a short silence.

Hugh had never taken his gaze from Alf during all this time. She could feel herself trembling under that intense black stare. She wanted to talk to him, but if he was here simply to tear her heart apart again . . .

She wasn't sure she'd survive a second time.

"Let me speak to you, Alf," Hugh said.

She swallowed, feeling as if her heart had climbed right up into her throat.

Megs gave a gusty sigh. "Oh, Godric, it makes me quite faint when you come over all lord-of-the-manor and master-of-the-circumstances, but you really shouldn't do it to a lady in such a delicate condition as I am."

St. John made an irritable sound under his breath and glanced up at his wife.

Who smiled beatifically at him. "Have I told you that Sophie was trying to say *bombast* today? I think that quite an advanced word for a one-year-old, don't you?"

"Meggie, it seems very unlikely that she's trying to say *bombast.*"

Lady Margaret's smile didn't waver at her husband's gently chiding tone. Instead it grew slightly wider. "Do you think so? Perhaps you ought to help me put her to bed and hear for yourself. And in the meantime His Grace and Alf can have a short discussion in my sitting room."

St. John's lips thinned as he locked gazes with his wife. They seemed to have some sort of wordless exchange, at the end of which St. John nodded abruptly. "A half hour only."

Megs took Alf's arm and quickly led her into the sitting room, still carrying baby Sophie.

"Good luck," she murmured, kissing her on the cheek. "Remember, he might be a duke, but he's a man, too. Just a man. I've found that they can make terrible asses of themselves sometimes." Megs stood back and regarded Alf seriously from eyes that matched her daughter's. "And Godric was right, you know, you *do* have choices. I wouldn't mind if you stayed with us for a very long time. Don't let that duke talk you into anything you don't truly want with his pirate mouth."

And then Megs was gone from the sitting room. Alf could hear her in the hall, saying something about bombast as her voice and St. John's faded.

She breathed in and out, feeling as if all her life, before and after, had narrowed to this one point in time.

Hugh walked in.

He looked horrible. He hadn't bothered with his wig, his eyes were shadowed, and he'd forgotten to shave. His right cheekbone was red and beginning to swell where St. John had hit him. He'd most likely have a black eye in the morning.

She wanted to run to him and wrap her arms around him and never let go.

Instead she clasped her hands together tightly so they wouldn't do anything daft. "Would you like to sit down?"

He ignored her invitation and kept walking toward her, big and broad and *here*.

"Alf," he said, just before he took her face between his palms and kissed her.

She couldn't keep her hands confined then. She sobbed and ran her hands over his shorn hair, his dear head, his neck, his shoulders.

"Why did you leave me?" he muttered against her lips as if he couldn't stand to pull away long enough to hear her answer.

"You paid me," she replied, her tears running into their open mouths. "You were done with me."

"I'll never be done with you, imp. Never." He crushed her against his chest, so close she wasn't sure if it was his heart or her own that she heard beating. "I paid you because I thought it was the honorable thing to do. And I thought you would like to go shopping while I was with Shrugg."

She pulled away—or tried to; he scowled and wouldn't let her move. "*Shopping?*"

Both of his cheekbones were reddened now. "You only had the clothes on your back. I thought you might like... *something*." He glowered at her. "I never meant for you to leave. I want you to stay with me forever."

He seemed sincere, but... "You were so stiff that morning. So strange and cold."

He closed his eyes. "I'm not like you." He laughed under his breath, but it wasn't a happy sound. "You grew up in desperation and squalor, and yet you're able to hope and dream. I don't quite know how you can, but I love you for it." He opened his black, black eyes, and she saw in them wonder and pain and vulnerability. "You're much more courageous than I am, imp. I've had everything material handed to me on a golden platter, and yet I find it... difficult to hope as you do. Even more difficult, I think, to trust."

"To trust me?" she whispered, feeling hurt.

"No, never," he said fiercely. "To trust *myself*. To trust in the future, I suppose. To open my hands and let go of the reins of control and simply trust that things—my life, my family, our happiness—will turn out well." He frowned down at her. "Do you understand?"

"No," she said simply, but she smiled to take away the sting of the word. "No, because if you say you love me then I believe everything *will* turn out well. It simply must. For I love you, too."

He laid his forehead against hers. "I do love you, heart

and soul and body, Alf, my imp. I love you now and forever, and I will trust and I will hope in *your* dreams and hope."

"That's all we need, really," she whispered.

He kissed her, so sweetly, like a promise, and when she opened her eyes he asked, "Will you marry me, Alf?"

And she said, "Yes, guv."

Which was when Megs burst in and clapped her hands and said, "Oh, good! I do love a wedding."

APRIL
OAKDALE PARK, NOTTINGHAMSHIRE

Iris smiled as she climbed the stairs to the nursery in Oakdale Park, carrying a small bag. It was quite early in the morning, and yet the big country house was buzzing with activity and excitement.

But then, it wasn't every day the Duke of Kyle was to be married to his true love.

Few knew of the secret wedding and fewer still had been invited. Aristocratic society could be very cruel and when Iris had realized that Hugh actually intended to *marry* Alf, she suggested a very tiny white lie. Iris and Hugh would simply not announce that they no longer had an understanding. After all, there had never been an official engagement. If others *assumed* that they still intended to be wed, well, that was their affair wasn't it? Alf had moved into Kyle House, but as she was a nobody, no one in society really took any notice.

Hugh and Alf had planned their wedding for the last three months and then decamped with the boys to Oakdale Park, Kyle's country residence in Nottinghamshire. Here they would wed in a small family ceremony and stay until well into fall—far from society. The news of the Duke of

Kyle's scandalous mésalliance would slowly filter back to the London gossips and no doubt cause quite a stir. But by September or October some other cause célèbre would've caught the scandalmongers' fickle attention and they could return to London.

That is what they hoped in any case, and really, Iris saw no reason why the plan shouldn't work.

After all, Hugh was certainly not the first duke to cause a scandal by marrying a penniless lady with no family or name.

Iris supposed she ought to be disappointed that it wasn't her wedding day, but really, she couldn't find it within herself to bother. She was very fond of both Hugh and Alf, and she loved the boys.

Which was why she had slipped away just for a moment from helping to dress Alf.

She paused on the upstairs landing, glancing out of the old diamond-paned windows. Oakdale was surrounded by an overgrown wood—quite a magical place—but sometimes she thought she saw movement in the trees.

Obviously she'd not spent enough time in the country.

Iris picked up her sunset pink skirts and continued her climb.

She could hear giggles when she neared the open door to the nursery.

Iris peeked in and saw Peter on the floor with the ridiculously named Pudding. He was getting dog hair all over his new dark-blue suit. Christopher knelt beside him. As she watched, the older boy rolled a wooden ball across the nursery floor. Pudding tumbled after it, caught it in her mouth, and then promptly ran away with her prize to hide under a chair.

Peter giggled.

Christopher, however, was of a sterner mind. "No, Pudding," he chided, peering under the chair at the puppy. "You're supposed to bring *back* the ball, not keep it."

He reached under the chair and pulled out the ball—with the puppy still attached, all four of her small paws firmly planted on the floor.

Peter rolled around on the floor, convulsing with laughter.

Iris cleared her throat.

Both boys looked up.

She smiled at them. "Pudding probably just needs more practice."

"Maybe," Christopher said doubtfully.

Iris glanced around the nursery. "Where are your nursemaids?"

"Milly went to fetch our breakfast, and Annie is polishing my shoes," Peter said.

"Ah." She noticed for the first time that Peter was indeed in his stocking feet. "Is Annie in your bedroom?"

"Yes," Peter said.

"Perhaps you should find her and see if she can brush your suit as well," Iris suggested.

Peter bent at the waist and looked down at himself. "Oh." He turned and trudged off in the direction of the boys' bedroom.

"I have something for you," Iris said to Christopher.

"You do?" He put the puppy down and straightened. In the past three months Christopher had lost most of his angry moods. He'd slowly become closer to his father and had started to smile more.

Iris had always thought that he resembled Hugh the most—the boy had Hugh's dark coloring, his black hair and eyes, and even his scowl and brooding air on occasion. But there were moments, like this one, when she caught a glimpse of Katherine in him. Something about the excitement in his face at the thought of a surprise. The wonder of the unexpected.

Katherine was a part of him, too.

Iris sat in a nursery chair and opened the bag she'd brought with her. She took out the slim red leather volume that she'd found in Christopher's bed so many weeks ago.

The boy's eyes widened when he saw it. "That's my mama's."

She nodded. "Yes, it is. I owe you an apology, Christopher. I found this in your room and I took it without permission. I'm sorry. I can only say that I miss your mother very, very much."

Christopher's lower lip trembled as he took the diary back. He opened the book and looked inside. "Some of the pages are missing."

"I cut them out," she said gently. "It's a private diary, and some of the things your mother wrote, she probably didn't want you to read. I've kept the pages, and when you are grown up and are a man, if you would like to read them, I will give them to you."

He nodded, still staring at the book. Then Christopher closed it and stroked the leather cover. "I didn't read it. I just liked having it because it was hers."

She reached out her hand, hesitated, and finally laid it on his shoulder. "I understand."

From the bedroom they could hear Peter's voice raised in argument. The poor nursemaid was apparently having difficulties in cleaning his suit.

Christopher darted a look at the bedroom and then at her.

"Lady Jordan?" he whispered.

"Yes, love?"

"When Father marries Alf today…" He trailed off as his brows drew together. It was an expression that reminded her very much of his father. He inhaled. "When they are married, will Alf be my mother?"

She bit her lip. "Do you want her to be?"

He was staring at the diary again, stroking the cover. "Maybe."

"Then maybe she could be," Iris said gently. "Or maybe she could just stay Alf. I don't think you need make up your mind right away, do you?"

He sighed, looking relieved, and shook his head.

Iris smiled and stood. "Then I suggest we finish getting ready. We do have a wedding to attend this morning."

And at that he grinned.

HUGH STOOD IN the yellow sitting room that stretched all along the back of Oakdale Park. The manor was ancient, a venerable residence that had reverted to the Crown when the previous owner died without an heir. Which might explain the curiously outmoded decor of the manor and the overgrown gardens. Katherine had hated the country and had never stepped foot in Oakdale Park.

Alf, in contrast, had half hung out of the carriage window the first time they'd driven up to Oakdale Park. Apparently it had been love at first sight, for she'd exclaimed over the vine-covered facade, the dark paneling in the entry hall, and the odd colors previous tenants had chosen for the rooms. When Hugh had made a vague reference to possibly clearing some of the overgrown trees near the manor, she'd been brought nearly to tears.

Who would've thought that a St Giles urchin would so love the country?

Now he waited impatiently beside an elderly bishop for Alf to come downstairs so that they could be married.

Finally.

His men, all in their best, stood beside him. Kit and Peter sat with their nursemaids and were behaving very well—

though Peter gave an impatient wriggle every now and again. St. John and his wife were in attendance, the wife already dabbing at her eyes in between chatting with Iris. Almost the entire manor staff—save for those involved with the wedding breakfast preparations—were lined up at the back wall to witness the wedding.

Behind Hugh, seated facing the rest of the room, was their surprise guest—the King. He wore a plum suit and white wig and otherwise looked quite ordinary—were one to miss the jewels that encrusted his buttons. Shrugg was a discreet—and rather scandalized—presence beside His Majesty. This was only the fourth time in his life that Hugh had met his father in person and he wasn't entirely certain how he felt about it.

Alf, of course, had been thrilled, and that, he supposed, was all that mattered.

The first time he'd married, Hugh remembered being nervous. And mostly looking forward to the wedding night and bedding Katherine.

This time . . .

Well, this time he was still looking forward to the wedding night, but it was much more than that with Alf.

He was looking forward to spending the rest of his life with her. To waking with her. To sitting across the dining room table from her. To taking the children to the fair and boating on the Thames with her.

To perhaps bringing more children, children they created together, into their family.

It wasn't the life he'd envisioned eight years ago when he'd wed Katherine. He certainly wouldn't be doing the diplomatic work Shrugg wanted him involved in. But this was the life he wanted. This was the life that brought him joy.

The door to the sitting room opened.

Hugh wondered vaguely if he would always feel this punch to the stomach on first seeing her.

Alf walked in. She was wearing a new dress—one of many he'd insisted she have made in the last months. Her wedding dress was white, with tiny purple embroidered flowers scattered all over the skirt, bodice, and sleeves. A thin line of embroidery outlined the square bodice and the elbow-length sleeves. And in her swept-up hair she wore the amethyst pins he'd given her as a wedding present.

She was beautiful, his imp.

Beside her were two little girls holding hands. Hannah and Mary Hope wore matching white dresses. Hannah was solemn and wide-eyed while little Mary Hope had her thumb in her mouth. The girls would be his wards after today.

A part of their family.

Hannah and Mary Hope marched between the chairs to take their seats with Peter and Kit and the nursemaids. Peter immediately leaned over and whispered something in Hannah's ear and the two giggled. Those two would bear watching.

But at the moment Hugh had eyes only for his bride.

Alf smiled, her lips trembling just a little, as she neared him, and he held out his hand.

When she laid her palm in his, he drew her near. "Are you ready, imp?"

"Yes, guv," she whispered, and he felt that soaring joy, that wild freedom, he'd once feared. This time, though, he knew his love for Alf was nothing to fear.

Alf's love brought only hope.

Epilogue

*The Black Prince looked at the golden-haired woman
sadly and whispered, "Why did you not listen to me?
You've doomed yourself to die."
She simply smiled at him and held out her hand. "Have
a little faith, my love."
The Black Prince stared into her golden eyes and placed
his hand in hers.
Still smiling, she led him to the flames, and when
he stiffened and balked, she merely looked over her
shoulder and murmured, "Faith."
He nodded and squared his shoulders.
Together they walked through the magical
fire . . . and emerged unscathed on the
other side.
The Black Prince blinked and looked back to where the
flames were now dying down. "But . . . how? I know of no
such spell or magic."
The golden-haired woman touched her fingertips to his
hard cheek. "Because I am White and you are Black
and together we are balanced. They never understood
that, my mother and your father. They saw only their
differences, not what they could have formed had
they tried."
The Black Prince stared at her in wonder. "You are very
wise. I think I should marry you and join our*

lines together. We shall form a new kingdom and
rule in peace."
The White Princess grinned and stood on tiptoe to kiss
the Black Prince. "I think so, too."
So the House of Black and the House of White were
joined together and became the House of Gray.
The new king and queen had a dozen children and too
many grandchildren to keep count of and they
did indeed live in peace and happiness for a very,
very long time.
And sometimes, at dusk, the king could be seen riding
out away from the prying eyes of the castle with a
golden falcon upon his arm, the jingle of bells singing in
the air....

—From *The Black Prince and the Golden Falcon*

Meanwhile...

Raphael de Chartres, the Duke of Dyemore watched from the cover of the woods as the wedding celebration spilled out into the overgrown gardens of Oakdale Park. His bay shifted restlessly under him and he patted her glossy neck absently. Guests mingled and laughed. Small children raced and tumbled in the weeds. And she smiled as Kyle bent his head and kissed her on the cheek.

She wore peach for her wedding. A pale shade the color of dawn or certain peony blossoms—or the blush on a woman's cheek when a man had maligned her honor. The dress was beautiful.

The flaxen-haired lady more so.

Ah well. She was the Duchess of Kyle now and she had her husband to guard and keep her safe. She was no longer his concern.

Rafe turned his mare's head and disappeared back into the dark woods.

THE SIZZLING MAIDEN LANE
SERIES CONTINUES...

A PREVIEW OF

Duke of Desire

FOLLOWS.

APRIL 1742

Considering how extremely dull her life had been up until this point, Iris Daniels, Lady Jordan had discovered a quite colorful way to die.

Torches flamed around her on tall stakes driven into the ground. Their flickering light in the moonless night made shadows jump and waver over the masked men grouped in a circle around her.

The *naked* masked men.

Their masks weren't staid black half masks, either. No. They wore bizarre animal or bird shapes. She saw a crow, a badger, a mouse, and a bear with a hairy belly and a crooked red penis.

She knelt next to a great stone slab, a primitive fallen monolith brought here centuries ago by people long forgotten. Her trembling hands were bound in front of her, her hair was coming down about her face, her dress was in a shocking state, and she suspected that she might smell—a result of having been kidnapped over three days before.

In front of her stood three men, the masters of this horrific farce.

The first wore a fox's mask. He was slim, pale, and, judging by his body hair, a redhead.

The second wore a mask in the likeness of a young man with grapes in his hair—the god Dionysus if she wasn't mistaken, which, oddly, was far more terrifying than any of the animal masks. He bore a dolphin tattoo on his upper right arm.

The last wore a wolf's mask and was taller by a head than the other two. His body hair was black, he stood with a calm air of power, and he, too, bore a dolphin tattoo. Directly on the jut of his left hipbone. Which rather drew the eye to the man's penis.

The man in the wolf's mask had nothing to be ashamed of.

Iris shuddered in disgust and glanced away, accidentally meeting the Wolf's mocking gaze.

She lifted her chin in defiance. She knew who this group of men was. This was the Lords of Chaos, an odious secret society composed of aristocrats who enjoyed two things: power and the rape and destruction of women and children.

These... *creatures* might kill her—and worse—but they would not take her dignity.

Although right now she rather yearned for her dull life.

"My Lords!" Dionysus called, raising his arms above his head in a theatrical gesture that showed very little taste. But then he *was* addressing an audience of nude, masked men. "My Lords, I welcome you to our spring revels. Tonight we make a special sacrifice—the new Duchess of Kyle!"

The crowd roared like the slavering beasts they were, but Iris blinked. The Duchess of...

She glanced quickly around.

As far as she could see in the macabre flickering torchlight, *she* was the only sacrifice in evidence and she was most certainly *not* the Duchess of Kyle.

The commotion began to die down.

Iris cleared her throat. "No, I'm not."

"Silence," the fox hissed.

She narrowed her eyes at him. Over the last three days she'd been kidnapped on her way home from the wedding of the true Duchess of Kyle, had been bound and hooded, and then shoved into a tiny stone hut without any sort of fire. She'd been forced to relieve herself in a bucket, and had been starved and given very little water. All of which had given her far too much time to contemplate her own death and what torture might precede it.

She might be terrified and alone but she wasn't about to go down without a fight. As far as she could see she had nothing to lose and possibly her life to gain.

So she raised her voice and said clearly and loudly, "You have made a mistake. I am not the Duchess of Kyle."

The wolf glanced at Dionysus, and for the first time he spoke, his voice smoky, "Your men kidnapped the wrong woman."

"Don't be a fool," Dionysus snapped at him. "We captured her three days after her wedding to Kyle."

"Yes, returning home to London from the wedding," Iris said. "The Duke of Kyle married a young woman named Alf, not me. Why would I leave him if I'd just married him?"

The wolf chuckled darkly.

"She lies!" cried the fox and leaped toward her, his arm raised.

The wolf lunged, seizing the fox's arm, twisting it up behind his back, and forcing the other man to the ground on his knees.

Iris swallowed, staring. She'd never seen a man move so swiftly.

Nor so brutally.

The wolf bent over his prey, the snout of his mask pressed against the man's vulnerable bent neck. "Don't. Touch. What. Is. *Mine*."

"Let him go," Dionysus barked.

The wolf didn't move.

"Obey me," the Dionysus said.

The wolf finally turned his mask from the fox's neck. "You have the wrong woman, a corrupt sacrifice, one not worthy of the revel. I have the right to claim her. She is forfeit to me."

Dionysus tilted his head as if considering. "Only by my leave."

The wolf abruptly threw wide his arms, releasing the fox and standing up again. "Then by your leave," he said, his words holding an edge of mockery. The firelight gleamed off his muscled chest and strong arms.

What would make a man with such natural power and grace join this gruesome society?

The other members of the Lords of Chaos didn't seem as sanguine at the thought of having their principal entertainment for the evening snatched out from under their noses. The men around her were muttering and shifting, a restless miasma of danger hovering in the night air.

Any spark could set them off, Iris suddenly realized.

"Well?" the wolf asked the Dionysus.

"You can't let her go," the fox said, getting to his feet. "Why the bloody hell are you listening to him? She's ours. Let us take our fill of her and—"

The wolf struck him on the side of the head, a terrible blow that made the fox fly backward.

"Mine," growled the wolf. He looked at the Dionysus. "Do you lead the Lords or not?"

"I think it more than evident that I lead the Lords," the

Dionysus drawled, even as the muttering of the crowd grew louder. "And I think I need not prove my mettle by giving you this woman."

The wolf was standing between Iris and the Dionysus and she saw the muscles on his legs tense. She wondered if the Dionysus could see that the other man was readying for battle as well.

"However," the Dionysus continued, "I can grant her to you as an act of...charity. Enjoy her in whatever way you see fit, but remember to make sure she can never tell others about us."

"My word," the wolf bit out.

He grabbed Iris's bound wrists and hauled her to her feet, dragging her stumbling behind him, as he strode through the mass of angry masked men. The crowd jostled her, shoving against her from all sides with bare arms and elbows until the wolf finally pulled her free.

She had been brought to this place hooded and for the first time she saw that it must be some sort of ruined abbey. Stones and broken arches loomed in the dark and she tripped more than once over weed-covered rubble. The spring night was chilly away from the fires, but the man in the wolf mask seemed unaffected by the elements. He continued his pace until they reached a dirt road and several waiting carriages. He walked up to one and without preamble opened the door and shoved her inside.

The door closed and Iris was left panting in the dark empty carriage.

Immediately she tried the carriage door, but he'd locked or jammed it somehow. It wouldn't open.

She could hear men's voices in the distance. Shouts and cries. Good Lord. She imagined a pack of wild dogs would sound the same.

She needed a weapon. Something—*anything*—with which to defend herself.

Hurriedly she felt the door—a handle, but she couldn't wrench it off—a small window, no curtains—the walls of the carriage—*nothing*. The seats were plush velvet. Expensive. Sometimes in better-made carriages the seats...

She yanked at one.

It lifted up.

Inside was a small space.

She reached in and felt a fur blanket. Nothing else.

Damn.

She could hear the wolf's voice just outside the carriage.

Desperately she flung herself at the opposite seat and tugged it up. Thrust her hand in.

A pistol.

The door to the carriage opened. The wolf loomed in the doorway, a lantern in one hand. She saw his eyes flick to the pistol she held between her bound hands. He turned his head and said something in a strange incomprehensible language to someone outside.

Then he got in the carriage and closed the door. He hung the lantern on a hook and sat on the seat across from her. "Put that down."

She backed into the opposite corner as far away from him as possible, holding the pistol up. Level with his chest. "No."

The carriage jolted into motion.

"T-tell them to stop," she said, her voice stuttering with terror despite her resolve. "Let me go now."

"So that they can rape you to death out there?" He tilted his head to indicate the Lords. "No."

He reached for her and she knew she had no choice. She'd seen how he moved, how fast and how ruthlessly.

She shot him.

The blast knocked him into the seat and threw her hands up and back, narrowly missing her nose with the pistol.

Iris scrambled upright. The bullet was gone but she could still use the pistol as a bludgeon.

The wolf was sprawled across the seat, blood streaming from a gaping hole in his right shoulder. His mask had been knocked askew on his face.

She reached forward and pulled it off.

The face that was revealed had once been as beautiful as an angel's but was now horribly mutilated. A livid red scar ran from just below his hairline on the right side of his face, bisecting the eyebrow, somehow missing the eye itself but gouging a furrow into the lean cheek and catching the edge of the upper lip on that side, making it twist. The scar ended in a missing divot of flesh in the line of the man's severe jaw. He had inky black hair and emotionless crystal gray eyes—though they were closed now—and she recognized him.

He was Raphael de Chartres, the Duke of Dyemore, and when she'd danced with him—once—three months ago at a ball, she'd thought he'd looked like Hades.

God of the underworld.

God of the dead.

She had no reason to change her opinion now.

Then he gasped, and those cold crystal eyes opened and he glared at her. "You idiot woman. I'm trying to *save* you."